GAMBLING
ON
LOVE
TRILOGY

CARA MARSI

Published by The Painted Lady Press

United States of America

Electronic Edition: November, 2017

ISBN: 978-0-9969811-0-1

Cover by Harris Channing

Formatting by Aileen Fish

Wedded in Vegas edited by BKR Editing Services

Cover copy created by BlurbWriter.com

Three couples
Three chances at love
What happens in Vegas...

Wedded in Vegas

When a sexy nerd asks a Vegas bartender out, she does what everyone else in Vegas does: she takes a chance...and learns some rolls of the dice take an unexpected turn.

Love by Chance

In Sin City, a couple, unlucky in love, gamble on each other. Win or lose?

A Very Vegas Christmas

A Las Vegas event planner in need of luck meets a mysterious guy who might be her winning ticket. Will his secret split them apart?

WEDDED IN VEGAS

CARA MARSI

A reluctant bride
A hot Hollywood actor
What happens in Vegas...

Bartending in Las Vegas is the means to an end for Analisa Barbero. As soon as she finishes school she can get her dream job as a teacher. With her hard-working single mom temporarily disabled, money is tight and the hours are long. Who has time for dating? But when a sexy nerd asks her out, Analisa does what everyone else in Las Vegas does: she takes a chance and says yes.

Some people come to Sin City to gamble. Some come to start over. And some come to hide out. Cole Lassiter is Hollywood's hottest property. Fed up with phoniness and paparazzi parasites, he just wants to be an ordinary nobody for a while. But when his deception causes a pretty bartender to lose her job, he makes her the kind of offer that can only happen in the city of make-believe: Marry him for one year in exchange for a house, money, and all-expenses-paid tuition for school. If she agrees, maybe the tabloids will finally give him a break.

Neither Analisa nor Cole thought love was in the cards for them. But what happens in Vegas doesn't always stay in Vegas. Is Analisa willing to gamble her future on a man who already deceived her once? Everyone in Las Vegas knows one thing: You have to roll the dice if you want to hit the jackpot. And love is worth the risk.

CHAPTER ONE

"Analisa, look sharp. He's here."

Analisa Barbero glanced sideways at her co-worker, Patti, and finished pouring the glass of wine for her customer. After acknowledging the customer's thanks, she turned to Patti. "Who's here?"

Patti moved close to whisper. "That hot guy who's been coming in here the past five days, the one who's sweet on you."

Like fine champagne, excitement bubbled through Analisa. She looked toward the entrance of the Capri Bar and Grille, one of the elegant bars in the Augustus Hotel and Casino. The five-star Las Vegas hotel boasted an eclectic clientele of celebrities and millionaires, many of them sexy, polished men who frequented the Capri. Analisa was used to them coming on to her. She took her job as bartender seriously and always fended off their advances with a smile. Her smiles helped get her nice tips too. She sure needed the money.

Despite the beautiful people who came in and out of her bar, none had affected her like Cody Lamont, who stood in the doorway until their eyes met, then sauntered toward her, his full lips tilted in a smile. She liked his friendly smile, his easy-going manner, his humor, the respectful way he treated her. She'd had customers treat her as their servant, but never Cody.

His looks weren't bad either. She thought of him as a sexy nerd, with his short black hair, and his intelligent brown eyes behind black-framed geek glasses. The ruggedness of his chiseled cheekbones and square jaw hinted at hidden depths of strength.

Her pulse jumped a notch when he sat at the bar in front of her. "Hey, Analisa, how's it going?"

My day just got better now that you're here. "It's been busy," she said instead.

"That's good, right?"

"Sure is. The usual?"

When he nodded, she pulled down a Pilsner glass from the overhead rack and filled it with the draught lager he always ordered.

"Thanks," he said with a smile when she slid his drink in front of him.

His smile dazzled as always, his teeth perfect and white in his tanned face. He'd told her he was a medical supplies salesman from Ohio, in Vegas for a conference. Considering the cloudy March weather in Vegas, and that it probably wasn't sunny now in Ohio, his tan surprised her. The blackness of his hair made her wonder if he dyed it, but he didn't strike her as a guy who would dye his hair or go to a tanning salon.

Analisa returned his smile as she scanned him. His white, button-down shirt, opened at the neck to reveal a scattering of fine light-colored hair, stretched across broad shoulders. She'd checked him out many times and knew the dark jeans he favored showcased his tight butt and his long legs that went on forever.

"You look nice," he said. "But then you always do. I like your hair down."

"Thanks." She resisted the urge to flip aside strands of her long hair that lay over her shoulders. She usually wore it pinned up, but this morning, running late, she hadn't bothered to style it.

Another customer sat at the bar, and she reluctantly left Cody to wait on the other man. She couldn't allow herself to get too close to Cody. When his conference ended, he'd go back to Ohio and she'd never see him again. Years ago she'd fallen deeply in love with a man whose work took him to Las Vegas on a regular basis. His betrayal had torn a hole in her heart. She would not let that happen again.

Busy with the crush of customers who'd come in for the bar's Happy Hour, Analisa couldn't spare more time to talk to Cody. Friday night in Vegas, the workers poured out of their buildings and casinos, and the tourists finished their sightseeing or were taking a break from gambling. Everyone wanted to party in Sin City. Everyone except her. She'd go home to the small house she shared with her mom, have dinner, then hit the books. In about eighteen months, she'd have her degree, and she could do what she'd always wanted—teach.

She snuck a glance at Cody. He'd finished his second beer and signaled her over. "Another?" she asked when she reached him.

"No. I'm fine." He drew a deep breath, then met her gaze. "What time do you get off work?"

"Six."

He cleared his throat. "Analisa, I was wondering. Would you have dinner with me tonight?"

She smoothed a hand down her black pants. The Augustus frowned on employees becoming involved with hotel guests, but Cody had told her he was staying at the MGM. She wanted to go out with him, and her mom would be glad to see her enjoy herself for a change. But if she went to dinner with him and they had a great time, his leaving would be harder on her. She didn't want to like him enough to miss him when he left.

"Analisa?"

He watched her, waiting.

Her trepidation warred with her desire to see more of him. She was overthinking, as Patti always told her. "I'd like that," she finally said.

Cody seemed like a genuine guy, but she had to be careful. She made it a rule not to get into cars with guys she didn't know well. If they stayed on the crowded Strip and she didn't get into a car with him, she'd be okay. "I have to go home to change. How about if we meet back here at seven-thirty?"

His smile kicked up butterflies in her stomach.

"Great! It's a date." He stood and placed several bills on the bar. "See you at seven-thirty."

She watched him as he walked away.

"He finally ask you out?" Patti said, coming up to her.

"Yes."

"You go, girl."

"Patti, I don't know. He seems really nice, but I have studying to do, and I'm scheduled to work all weekend. I don't want to get to know him better when he won't be here long."

"Overthinking again, girl. You'll fit in the studying. Go out and have some fun."

"I guess you're right." Analisa scooped up the bills Cody had put on the bar. As usual, he over-tipped. Way over.

CARA MARSI

CHAPTER TWO

Nervous as an underage kid at a bar with a fake ID, Cody punched the elevator button for the lobby and his date with Analisa. For the hundredth time, he wondered what the hell he was doing, getting involved with her. From the first moment he'd seen her at the Capri, he'd zeroed in on her like a laser. Sure, she was beautiful, but she had a gentleness that spoke to the part of his heart that still believed in the goodness of people. She treated him as a normal guy, just what he wanted. So why did he feel so damn guilty? He'd tell her the truth tonight.

He stepped off the elevator onto the marble-floored lobby of the Augustus Hotel. The Capri was situated in a corner of the lobby. Tourists posed for pictures next to the magnificent, world-renowned glass sculpture that dominated the area. People from all parts of the country and the world bustled through, intent on having a good time. All he wanted was to hide out, if even for a little while, from the chaos that had become his life.

Spotting Analisa waiting for him in front of the Capri, he smiled as happiness, something he didn't have much of these days, surged through him. He worked with the most beautiful women in the world, yet none possessed Analisa's inner beauty.

She'd traded her working uniform of black pants, white shirt, and flats for a short, dark green skirt that hugged her hips and flared out gently at the knees, revealing slim legs. Her sweater in varying shades of green stretched across her lush breasts. Her high-heeled brown sandals made her legs longer and even more appealing.

"Settle down, boy," he whispered to himself. "This is only a date." Once she found out the truth, it might be their last one.

<><><>

Analisa's heart stuttered as she watched Cody strolling toward her. He'd changed into tailored black pants and a tan shirt, perfectly ironed. For a medical supplies salesman, he dressed elegantly and stylishly, a model who'd stepped off the pages of a men's fashion magazine.

Cody let out a low whistle when he reached her. "Wow! You look great."

"Thanks. So do you."

He leaned closer. "Flattery will get you everywhere."

Joyous laughter erupted from her.

"Where to?" he asked.

"There's a cool French bistro a short walk away. I know the manager and I made a reservation." The bistro served good food, and the prices weren't too extravagant. Analisa assumed Cody made an average salary, and she didn't want to take him to an expensive place he might not be able to afford.

"Sounds good." He cupped her elbow as they turned to exit the hotel.

When they approached the glass doors that led to the Strip, the hairs on Analisa's nape stood on end. She twisted to look behind her. Hailey Appleton, daughter of one of the hotel's owners, stared at Analisa and Cody. The phrase "if looks could kill" ran through Analisa's mind. She'd only met Hailey a few times. She couldn't imagine why the beautiful socialite would be glaring at them with rigid, angry features.

Later, seated at a white-clothed table on an enclosed veranda that overlooked the Strip, Analisa vowed to enjoy every minute in Cody's company. Like a high roller, she'd throw her dice and rake in whatever fun came her way. When he ordered the most expensive bottle of wine on the menu, she hid her surprise. His clothes and manners showed exquisite taste. Maybe he made more money than she assumed.

While they waited for their food and enjoyed the rich burgundy wine, Cody leaned closer and met her gaze. "Tell me about Analisa Barbero. Do you like being a bartender? What other interests do you have? I want to know all about you."

She laughed. "I hate to disappoint you, but I have an ordinary life. I enjoy bartending. The money's decent and I like people. Most of my customers, like you, are great. For the past six years, I've been going to night classes at UNLV. I graduate in about eighteen months, depending on how many classes I can handle."

"I'm impressed. Carrying a fulltime job and school is a heavy burden."

"It's hard, but I'm working toward something I've always wanted."

"What's that?"

"I want to teach. There are areas in Las Vegas where kids are practically living on the streets and have little access to decent food or clothes. Education is the only way out for them. I want to do what I can to make their lives better."

"I'm doubly impressed." He lifted his wine glass in salute. "To you. Not only are you beautiful, but you're intelligent, warm, and ambitious."

Her face hot, she clinked her glass with his.

"It's your turn," she said. "Do you like your work?"

He glanced away and sipped wine before turning back to her. "It's okay. It pays the bills."

Frowning, she studied him. The tightness in his face and voice told her he hid something. A ball of dread gathered in her chest. He'd told her he wasn't married. She'd believed him. There was no telltale line on his fourth finger left hand that would indicate he usually wore a ring. Lots of married men came to Vegas and pretended they were single. She'd taken a chance on Cody. She hoped she weren't too naïve, too trusting.

During the delicious dinner, Analisa's doubts began to dissolve. Cody made her laugh with his stories of growing up the youngest of six. The love he felt for his family shone through his words and the softness in his eyes.

As they shared dessert, a luscious crème brûlée, she said, "Your family sounds like such fun. I'm an only child. I always wanted siblings."

"Your parents didn't want more kids?"

She blew out a breath. "My dad walked out on my mom when I was three. Mom worked several jobs at a time through my childhood. Her latest job was on the housekeeping staff at the Augustus. She slipped on something a guest had left on the floor and tore a rotator cuff so badly she needed surgery and rehab. She can't lift anything heavier than a dust cloth so she won't be working for a while."

Cody reached across the table and put his hand over Analisa's. "That's rough. So you're supporting her and yourself? And going to school?"

"Yes, but I can handle it. Mom gets a little bit from worker's comp, so that helps."

He shook his head. "You are one terrific woman."

"Thanks, but I'm doing what millions of people do every day." Uncomfortable talking about herself, she dipped her spoon into the creamy dessert.

"Where I come from, there aren't too many women like you," he said.

"In Ohio? That's strange."

He didn't answer but signaled their waiter for the check.

Cody held her hand as they walked back to the Augustus where she'd parked her car. At his touch, warmth and contentment covered her like the Vegas sun in summer. The hordes of people crowding the sidewalks and shouldering by them faded. The cool air drifted over them, bringing the scents of the desert mingled with the flowers that grew in pots along the sidewalks.

She liked Cody a lot, yet doubts assailed her. From the first moment she'd seen him, she knew there was something different about Cody Lamont. Polished and sophisticated, he didn't strike her as an ordinary working stiff. He had a charisma that attracted others. Analisa saw the way people, men and women, reacted to him everywhere—along the Strip, in the restaurant. He was good-looking in a laid-back kind of way, yet he turned heads.

When they got to her silver Kia, a car she'd bought used several years ago, she unlocked the door, then turned to Cody. "Thanks for dinner. I had a great time."

He stepped closer. "Me, too. Will you go out with me tomorrow?"

Inhaling his scent of spice laced with the outdoors, she fought the urge to grab him and kiss him. "Isn't your conference over?"

"It is, but I'm staying a few more days."

The more she saw him, the more she liked him, despite her

doubts. She'd miss him when he left. She didn't want to miss him.

"I have to work tomorrow night," she said.

"After work?"

Fear of losing her heart to a man she'd never see again made her hesitate. "I'm not sure."

He reached into his pants pocket and pulled out his phone. "How about we exchange numbers and you can call me?"

"Okay." No harm in that.

They entered their numbers into each other's phones. "I guess I'd better go." She stuffed her phone back into her purse, opened her car door, and threw her purse onto the seat.

"Analisa," he whispered.

She turned to him. His eyes had darkened. He bent and took her lips in a gentle kiss, giving her the choice. His kiss caressed and seduced. He tasted like wine and sugar. His lips firmed over hers. Standing on her toes, she pressed against his taut frame and wound her arms around his neck. He groaned softly.

His deep, drugging kiss possessed her. Fire, like aged bourbon, raced through her veins. She opened to him, giving more of herself, wanting more of him. His tongue, hot, demanding, probed her mouth. She melted into him.

When they finally pulled apart, he cradled her face between his big hands. "I need to tell you something."

"What do—?"

Laughter and the flash of bright lights made them jump apart. Blinded by the lights, she shielded her eyes.

"Is this the new lady in your life, Cole?" a man shouted.

"Is she why you're in Vegas and in disguise?" a woman shouted.

Blinking, Analisa backed up against her car. "Cody, what's going on?"

He moved in front of her, blocking her from the group of five men and women with cameras. "Don't worry, Analisa, it's just the paparazzi. They're annoying but they won't hurt you."

"Paparazzi?" she croaked.

"Cole, look this way," one of the men called out.

"Why do they keep calling you Cole?" Analisa asked.

"Leave us alone," Cody snapped to the group confronting

them.

"Lassiter, you're news, dude," one of the men said before more flashbulbs went off.

"Cole? Lassiter? As in Cole Lassiter, the movie star?" Analisa forced the words out in a hoarse whisper.

Cody/Cole turned to her and cupped her shoulders. "I'm sorry. I'm really sorry."

"What is this?" she asked. "Are you using me to research a movie? Slumming it?"

"No, nothing like that. Go home. I'll call you."

She slid into the car and he shut the door. With shaking hands, she turned on the ignition and backed out. The photographers scurried out of her way. As she headed out of the garage as fast as was safe, she glanced into the rearview mirror. A stricken-looking Cody/Cole stared at her car.

She'd just had a date with Cole Lassiter, the hottest movie star in Hollywood? It couldn't be. Cole had longish blond hair, and blue eyes, and he didn't wear glasses. As she exited the garage onto the Strip, she remembered the blond chest hair peeking from the vee of his shirt. Dying his hair black and wearing brown contact lenses would be easy for someone with his resources.

She pounded a fist on the steering wheel. Cole Lassiter had lied to her, had taken advantage, had played her. She wanted to turn around, find him, and slap him on that beautiful, lying face.

CHAPTER THREE

After a night of restless sleep, punctuated by nightmares of flashbulbs going off in her face, Analisa woke with a headache. Pressing her hand against her forehead, she slid out of bed. She would never see Cody/Cole again, and that was fine with her. Why did he do it? She liked Cody, thought he was a genuine guy, sincere and considerate. Maybe he was in disguise to research a movie role; maybe he wanted freedom from a life lived in the public eye. He should have been honest with her. Guys had lied to her before. She didn't like lies and wouldn't put up with them. Her head hurt too much to think about it.

Her shift didn't start until noon so she had time to study before work. If she could concentrate enough. She threw a robe over her pajamas and went into the hall. Before going downstairs, she peeked into her mother's room. Seeing her mom asleep, Analisa closed the door softly and padded down the stairs of the rental townhouse she and her mother shared.

When Analisa opened her front door to retrieve the morning paper, Mrs. Myers from across the street waved to her.

"Good morning," Analisa called out.

"It must be a very good morning for you," Mrs. Myers shouted, a smirk on her face. She waved her newspaper. "What's he like?"

A sinking feeling settled over Analisa. "What's who like?"

"You know. The movie star. That Cole Lassiter is one hot dude."

Hot dude? Coming from seventy-five-year-old Mrs. Myers,

the statement might have been laughable. Analisa wasn't in a laughing mood.

She started to respond when two news vans wheeled around the corner and stopped in front of her house. Two women with mics jumped out of the vans, followed by men with cameras. "Analisa," the women shouted. "Are you and Cole Lassiter a couple?"

Feeling dizzy, Analisa scurried back into her house and slammed the door shut. Breathing heavily, she leaned against it. She threw the newspaper onto the floor. No way did she want to see pictures of her and Cole/Cody, that lying snake.

Pounding on the door made her heart race. "Go away!" she shouted.

"Ana? What's going on?" Her mother, a frown on her face, hurried down the stairs.

Holding back a scream that threatened to explode, Analisa said, "Mom, we need to talk."

<><><>

"What the hell were you thinking?" Cole's publicist, Teresa Mack, an unlit cigarette in her hand, paced the living room in the penthouse suite at the Augustus Hotel. Her voice, raspy from years of smoking, grated on Cole's already frayed nerves.

She and his agent, Brian Crenshaw, had flown in from Los Angeles that morning after Cole called them. They were experts at damage control, and Cole needed to control the harm he'd done to Analisa.

He smoothed a hand over his short hair. He disliked having his hair this short, but it had been necessary to go incognito. Lot of good that had done him. His antipathy of the whole Hollywood bullshit—the constant photographers, the women who wanted him only for how he could advance their careers, the rampant greed and phoniness—had driven him to come up with his harebrained scheme. His self-indulgence had hurt Analisa.

"Sit down, Teresa. You're making me nervous," he said.

"I can't sit. I need to walk to think."

"Have a drink," Brian said from the bar where he'd poured himself a whiskey. He held the bottle out. "Both of you take a drink and settle down."

Cole shook his head, but Teresa nodded, and Brian poured

her a few fingers of the alcohol. She slugged it down and slammed her glass onto the walnut-topped bar. "What the hell were you thinking?" she repeated. She stalked over to Cole and ruffled his hair. "You cut that beautiful hair and dyed it this awful color."

Her whiskey and tobacco-laced breath wafted over Cole and he took a step back. "I wanted time away from movie star Cole Lassiter, time to be an ordinary guy. I'm sick of reading lies about myself in the tabloids, of getting roles based on my looks, sick of gratuitously having to remove my shirt in most every movie."

Brian chuckled, and glass in hand, sauntered out from behind the bar. "Cole, you're Hollywood's hottest property. You may not like being a sex symbol, but you've made us and yourself tons of money. You never have been, nor will you ever be 'an ordinary guy'. Not with your looks and talent."

"We'll fix this," Teresa said. "You look like a fool hiding out in disguise, and in Las Vegas of all places. We'll make this escapade work for us." Like a caged panther, she circled the room.

Cole clenched a fist at his side. "I didn't bring you here to make things work for us. I don't care about myself. My career is strong. If anything, this 'escapade' will enhance my street creds. I've hurt the sweetest woman I've met in the ten years since I left Ohio. She doesn't deserve this sort of attention or to have the paparazzi stalk her. We need to call off the vipers."

Brian perched on one of the barstools. "She's a grown woman, Cole. She'll handle it. You need to run things by us before you go off on your own."

Teresa stopped pacing and studied Cole. "I saw pictures of you in disguise. I almost didn't recognize you. How did the press get wind of this?"

"Hell if I know."

"Anyone besides you in on this little scheme?" Brian asked.

"Only the owners of the Augustus, Gordon and Appleton, but I swore them to secrecy."

Brian frowned. "I know those guys. They're discreet. How the hell did the press find out?"

Feeling the beginnings of a headache, Cole strode to the small refrigerator behind the bar, opened it, yanked out a bottle of water, and unscrewed the cap. He took a long draught of the water and set the bottle down, then leaned against the bar. The hard walnut dug into his back, as if punishing him for what he'd done. "Let's discuss what's important. I hurt Analisa and I need to make things right with her."

"Analisa? That's her name?" Teresa said. "You got a last name?"

"Barbero."

"Latina?" Brian asked.

When Cole nodded, Teresa smiled.

"This is good," she said. "You're dating a Latina. Your fan base will increase with that community. Why didn't I think of this? It's genius."

Red-hot anger propelled Cole away from the bar and to Teresa. "You. Will. Not. Use. Analisa. It's bad enough I lied to her and put her in this position. Call off the paparazzi. You have contacts. Promise them something else, anything. I want Analisa kept out of this ugliness."

Scrubbing a hand down his face, he backed away. "I owe her an apology."

CHAPTER FOUR

Analisa managed to push her way through the half-dozen or so reporters outside her house and get into her car. She doubted her manager would consider fighting through a gauntlet of paparazzi as a good reason to be late for work.

The reporters jumped into their vans and followed her, a motley caravan winding slowly down the Strip. Knowing a back way to the Augustus, she outmaneuvered the reporters and found a parking spot in the Augustus garage. As she hurried to the elevators, several vans careened into the garage. When the vans jerked to a stop, reporters dove out and chased her. She ran to the elevators with them in hot pursuit. The comfortable shoes she wore for work made running easy. She punched the elevator buttons and was rewarded with the doors sliding closed before the reporters could reach her.

She made it to the Capri with no one on her tail. Patti, her eyes wide, ran over to Analisa. Thankfully, only a few customers sat at the bar. Analisa hoped she'd evaded the reporters. If they knew where she worked, the place would be a mob scene.

She signaled Patti for quiet and gestured for her to follow her through the door behind the bar to the employees' locker room.

When they got inside, Patti grabbed her arm. "Oh. My. God. Cody is Cole Lassiter. How could we have not known?"

With a wry smile, Analisa freed herself from Patti's death grip, opened her locker and stuffed her purse inside, then faced Patti. "He's an actor. His disguise was good, and everything he said and did was merely playing a part." Anger pounded in her chest, and she drew in shallow, too-fast breaths. "He used me. He must be laughing at how naïve I was."

"He seemed really into you," Patti said, confusion in her eyes. "Sure, he's a great actor, but I don't think he was acting. He likes you. Maybe he has a good reason for wearing a disguise."

Analisa put up a hand. "Don't make excuses for him. It's been a nightmare. The paparazzi won't leave me alone. I feel like such a fool. Not knowing who he really is put me on the spot. I'm an ordinary working woman. I can't handle people following me around, and I don't want to."

"I know you're upset, but think of this as your fifteen minutes of fame. Enjoy it."

"I don't want fame for even fifteen seconds." Analisa pushed hair out of her face. "We've both seen our share of celebrities who come into the Capri and only want to relax with a glass of wine or a beer. But they can't because their fans follow them and harass them for autographs and selfies."

"Those celebrities get paid big bucks for what they do, and being constantly in the public eye is part of doing business," Patti said.

"I don't get paid big bucks to put up with it."

"Forget all that for a minute. How was your date with Cole?"

At Analisa's narrowed-eyed look, Patti fanned herself with her hand. "Cole or Cody, the man is hot."

Analisa bit down on her lip. "He's a liar. Like lots of men." She swallowed the lump that had formed in her throat. "I hate to admit it, but I had a good time. With Cody. I can't tell you what Cole is like because he didn't make an appearance until the paparazzi found us."

Sympathy softened Patti's eyes. "This will blow over. We need to get back out there. Hopefully we'll be so busy you won't have a chance to think about Cody/Cole."

Analisa knew she wouldn't be able to put Cole out of her mind for a very long time.

When they came out of the employees' locker room, Tony, her manager, and Louise Thurston, the head of HR, waited, both tight-lipped.

Dread rooted Analisa to the spot. *This can't be good.*

"Analisa," Louise said. "I need to speak to you in my office.

Now."

Tony shook his head and shrugged when Analisa turned to him.

Louise stomped out.

With a black cloud hovering over her, Analisa followed Louise. As she hurried across the lobby to catch up with the older woman, other employees and some hotel guests turned to stare. Her friend Laney, working the concierge counter, watched Analisa and Louise with wide eyes.

"There she is!" someone shouted. Analisa pivoted to see a horde of reporters and camera operators running toward her. She sprinted to the elevator where Louise held the doors open. She slipped inside, and the doors closed before any of the reporters could get in.

When they got to Louise's office, the other woman gestured for Analisa to sit in the chair in front of the desk. Her heels clicking on the tile floor, Louise walked to her large desk and sat behind it.

Close to sixty years old, Louise wore her blond hair short. Red-framed glasses, in the latest style, rested on her small nose. Her pale skin, smooth and flawless, testified to the expertise of her cosmetic surgeon.

Analisa had always liked Louise. The older woman treated her entire staff with kindness, their mother hen.

Louise steepled her fingers in front of her and stared at Analisa until Analisa began to fidget, feeling like an unruly kid sent to the principal's office.

Resting her palms on her desktop, Louise said, "I like you, Analisa. You're one of my best workers, conscientious, hard-working, always on time. I don't believe you've taken one sick day in the eight years you've been here."

"I haven't."

Louise sighed. "What I have to say is very difficult. We frown on employees dating our guests, but we have no hard and fast rule against it. However, we expect our employees to be discreet in all of their social interactions that might reflect badly on the Augustus. Mr. Appleton is very displeased at the unsavory publicity you've brought to this establishment."

Analisa dug the nails of one hand into the palm of the other and leaned forward. "What are you saying, Louise? I didn't know the man I went out with last night was a celebrity. He told me he was staying at the MGM."

Louise smiled, slowly, sadly. "Mr. Lassiter is a guest in our penthouse suite. If it were up to me, I'd reprimand you and let it go. But Mr. Appleton wants you fired."

Analisa opened her mouth to speak, but no words came out. She clutched the edge of the chair. Mr. Appleton wanted her fired? His daughter, Hailey, had watched Analisa and Cole last night as they left the hotel for their date. Foreboding crawled up her spine, making her shiver. "Fired?" she squeaked out.

"I'm afraid so. We're prepared to give you two weeks' severance and pay your health benefits for two weeks. I'm sorry, Analisa."

"But—but, Louise. My mother is still in rehab for her rotator cuff. Her workers' comp doesn't pay as much as her salary. I need my job."

Louise stood, signaling the end to the meeting.

Analisa stayed seated. "No, I can't accept this. It's totally unfair. I did nothing wrong. I've been a good, loyal employee for eight years. Let me talk to Mr. Appleton. I'll make him understand."

"I went to bat for you with Mr. Appleton. I begged him to give you another chance, but he's adamant. Please clean out your locker." Louise's features softened. "I wish you luck."

Analisa stood and stumbled out on shaky legs.

She had no job, no income, no savings.

Fired.

CHAPTER FIVE

He shouldn't be doing this. He'd only give the paparazzi more fodder. Analisa wouldn't pick up his calls. Cole had to see her, to try to make it up to her. Finding her address proved easy through his contacts at the Augustus. Teresa and Brian, planning to stay a few days to keep an eye on him, had taken suites at the hotel, leaving him alone in the penthouse. They'd be furious at him for taking matters into his own hands. He wouldn't be the man his mom had raised him to be if he didn't apologize to Analisa in person.

Instructed by his car's GPS, he swung a left out of the Augustus' garage onto the Strip. The houses got seedier as he headed toward North Las Vegas. The woman he'd come to know and like didn't reflect the poverty and hopelessness he saw around him. Not only was Analisa beautiful, with her creamy olive skin and long, curling black hair, but she carried herself with pride. Her big, gold-flecked brown eyes, framed by thick lashes, shone with intelligence.

He'd enjoyed talking with her whenever he'd come into her bar. In the time he'd been hiding out in Vegas in a futile attempt to escape the constant need to be on, to be Cole Lassiter, star, Analisa had brightened his days. When he'd first laid eyes on her behind the long stainless steel bar, she'd radiated honesty and guilelessness.

They'd had a good time at dinner last night. A part of him had known he shouldn't get too friendly with her, that his sojourn to Sin City would soon end. He liked her company, her infectious laugh and smile. And he hadn't thought of the harm his deceit could cause.

As soon as he turned down her street, he didn't need to search for her house number. The news vans parked outside made it obvious. He gripped the steering wheel and gritted his teeth. Photographers and the media were a part of the life he'd chosen for himself. He always tried to be gracious to them. He didn't feel gracious today.

When he pulled his Ferrari into the driveway behind her Kia, reporters and photographers rushed him, mics extended and flashbulbs popping. He pushed the car door open and climbed out, holding up his hand to keep them at a distance.

"Is Analisa Barbero your new girlfriend? Will you take her to L.A. with you? Is it serious between you?" several voices shouted.

Cole inhaled a deep breath, then blew it slowly out. "I promise I'll give you a statement later, but only if you leave right now. Analisa doesn't deserve your harassment." His jaw clenched, he waited.

"Where and when will you give us this statement?" a reporter asked.

"Tonight at the Augustus. Check with my publicist." He hoped. He'd have to call Teresa as soon as he finished here.

"It's a deal," one of the photographers said.

"Now, leave, all of you." Cole waved them back.

Arms folded, he stood next to his car until the news vans left. He swallowed around his suddenly dry throat. Getting rid of the paparazzi was the easy part. Now, he had to face Analisa.

He walked to her door feeling a target on his back from the stares of the neighbors he'd noticed peering at him from their windows. He knocked hard and waited. The vibration loosened some of the peeling paint on the door. No answer. He knocked again. This time, he heard voices. One, an older-sounding woman, said, "Ana, open the door. See what the man has to say. He sent away those reporters, didn't he?"

Then Analisa's husky tones. "It's his fault they were here in the first place."

He knocked again. "I can hear you. I know you're in there."

"Open the door or I will," said the other woman.

The door flew open. Analisa, dressed in her work uniform of black pants and white shirt, stood there like an avenging angel. Anger flashed from her red-rimmed eyes. She'd been crying.

Regret that he'd caused her pain squeezed his heart like a vise. "May I come in?" he asked from the other side of the screen door.

She narrowed her eyes, but stepped back to let him open the screen door and slide inside. She quickly closed both doors and faced him.

"Why are you here?" Her voice rose with agitation.

He raked fingers through his short hair.

"I see you got rid of the glasses and the brown contacts," she said. "I guess you think I'm stupid for not recognizing the famous movie star Cole Lassiter."

"No, I don't." This would be harder than he thought.

"Forgive my daughter's bad manners," a female voice said from behind Cole.

He whirled around to a middle-aged woman, petite and trim, with short curly hair and big brown eyes that mirrored Analisa's.

She stepped toward him, hand outstretched. "I'm Rosa Barbero, Analisa's mother."

Cole took her hand in his. Her gentleness and friendliness dissolved some of the tension in the room. "Cole Lassiter."

Smiling, she withdrew her hand. "I know who you are." She tilted her head to study him. "I like your hair better long and blond."

"Mother! Cole is not here on a social visit."

He turned back to Analisa.

"Why *are* you here?" she asked.

"To apologize."

She pinned him with a fierce glare and folded her arms across her chest. "So you think an apology will erase the hell you put me through? I lost my job because of you."

Her words hit him with the power of a fist in his gut. "What? Why?"

She moved away from the door, but kept her stance rigid. "Mr. Appleton didn't like the publicity I gave the hotel."

"How about some iced tea, Mr. Lassiter?" Rosa asked.

"Not now, Mom."

Cole smiled at Rosa. He needed the mother on his side. "I'd love some, Mrs. Barbero. Thanks."

She dimpled. "Call me Rosa."

"Only if you call me Cole."

"Mom, again, this isn't a social visit," Analisa said.

"Calm down, Ana. I'll get your iced tea, Cole. Please, have a seat."

"Thanks, but I prefer to stand."

When Rosa left the room, Cole met Analisa's gaze. "I'm truly sorry for what I put you through. I had no idea they'd find me or that you'd get fired. What can I do to make it good?"

Her eyes sparked brown-gold fire. He had the insane impulse to take her into his arms and kiss her senseless. That would get him a punch in the mouth.

"You lied to me, Cody, or Cole, or whatever your name is." She marched past him into the small living room and spun around to face him again. "A medical supplies salesman from Ohio? The youngest of six kids? You must have had a good laugh at my expense."

Hurt had replaced the anger in her eyes. Forget kissing her, he wanted to hold her and soothe her and make things right for her. "I started to tell you the truth last night, right before the paparazzi attacked us. I should have told you long before that."

"Yes, you should have."

Rosa entered the room carrying a large glass of iced tea and handed it to him. "I'll leave you both for now," she said, walking toward the stairs.

Cole took in the small room as he sipped his drink. With its worn-out sofa and non-matching chairs, the scratched coffee and end tables, he doubted even a set designer would use the furniture as props to depict a poor family. Despite the threadbare décor, the place was clean and tidy. Times were hard for Analisa and her mother, and he'd made things worse for them.

He placed his glass on a small table and faced Analisa. "Not everything I told you was a lie. I am from Ohio and I'm the youngest of six. My family is large and loving. We gather together every Christmas at one of our houses. My family keeps me grounded."

Her lips in a straight line, she tapped her foot. "And I'm

supposed to forgive you because not everything you told me was a lie?"

Her features softened, giving him hope.

"Why did you pretend to be someone you're not?" she asked.

When he moved closer, she backed away. He stopped. "I'm a jerk for lying to you. I hadn't meant to hurt you. I like you, Analisa. A lot. I enjoy being with you. You're beautiful and real. I don't see many unpretentious people in my line of work. I came to Vegas incognito to get away from the rat race in Hollywood." He released a bitter laugh. "Guess I wasn't so clever after all. Someone found out."

"You came here for your own selfish reasons with no thought for others. Because of you I have no job and I'll be forced to drop out of school." Her nostrils flared. "And you'll go back to Hollywood and your privileged life."

She pushed hair back from her face with a shaking hand. "We have no union at the Augustus, and Nevada is an 'at-will' state, which means an employer can fire an employee for any reason. I might have a case, but I can't afford a lawyer, and litigation could take years. Mr. Appleton is a powerful billionaire. I can't fight him. I need a job now."

Her eyes filled, and Cole stepped forward, ready to take her into his arms, then halted at her tense features.

"I don't know if anyone else will hire me," she said. "Vegas can be like a small town where everyone knows your business. Mr. Appleton carries a lot of weight here." She laughed, a bitter sound. "My business is splashed all over the tabloids."

He grabbed his drink and took a long swig as if he could wash away his guilt at what he'd done to this kind woman. "Let me see what I can do. Only two people knew I was here and staying at the hotel—the owners, Appleton and Gordon. I'll talk to them." He shook his head and set his glass down. "They wouldn't betray my trust, but someone spilled to the press. I'll get to the bottom of this, see if I can get your job back."

"I don't need any favors from you. I'm not sure I want to work there anymore, not after this." She tipped her head toward the door. "You need to leave."

"I'll make it up to you, Analisa. I promise."

"Done enough. Out."

CHAPTER SIX

Analisa slammed the door shut behind Cole and leaned against it, pressing a palm to her trembling stomach. Her dreams had turned to nightmares. She didn't see how she could continue at school. Maybe she could get a job at one of the dive bars. The last dive bar she'd worked at paid barely enough to put food on the table. She had her mom to support now, and medical bills that would take years to pay.

When Cole had mentioned Appleton, the image of Hailey Appleton staring at her and Cole with malice imprinted itself on Analisa's mind. Maybe Hailey knew about Cole staying at their hotel and leaked to the press. Analisa couldn't imagine why the hotel heiress would do such a thing.

A single tear slipped down Analisa's face. She'd really liked Cody Lamont, the gentle, funny guy who enhanced her day whenever he came into her bar. She didn't like Cole Lassiter, the liar who'd destroyed the life she'd built. Eight years ago, another liar had devastated her and shattered her heart. She'd been careful since then, but Cody Lamont had tempted her to open her heart again. She massaged her temple. She sure could pick them.

Her mother came slowly down the stairs. "Is he gone?"

Analisa nodded and rushed to help her. Cupping her mom's elbow, she led her into the living room and helped her sit on the old brown sofa, something they got years ago at a thrift store.

"You need to rest, Mom."

Rosa waved a hand. "I'm not an invalid." She sank onto the

cushions. "I think Cole truly feels sorry for what he did."

Analisa rolled her eyes. "Don't make excuses for him, Mom. What he did is reprehensible. He caused me to lose my job."

Rosa chuckled. "He's not as bad as you think. I saw the way he looked at you. He's a young guy who wanted to get to know a wonderful, smart woman."

"For God's sake, Mom, he's a liar." Analisa's old hurts flared up, constricting her chest. "Remember Brad."

"That was a long time ago, and Cole is not Brad. I told you Brad was a bad gamble, but you took a chance on him anyway."

"And I lost." Fighting for calmness, Analisa gathered her hair into a ponytail, then released it to trail over her shoulders. Her mom had warned her against Brad, but in love for the first time, Analisa had ignored her.

"I like Cole's movies," Rosa said. "And he's so handsome."

Analisa liked Cole Lassiter's movies too. She liked him as Cody. She couldn't deny his extraordinary looks.

She didn't like his lying. She couldn't forgive that.

<><><>

Cole's publicist had managed to score a meeting room at the hotel for his press conference that evening. Social media and the gossip shows speculated *ad nauseam* about the mysterious brunette Cole had been photographed kissing.

He had talked with Appleton about giving Analisa her job back, but Appleton had been adamant that his decision stood. Appleton had been cool to him, and Cole suspected there was more to Analisa's firing than the other man wanted to reveal.

With time before the press conference, Cole sat in front of the floor-to-ceiling windows in the penthouse nursing a glass of the hotel's famous lemonade. The Vegas Strip, in all its brash splendor, spread below like the panoramic lens of a camera. In the distance, the Stratosphere's needle thrust into a cloudless blue sky.

The Wynn's golf course popped in a sea of green against the brown-gray mountains on the horizon. The fountains of the Bellagio, out of his view, would spring forth in all their watery, musical brilliance this evening. To him, Vegas felt more real than L.A. Vegas didn't pretend to be anything other than what was—an adult playground where dreams were made and crushed.

What happens in Vegas stays in Vegas. He repeated the clever marketing tag to himself. What he'd done sure hadn't stayed here.

Damn, but he hated all the Hollywood bullshit. Didn't people have anything better to do than talk about his love life? He chuckled without mirth. What love life? His last serious relationship had ended badly a year ago. While living with Cole, Jennifer Brady had started an affair with the married director of the film she'd been shooting, a man thirty years her senior. Jennifer had fooled Cole. He'd thought her honest and real. Turned out, she hid her naked ambition better than most. She'd broken up the director's long-time marriage, and was now engaged to him. She'd also gotten the lead in an important new film, directed by her fiancé.

Cole tossed back the rest of his drink. Everyone had an angle.

Everyone except Analisa. Her goodness spoke to the part of his soul still untainted by the sharks in Hollywood. His parents and siblings would like her.

Cole jerked upright as a thought, like the proverbial lightbulb, went off in his head. He knew how to help Analisa, and maybe himself. If he could convince her. He glanced at the wall clock. He didn't have much time.

He grabbed his phone and called down to the garage for his car. With a hopeful spring in his movements, he slipped on his leather jacket against the March chill and left the penthouse.

He had a woman to win over.

Cole let out his breath at the quiet when he turned down Analisa's street. True to their word, the paparazzi had left the area. He tightened his hand on the gear-shift knob, hoping all would go well now so he'd have some big news for the press later. Mostly, he hoped his plan would help Analisa.

When he pulled into her driveway, he saw movement behind the front curtains. Busted! Anxiety clenched his stomach. He had a lot of convincing to do. First, she had to let him in.

As he exited his car, shouts from up the street drew his attention. Anger propelled him to run toward the noise. A group of young teens was throwing rocks at a black kitten. The poor creature was running in circles, trying to avoid the missiles.

"Stop it!" Cole shouted as he got close. He scooped up the

trembling kitten and held it against his chest. "It's okay," he crooned. "You're safe now."

He glared at the nearest kid, one with a rock ready to throw. "Drop the rock. Now," Cole said in the harsh tones he'd used as the superhero in his last action picture.

The kid dropped the rock. Cole's gaze canvassed the group, locking eyes with each boy. "Are you proud of yourselves? Hurting a defenseless little cat? Didn't your parents teach you to be kind to animals?"

"Someone dumped that cat off here coupla days ago, mister," one of the kids said. "My mom said not to feed it 'cause it would hang around. No one wants it here. We were just having fun."

"Yeah," said another. "It would have starved to death anyway."

"You would let a poor, helpless creature starve?" At Cole's glower, they moved back. "What kind of jerks are you?"

Rage coiled his insides. No wonder the world was in such a sad state with kids like this. Dismissing them with a look of disgust, he held the kitten close and strode toward Analisa's house. After several knocks, she opened the door.

Her beauty stole his breath. Her curling midnight hair cascaded past her shoulders. The yoga pants and top she wore hugged her lush curves. Her amazing eyes, shuttered and red-rimmed, tore a hole in his heart.

"What do you want?" Her voice and tight features communicated her distrust of him. Her eyes widened when she noticed the kitten he held. "What are you doing with a kitten?"

"I saved it from some thugs who were about to kill it. Can I come in?"

She opened the screen door, reached out, and took the kitten from him, hugging it to her. "The poor little thing." Turning away from the door, she motioned for Cole to enter.

Rosa pushed up from the sofa when she saw him. "Hello, Cole."

"Hello, Rosa. Good to see you again."

"Mom, look at this dear kitten. Cole said kids were trying to hurt it."

"Poor baby. Let me have it. I'll take it into the kitchen and give it some milk."

"May I sit?" Cole asked when Rosa left.

"Suit yourself," Analisa said.

He sat on the sofa, while she perched on the edge of one of the chairs that flanked it. Hands clasped on her lap, she stared, unblinking, at him. "What do you want?"

"Hear me out. Please. I talked to Appleton but I couldn't change his mind about your job. I've come up with something that might help us both."

Silent, she studied him with cool, gold-brown eyes.

Rubbing a hand over his hair, he swallowed. "I like you a lot. We get along well, or we did before all this happened."

At her continued silence, he said, "I think we should get married."

CHAPTER SEVEN

Analisa's brain refused to function. She'd imagined Cole Lassiter, hot movie star, world-class liar, had asked her to marry him.

She jumped up from her chair. "Are you crazy?" she managed when she found her voice. Keeping her voice low so her mom wouldn't hear, she said, "Why would I marry you? Why would you even suggest such a thing?"

He stood too, his deep blue gaze holding hers. "I've given this a lot of thought. It can work. My selfishness caused you to lose your job, a fact that will haunt me for a long time."

"Haunt you? It'll do a heck of a lot more to me. Maybe you should have been honest with me from the first."

Regret flashed across his face. "I should have been." His assessing gaze made a sweep of her poor excuse for furniture. "You work hard. I admire what you do, carrying work, school, and helping your mom. I don't mean to offend, but it's obvious you could use money."

Analisa bristled. "We don't want your charity. Mom and I might struggle financially, but we don't need a Hollywood actor to ride in on his white horse and rescue us."

He took a half-step closer. "You're one of the kindest women I've ever met. I trust you. I like being with you, and I think you like being with me. We can make this work. My plan can help both of us."

"Seriously? How does marrying me help you?"

"I'm tired of my strings being pulled like I'm some sort of

puppet. My publicist fixes me up with women I barely know to keep my name in the tabloids." He barked a brittle laugh. "After all, bad publicity is better than no publicity. I'm sick of getting beefcake roles, of being paraded around because of my looks. I'm lucky to have made it big in a soul-eating business, and I'm appreciative, but I worked hard to get where I am, and I want to be taken seriously. I'm a good actor."

"You're more than lucky. You're blessed. Most actors don't make a living at it. Most men would die to date the women you're paired with." Analisa frowned. "Your relationship with Jennifer Brady was a sham?" As soon as the words were out, she wanted to bite them back. She didn't care about his affairs with other women, and she didn't want him to think she did.

"My relationship with Jenn started out as a publicity stunt, but it developed into something more."

Analisa raised an eyebrow. "Until she ditched you."

He smiled, his first genuine smile since he'd gotten there. "Yeah, well, I'm over that, but it took a while."

"According to the tabloids and gossip sites, you got over her quickly."

"Another story planted by my publicist." He began to pace the small room, appearing deep in thought. Stopping, he turned to face Analisa again. "I want to live my life the way I see fit. If we marry, my publicist and the studio will stop pairing me with women I have nothing in common with. Maybe the tabloids and social media will leave me alone to focus on my acting career with better parts that have nothing to do with my looks. Hopefully I'll get a chance to move on."

"Move on?"

"I want to try my hand at directing. Until Hollywood sees me as more than a pretty boy, a playboy, a money machine, the powers that be won't give me a chance to prove I'm much more."

"So you marry me and they leave you alone?"

"That's the hope."

"What do I get out of this marriage?" What he offered could be called a business arrangement, and she hated to admit his so-called proposal intrigued her.

His eyes softened. "Do you owe medical bills for your mother?"

She nodded. "A lot."

He stopped in front of her until they were a whisper apart. His warm breath fanned her face. She held her ground.

"Here's my proposal," he said. "We stay married for one year. At the end of that year we divorce. I pay you five-hundred-thousand dollars when the divorce is final. Meanwhile, I pay your tuition to attend school full-time so you can graduate sooner, and I pay off your mom's medical bills. I hire the best physical therapist I can find to make home visits to treat your mother. I'll buy you a house in Vegas, in a secure neighborhood. When the year is up, you'll keep the house. With the right treatment, your mom will be better than she was before her accident, and she won't ever have to work again, unless she wants to. You'll earn your degree and you'll be debt-free. It's a win-win for everyone."

Analisa chewed her lip and glanced away to the thrift-store painting hanging over the sofa. The paint peeled in places on the frame, like her life, peeling away in front of her eyes. She had to be crazy to even consider Cole's offer.

"We'll sign a contract and make it legal," he said, drawing her attention. "You'd be surprised the number of marriages in some wealthy circles that are little more than business deals. I know people in Hollywood who have contract marriages, including one top actor who hides the fact he's gay by marriage to an accomplished woman." He shook his head. "Not something I agree with. I think a person should be true to himself, but my point is it's done more often than you think."

"I'm not in one of your wealthy circles, and I certainly don't know anyone in a contract marriage. This is the twenty-first century. No one makes marriages of convenience anymore."

She looked toward the kitchen, hoping her mom, busy with the kitten, couldn't hear them. A single parent since Analisa was three, Rosa had worked hard, holding down several jobs at once, to provide a home for them. Her mother didn't have a social life, didn't do anything for herself. Rosa deserved a decent house, topnotch treatment for her injury, a better life. Her mom was fifty years old. Once her rotator cuff problem was fixed, she'd go back to housekeeping, a job with no pension. She'd most likely work until she was seventy or older, if her health allowed. They had no savings. Cole offered them a house, something to build on, a way to dissolve some of the stress in their lives, and security. Still, it was a crazy idea.

Truth be told, Analisa was bone-weary from carrying the heavy loads of work, school, and caring for her mother.

When she turned back to Cole, his intense gaze pinned her as he waited for her answer. His radical proposal could work. She could give her mom freedom for the first time in her life. That freedom came with a price.

"I hate being hounded by the press, hate seeing my name in the tabloids and on the gossip sites," she said. "If I marry you, the paparazzi won't leave me alone. I've seen how you celebrities have no private lives. I don't want that. Can you guarantee me privacy?"

"I can't promise, but I'll do what I can to protect you. If we marry, we'll soon be old news and the gossipmongers will leave us alone. I hope."

"This will be a marriage in name only, right?" Analisa said. "Nothing physical. I won't be the star in your fantasy."

His gaze drifted to her mouth and back. The desire she saw reflected in his eyes upped her pulse a few notches. She licked her lips, remembering the kiss they'd shared. She could still feel his mouth on hers, his heat.

"The only way I'll agree to this is if it's a marriage in name only," she said.

He continued to stare at her, then visibly relaxed. "Agreed. I won't be around Vegas much anyway. I'll be on location in Prague soon, and I have obligations in Los Angeles. So is it a deal?"

"Deal."

He reached out his hand to shake hers. She hesitated, then gripped his hand firmly before releasing him.

His lips tilted in a sympathetic smile. "I'll have my lawyers write up a contract and I'll have my assistant start looking for a house in the area. I need your agreement on one more thing. I'm having a press conference in a few hours. I want to announce our pending marriage. Okay with you?"

The paparazzi already knew who she was. Her marriage to Cole would change her life, which hadn't been so wonderful anyway. She didn't have anything to lose.

She shrugged. "We might as well start this thing now."

He gripped her shoulders and pulled her closer. She inhaled his faint scent of soap.

"You won't regret this, Analisa. I promise. It'll work out." His gaze searched hers, and she had the feeling he wanted to say more. Then he released her and stepped back. "I'll call you later." He strode out.

She grabbed the chair back for support as the full impact of what she'd done shot through her with the force of a bullet.

Soon she would be Mrs. Cole Lassiter. Heaven help her.

CHAPTER EIGHT

Cole held up his hand, signaling the reporters for quiet. "I promised you an exclusive, but I can't talk if you keep shouting."

He waited for silence, then began speaking. "In a few days, I'll be getting married."

Pandemonium again. "Is it that bartender?" someone called out.

Cole clutched the edge of the podium, fighting his anger. "Her name is Analisa Barbero, and she's one of the kindest women I've ever met. She deserves your respect."

"Did you meet Ms. Barbero at the bar where she worked?" another asked.

Cole nodded. "We struck up a friendship that turned to love." This was one of his most important acting jobs ever, and he hoped, for Analisa's sake, the public would never learn the truth.

"Let me finish," Cole yelled above the shouting that had started again. All quieted as twenty pairs of eyes turned to him. "My fiancée and I request privacy. She's not used to the limelight and I don't want you bothering her."

"Where will you be married?" a reporter asked.

"Here in Vegas."

"Where in Vegas?" from another.

Cole laughed. "I'm not crazy enough to tell you."

"When is the wedding?"

"In a couple of days." Las Vegas had no waiting period for marriage licenses. He and Analisa would go to the marriage license bureau tomorrow. The contract would be ready for them to sign tomorrow also. His friend Marissa had offered her compound for the wedding. Even if the paparazzi found out the location, Marissa's place had more security than the White House.

The reporters yelled out more questions, but Cole shook his head and backed away from the podium.

Teresa, standing next to him, took his place. "We're done here," she said to the reporters.

Mumbling their disappointment, they filed out of the room. Cole headed for the door with Teresa. Hailey Appleton waited for them, her arms folded over her substantial chest, and her collagen-enhanced lips in a straight line.

"I'll catch up with you, Teresa," he said.

"Hey, Hailey." He and Hailey had dated for a short while a few years ago. Cole broke it off when he got tired of dealing with her temper tantrums. Too self-absorbed, too demanding, she sucked all the energy from him. They'd remained friends, or so he believed.

"You're marrying that little bartender?" Hailey said. "Slumming it, aren't you?"

The bitter vitriol coming from her made him jerk his head back. "Analisa is a wonderful, intelligent person. I won't let you talk about her like that."

"She worked for my father. He fired her. She's nothing."

Cole stepped closer. "Stop it, Hailey. I thought you were my friend."

"Friend?" Her icy green eyes softened and she wrapped her fingers around his forearm. "I've always wanted to be much more than that to you."

He freed himself from her grip. "You want what I can't give."

"That little Latina barkeep can?"

Of course. He should have realized it. He narrowed his eyes. "The only ones who knew I was here incognito were your father and Gordon. Your father told you, didn't he? You're the one who tipped off the paparazzi."

Her eyes hardened to emerald chips and she glared at him. "I wanted to embarrass you and that hussy, and scare her away. You were mine before she came along."

"Hailey, I was never yours. We only dated for a short time and that was a while ago." He chuckled. "Your little plan backfired, didn't it? I'm marrying Analisa." Leaning toward her, he said, "Leave me, and especially Analisa, alone." He pivoted on his heel and stalked away.

<><><>

Analisa hadn't been sure she ever wanted to marry, not trusting men after her father's abandonment and after Brad's betrayal. If she had thought about her wedding, it sure wouldn't be like this—marriage that was a business deal to a man she hardly knew. She wasn't in love with Cole so he couldn't shatter her heart. This contract marriage might work out for her.

She stood in front of a judge and next to her husband-to-be in the sprawling living room of the palatial mansion belonging to Marissa, a singer adored around the world. Luckily, the singer was out of town, or Rosa, who grinned like a kid on her first trip to Disneyland, would have swooned into a dead faint.

Cole's agent Brian and his publicist Teresa stood as witnesses, while Marissa's butler and Rosa watched. Cole had assured her that his agent and publicist didn't know about their marriage agreement. Analisa hadn't told her mom about it either. Thankfully, Rosa hadn't overheard Analisa and Cole when he'd first proposed the contract idea. Rosa, despite her husband's desertion, still believed in love and happy-ever-after. She thought Analisa and Cole had fallen madly in love at first sight. Guilt she hadn't told her mother the truth nagged at Analisa. Someday, probably after they divorced, she'd tell her. Not now, when Analisa had so much else to deal with.

After a short ceremony, the judge pronounced them husband and wife. Analisa twisted the plain gold band Cole had slipped on her finger. A gold band symbolized everlasting love, but for her, it meant a business arrangement. Fear and anxiety clogged her throat.

While the butler showed the judge out, Teresa and Brian helped themselves to drinks behind the bar. Cole turned to Analisa. "I'd like to take you and Rosa to lunch. I made reservations at the Orchid." He named one of Vegas' top restaurants.

"I've always wanted to go there," Rosa said.

Analisa pressed a hand to her stomach. "Mom, we'll go there sometime. I promise. But not yet. I want to go home." She hadn't eaten anything all day. Now, at two in the afternoon, her stomach churned, making her nauseous. Hungry as she was, she couldn't bear the thought of facing the paparazzi, who would find them when they went anywhere in Las Vegas.

Her mother smiled despite the disappointment that flashed over her features. "I understand, Ana. We will go some other time."

Cole's smile included both women. "I'll take you there someday. It's probably best we stay out of the public eye for a time." He touched Analisa's arm. "Paparazzi will be camped out at your place. I need to get back to L.A. right away. I've arranged for you and Rosa to stay in my suite at the Augustus. The hotel's security will protect you. You can order whatever you want from room service."

Frowning, Rosa looked from Cole to Analisa. "You're newlyweds, and Cole has to go away? What about a honeymoon?"

"I have contractual obligations with the studio," Cole said. "Analisa and I will have our honeymoon a little later."

Bristling that he'd made the decision about where they'd stay without consulting her, and now promising her mom they'd have a honeymoon, Analisa squared her shoulders, ready to protest. Realizing Cole was right about the house, she relaxed her stance. She and her mom couldn't go back there, not ever. As for a honeymoon, Cole could dream on. It would never happen.

"What about the kitten?" Rosa said. "We can't leave her alone."

Cole smiled, that devastatingly sexy smile that made Analisa's knees turn to jelly despite her unease.

"I had the kitten taken to the suite earlier," Cole said. "We've got food and a litterbox for her. She's waiting for you now."

Rosa's lips tilted in a smile. "Cole, you think of everything. Thank you."

Cole had completely charmed her mother.

He glanced at Analisa. "I've had my people out looking for a house for you and Rosa. They found one I think will be perfect. We settle in a few days, and you can move in as soon as it's ready. If you don't like it, we'll find another place."

"You certainly do think of everything." Analisa couldn't keep the sarcasm from her voice. "Maybe you could have asked me what type house I'd like." She wanted to swallow her words. Cole was paying for the house, for everything for the next year. She'd always taken care of herself. Her independence warred with her new normal.

His eyes softened. "I want you to be comfortable and happy, Analisa. Rosa too. I didn't want to argue the limitations you might have placed on me. This will all work out. Don't worry."

"I'm not worried," she lied.

CHAPTER NINE

Two weeks later, Rosa, Analisa, and the black kitten moved into the rambling house in one of the city's most elite gated neighborhoods. Rosa and Analisa took only their clothes and a few personal items, including family photos. Saddened and embarrassed at their meager belongings, trepidation rode with Analisa in the stretch limo taking them to the new house.

Cole's personal assistant, a middle-aged woman named Mary, coordinated the move. Analisa had liked the no-nonsense Mary from the first. Seated in the back of the luxurious car, Rosa and Mary chatted like old friends. Analisa stroked the kitten, asleep on her lap, and tried to relax. She'd never seen her mom smile so much. That almost made her rash decision bearable. She'd always been a person who thought things out, but she'd rushed into this marriage on impulse. She crossed her fingers, hoping she hadn't made a huge mistake.

They pulled up to the community where the house was located. The limo driver rolled down his window and handed a card to the guard on duty. The gates slowly opened and the car slid through. After a few turns, the driver pulled into a circular drive fronting a stone and stucco two-story house. In the center of the circle, water spouted from a fountain adorned with marble Ancient Roman-style nymphs.

Rosa put a hand to her face. "Oh, my."

Analisa widened her eyes. A fountain? Surely, she was dreaming and would soon awaken.

"I hope you like the house," Mary said.

"What's not to like?" Rosa said.

The limo driver opened the passenger door and the three women slid out. Analisa held the kitten to her chest. Like a baby, the tiny cat settled down and closed its eyes again.

Mary smiled at Analisa and Rosa. "The house came furnished, but Cole will buy new furniture if you prefer."

As they walked toward the marble steps, the wooden double doors opened and a tall, distinguished-looking sixtyish man dressed in a suit stood there. He smiled as they approached. "Hello, my name is Bennett. Welcome." He spoke with a British accent that reminded Analisa of the aristocratic Crawley family in the TV series *Downton Abbey*.

"Bennett takes care of Cole's household in Malibu, and now here," Mary said. "He's also Cole's chef."

Analisa swallowed. They had a chef? A British one at that. Remembering her manners, she smiled and held out her hand to shake his. "Hello, Bennett, I'm Analisa Bar...Lassiter, and this is my mother, Rosa Barbero."

He bowed slightly, his gaze lingering on Rosa. "Pleased to meet you both, Mrs. Lassiter and Mrs. Barbero."

"Call me Rosa, please," her mom said.

"Call me Analisa." They'd never had servants, and Analisa couldn't live in a house where everyone was so formal. She didn't know if she could deal with servants either.

Bennett, looking every bit the royal, said, "It wouldn't be seemly for me to call you by your given names."

"Please, Bennett, don't stand on formality," Analisa said.

"I will call you by your given names in private, but in front of others, I cannot."

"Fair enough," Analisa said.

Bennett nodded and opened the doors wider so they could enter, then stepped inside and closed the doors. "Mary will show you around. Please excuse me." He headed to the back of the house.

Mary led them into a spacious, open living room which could have held their entire rental townhouse. Pale wood floors gleamed in the sunlight that streamed through the Paladin-style windows. Most houses in Vegas had either tile flooring or carpets as wood tended to buckle in the extreme heat. Many high-end houses, where the owners could afford the astronomical cooling bills, had hardwood floors.

Furnished with a beige leather sectional and chairs, and a free-standing fireplace, the living room could have graced the pages of *House and Gardens* magazine. The rooms needed pops of color Analisa thought as Mary took them through the downstairs that included a formal dining room with a crystal chandelier hanging above a white glass table. Comfortable-looking chairs covered in white leather flanked the table.

Two smaller crystal chandeliers hung over the white granite island in a kitchen the size of the Capri Bar & Grille. A wall of floor-to-ceiling windows opened to a deck and framed an Olympic-sized pool, the blue-green water shimmering in the sunlight.

"Ana, think of all the meals I can cook in this kitchen," Rosa said, her delighted gaze scanning the vast room.

"Bennett does all the cooking," Mary said. "You won't have to cook or clean. We have a cleaning staff, and a gardening staff."

Rosa shook her head. "Not cook? What will I do all day? I love to cook. I will take care of the meals."

"Are you sure, Mom?" Analisa asked.

"Of course."

When her mother got that "do what I say or else" look, Analisa knew not to argue. She turned to Mary. "I guess Bennett won't have to do any cooking."

Mary smiled. "I'm sure if that's what you want, Cole will make it happen. Bennett's possessive about his kitchen, but he is Cole's employee. Let me show you the rest of the house."

<> <> <>

Three weeks. It had been three weeks since Cole had seen his wife. Analisa Barbero Lassiter. Funny how he'd started thinking of her as his wife. He barely knew her, but he missed her. He called her almost every day. Just hearing her voice helped calm him after a brutal day of filming. Although their conversations were stilted, he liked to believe she'd begun to warm toward him.

Like a movie monster, regret stomped on his pleasant thoughts as he strode to his car in the studio lot. As Cody

Lamont, he and Analisa had had a promising relationship, friends with a lot in common. And maybe on their way to being more than friends. He got hot every time he thought about the kiss they'd shared before they'd been so rudely interrupted by the photographers.

Damn Hailey! Before the paparazzi upset Analisa's world, he'd been ready to tell her the truth, to tell her how much he liked her and that he wanted to see her again, to know her better. Then the whole debacle with the paparazzi destroyed his plans. He decided not to tell Analisa that Hailey had tipped off the press. It would only upset Analisa, and she had enough on her plate.

Waving to the guard, he pulled away from the studio and adjusted his sunglasses against the glare, his thoughts swirling with plans to let Analisa know the real Cole Lassiter, the kid who grew up in Ohio with a family straight out of *Leave It to Beaver*. He needed Analisa's friendship and approval to combat fame's corruption.

He headed to the freeway and his house in Malibu. Filming had been put on hold a few days while the leading lady got over her bout of the flu. He'd use the time to go to Las Vegas to see his wife.

CHAPTER TEN

Analisa pulled into the driveway of the new Vegas house after her classes. When she saw Cole's Ferrari parked there, her pulse double-timed, and she sat in the car for a while to compose herself.

She entered the house to laughter coming from the kitchen. Setting her books and jacket on a chair, she headed toward the sound. Amazement halted her steps in the doorway.

Her mom and Cole sat together at the center island, like two old friends enjoying each other's company. Rosa drank from a glass of wine in front of her, and Cole dipped his spoon into his soup bowl. The chicken tortilla soup Rosa had made earlier, Analisa guessed.

Her mother noticed her and gestured toward Cole. "Ana, look who's here."

Cole turned around, and his gaze locked with Analisa's. He slid off his stool and closed the distance between them, his eyes glinting with a light that incited an answering spark in her.

"Analisa. I've missed you." With gentle fingers, he brushed hair back from her face. The tenderness of his touch made her heart flutter.

Cole was an actor. The attention he showed her could be an act for Rosa's benefit.

He bent and kissed Analisa, gently at first. Then his lips firmed over hers, taking on a hunger and urgency that lit her insides. She tried to remain stiff in his arms, but his kiss melted her resistance and she pressed against him, wrapping her arms around his waist.

When they pulled apart, Cole's expression of wonder shot adrenaline through her veins. His kiss had been no act.

Rosa coughed, getting their attention. "I'm going to my room and leave you newlyweds alone." She stood and reached down to scoop up the mewling kitten twining around her ankles. With a sly smile, Rosa waved goodbye and left.

Cole gave Analisa his sexy grin that showed even white teeth. "Would you like some of this delicious soup? Your mom's a great cook."

"No, thanks. I had some before I left for school, and I'm not hungry. Mom's chicken tortilla soup is my favorite though."

He took her hand and led her to the counter. "Keep me company while I finish my bowl."

Analisa slid onto the stool next to him. He picked up the bottle of wine and a crystal glass from the counter and held them out to her. At her nod, he poured her some wine.

"House okay?" he asked. "Change anything you don't like. If you want different furniture, Mary will help."

"This house is a dream," Analisa said. "Mom has already taken over the kitchen." She shook her head. "To the dismay of Bennett."

"Bennett trained with one of the top chefs in the world, and he helped design the kitchen in my Malibu place. I hope he and Rosa can come to some sort of compromise. I don't want to have to choose between them."

"Me neither, but Mom is stubborn."

"Beneath Bennett's aristocratic bearing, he has a spine of steel." Cole grinned. "I see a fight brewing."

"God, I hope not." Noticing Cole's empty bottle of beer, she jumped up and went to the refrigerator for another. She placed it in front of him, and was rewarded with one of his smiles.

"Guess being a bartender never quite leaves me," she said with a shrug.

He patted her stool for her to sit again. "How have you been, Analisa?"

The way he said her name, like a caress, unfurled a ribbon of heat in her stomach. She understood why so many women swooned over Cole Lassiter. She took a sip of the wine, trying unsuccessfully to cool her rising libido. "I've been busy with school, which is almost over for the year. I'm not sure what I'll do this summer."

"Come to Malibu when school's out. I'd like that."

She ran her finger over the rim of her glass. Summer at the beach with Cole. The thought conjured up erotic images of making love in the moonlight with the swell of the nearby ocean as music. Warmth flooded her. She should refuse his offer. "I'll think about it."

"You and your mom could use a break. There's nothing like the ocean to relax you."

"We'll see. How long do you plan on staying here now?" Her emotional side wanted him to stay for a long time, but her rational side knew it would be best for her self-preservation if she didn't spend much time with him. She wrapped her fingers around the stem of her glass, fighting her warring factions.

His eyes teased. "Trying to get rid of me?"

"Of course not." The heat that spread over her face told her she blushed.

Chuckling, he went back to his soup. Finished with it, he pushed the bowl away. "I'll be here a few days. We had to stop filming while Lois Flynn recovers from the flu."

"That's too bad about Lois Flynn. She's one of my favorite actors. Do you like her?"

He nodded. "Very much. She's good people. There's a reason she's called 'America's Sweetheart.'"

"Have you ever dated her?" The words slipped out.

"Her husband wouldn't approve if I put any moves on her."

Analisa smiled, releasing the surprising tension that had risen at the thought of Cole and Lois Flynn together.

Cole lifted his beer to his mouth and studied Analisa. He took a swig and set down the bottle. "Shooting is about to wrap up in L.A. We finish filming in Prague."

"Prague? For how long?" Although Cole hadn't come around since the wedding, knowing he was a short plane ride away in Los Angeles had somehow comforted her.

"A few weeks, give or take." His blue gaze locked with hers. "I don't want to be away too long. I hope to convince the director to shoot my scenes first so I can be out of there and back to you."

He sounded sincere. Years ago, she'd been with someone who'd put on a good act of being a man in love. She wouldn't fall for that again. "Cole, you can drop the pretense of being the doting husband. There's no one else here. We have a contract that benefits us both, but don't pretend you miss me when we're apart."

"I'm not pretending." At her narrow-eyed look, he held up a hand. "Okay. Enough said."

He began peeling the label from his bottle, not looking at her. "Maybe you could come with me to Prague. Is your passport up-to-date?"

"I don't have a passport. Never had need for one." Disappointment and relief coalesced in her. Disappointment she couldn't go with him, and relief she couldn't. Time with Cole in a foreign country would be too much for her already shaky willpower. "We don't have to go to a foreign country to convince others our marriage is real."

He raised his gaze to hers. "We don't, but we like each other, so why not spend time together?"

She plunked her glass onto the counter. "We liked each other before I knew who you were. I get a lot out of this contract, which I agreed to mostly to help my mom. I can't forget you lied to me and caused me to lose a job I loved."

<><><>

Regret stabbed Cole in the gut. "I was a selfish jerk to lie to you," he said. "We were on our way to being friends and I blew it. I hope you can give me another chance to be your friend. You're doing me a favor with this contract. I'd like to take you places you've never had the chance to go. I'll have Mary move on expediting a passport for you. Then you can go with me another time we film on location. Will you do that?"

"I've never been on a movie set. I'll think about it."

He shifted on his stool, anxious to change the subject and see her smile. "Did you name the kitten yet?"

Analisa jerked her head up and frowned. "Blackie."

"Blackie? You can do better than that."

"What would you name her?"

"Something strong." He snapped his fingers. "I've got it! Killer."

"Killer? She's a sweet girl."

"Why not? It's irony. A killer name for a gentle cat."

Analisa rolled her eyes. "Another thing for me to think about."

"Now that we've settled that important issue, I need to go over some things before I head back to L.A. and then Prague. Strictly business stuff."

"Okay."

He poured the remaining small amount of wine into her glass, then grabbed his half-empty beer bottle. "Let's go into the living room."

They sat at each end of the leather sectional. Analisa set her wine glass on the tiled coffee table and toed off her shoes, sensible, plain flats, and snuggled into a corner of the sectional. She looked relaxed. That was a start.

Cole glanced from her shoes to her face. "You can buy yourself new clothes and shoes, and anything else you want. Mary gave you the credit card, but she said it hasn't been used yet."

"I don't want to take anything more from you than what's in our agreement."

"Damn it, Analisa." He shook his head. "Sorry. Let me do things for you. The card is yours. I want to do this for you and your mother."

"We're fine."

"I like that you're independent, but don't be too resistant. If you won't buy anything for yourself, take your mom on a shopping spree. I bet Rosa will like it."

Analisa grabbed her glass and finished off her wine before meeting his gaze again. "Mom is having a ball here, and that makes me happy. She's worked hard most of her life. I'll use the card for her. I can take care of myself."

He took a long draught of beer, plunked the bottle down, and leaned forward with his hands on his knees. "This isn't a one-sided deal between us. I may need you more than you need me. It gives me pleasure to help you and Rosa. You've got a responsible head on your shoulders."

"How can you need me more?"

"Since we married, the tabloids don't print as many bogus

stories about me, and most of the paparazzi have moved on to more interesting celebrities, although they still follow me around Los Angeles. I told my agent now that I'm married, he has to find me more serious roles, and to reject anything that has me taking my shirt off. My publicist doesn't try to fix me up with women interested only in furthering their careers through me. I love acting, but I hate all the phoniness and bullshit that comes with it." He waved a hand at the room. "Enjoy yourself. I don't believe any of this will corrupt you and change you from the good person you are."

He slid back in his seat and crossed his legs at the ankles. "If you need anything while I'm away, call Mary. You have my cell number. Call me any time of the day or night." When she remained silent, he said, "Call me just to talk. I'd like that."

Analisa nodded. "We'll be in good hands with Mary and Bennett."

Not the response he wanted. He'd hoped she'd agree to call him. It would take time for her to realize they could be friends. He was a patient man.

Cole sat straighter, effecting a more businesslike demeanor. "Bennett will take care of the house. He handles any problems with the cleaning staff and the grounds people."

"Got it." Analisa's gaze spanned the room and she frowned. "We need some color here. It's too sterile."

"I have a florist on retainer. He can supply fresh flowers every week, or more. Tell Bennett what you want and he'll call him."

"Okay."

Their eyes met and held. The atmosphere in the room became charged, thick with sensual tension. He wanted to pull her into his arms and kiss her senseless.

As if she read his thoughts, she stood. "Is that all? Anything else?"

"Nope. We're good. I'll be here a few days so if I think of anything, I'll let you know."

"I'd better go to my room. I have studying to do." She turned, then stopped and faced him. "I'm in the master suite. Is that okay? Where will you sleep? Bennett and Mom have rooms on the first floor so they won't know we're not sharing a room." Her eyes widened. "What will the cleaning staff think when they see we're in separate rooms?"

He stood and strode to her. Running his palms down her arms, he drew her close. "I'd prefer to share a room with you." When she stiffened, he said, "But that won't happen. I had Bennett put my things in the room next to yours. Don't worry about him or the cleaning crew. I hired the best. They're discreet."

They stared at each other for long minutes. She licked her lips. His gaze traveled to her mouth. Her full lips parted, begging for his kiss.

"Analisa," he whispered in a thick voice.

She swayed toward him.

Good sense overrode his carnal desires. He wanted to be her friend, not scare her away. He stepped back. "You'd better go before we do something we'll both regret."

She turned and marched out of the room.

CHAPTER ELEVEN

Analisa stretched out on the chaise lounge by the pool and lifted her face to the sun. After a large breakfast of scrambled eggs, ham, toast, and coffee, prepared by Bennett over Rosa's objections, Analisa felt lazy, and she needed the rest.

She'd had an uneasy night, dominated by erotic dreams of Cole. Knowing he slept in the next room only made her edgier. Her desire for him grew every day. She was a healthy, red-blooded woman and he was a red-blooded, alluring man. They were married. They could make love. She'd seen the desire in his eyes when he looked at her, but she'd felt something more in his kisses, an underlying tenderness that pulsed hope and need through her, and also fear. She should be relieved he'd rejected her last night, but instead she felt...deprived. If they made love, she could fall for him, deeply. She'd had her heart broken once. Once was enough.

Although wearing sunglasses, she put up a hand to shade herself from the relentless sun, her thoughts focused on Cole. The more she got to know him, the more she saw glimpses of Cody, the warm-hearted guy she'd been drawn to from the beginning. Liking Cole could be more dangerous to her heart than desiring him. She hadn't seen him all morning, and she assumed he still slept.

Needing to cool off from the burning sun and her own burning needs, she stood and whipped off her sunglasses. Dropping them on a table, she adjusted her bikini, then dove into the pool. She swam the length of it twice, enjoying the cool slide

51

of the water on her overheated body.

Tired from the exercise, she floated on her back, eyes closed, cradled by the gentle hold of the water. A splash behind her made her flounder and swallow water. Coughing, she stood and pushed her hair back. And came face-to-face with Cole.

He gripped her upper arms, steadying her. "I'm sorry," he said. "I didn't mean to startle you."

"What are you doing here?" she sputtered.

"Swimming. How about you?"

"You know what I mean."

Laughing, he held up his hands. "The pool's big enough to share."

"You scared me." *And you look too damn good.* Not fair. Muscles flexed on his bronzed, sculpted chest, glistening with droplets of water. Below the surface of the clear water, she could see his swim trunks riding low on his slim hips, and his long, perfectly formed legs. The cool water couldn't flush away the flaming heat that spread through her body.

"I saw you from my bedroom window and had to join you," he said. "How about a race from one end to the other? I could use the exercise."

"Race?"

"Sure. I warn you, I'm a fast swimmer."

"Bet I'll beat you."

His mouth tipped in a smile. "What will you bet?" At her silence, he said, "If I win, you have to kiss me. If you win, no kissing." He bent to whisper in her ear. "Unless you want to kiss me."

She lifted her chin. "Smug, huh? I'll win, and there will be no kissing."

"You're on."

Analisa cut through the water as fast as she could, but Cole, stronger, with longer legs, beat her. With a self-satisfied grin, he waited for her at the other end, arms folded across his impressive chest, and his back against the side of the pool.

"Okay, you're fast," she said. "So what?"

His eyes darkened and he reached for her. "I'm cashing in on my bet."

His nearly naked wet body molded to her as his lips

descended on hers. Her breasts strained against the small bikini top, wanting release. She drank in his warm, spicy scent mingled with the chlorine of the pool. Cole's lips coaxed and teased, urging her to give more. When he sucked her lower lip, she moaned and curled her arms around his neck.

Cole left her mouth to trail sizzling kisses down her throat. Analisa clung to him, wrapping one leg around his. His erection, hard and hot, pressed against her. When he kissed the tops of her breasts, she uttered tiny cries she barely recognized as her own.

He pulled away and looked at her. At the yearning in his eyes, she gripped his shoulders, afraid her legs wouldn't hold her.

"Cole," she managed.

Voices from inside the house snapped her to reality. She stepped back.

"My mom and Bennett are in the house. What if they see us?" At least they were in a gated community with lots of shrubbery, which kept away the paparazzi.

"We're married."

She shook her head. "A contract marriage. What was I thinking?"

"Neither of us was thinking."

"I need to go."

Cole pulled her closer and brushed his knuckles along her face. The tenderness shining from his eyes drenched her with longing.

"Spend the day with me," he said. "Let's do something fun."

When she hesitated, he said, "I promise no kisses. Just two friends enjoying the day together. What do you think?"

She should refuse, should keep to the terms of their business agreement. "Okay," she found herself saying.

"Great. How do you feel about Hoover Dam?"

"I've been there a couple of times."

He smiled that lazy grin that made butterflies zing in her stomach.

"But you've never seen it with me," he said.

She laughed. "True."

"Let's get out of here and get dressed. We've got a date."

When she narrowed her eyes, he said, "No date. Friends

only."

CHAPTER TWELVE

Analisa clutched Cole's hand as the elevator descended five-hundred-thirty feet through the rock wall of Black Canyon at Hoover Dam. She and Cole were pressed into the back behind a class of middle-schoolers. Elevators always unleashed a trace of claustrophobia in her, and this seventy-second ride into the bowels of the Earth made her especially queasy.

Cole looked down at her and smiled. "Almost over."

She relaxed her shoulders as the elevator came to a stop and they exited into a construction tunnel built in the 1930's. The tunnel led to a viewing platform atop one of the four pipes that transported nearly ninety thousand gallons of water a second from Lake Mead to the generators. Despite her resolve to keep a firm rein on her emotions where Cole was concerned, being here with him made her heart pound with the beat of the generators and her happiness surge like the water gushing through the pipes.

She'd let down her guard with Brad and bore the humiliation that so many others knew of her naiveté and his betrayal. She would not allow that to happen again.

She slid a glance at Cole. Wearing a baseball cap pulled low, and with a few days' growth of golden stubble on his chin, he could pass for any ordinary tourist. Only he wasn't so ordinary. His natural charisma drew looks from those around him. Some of the kids recognized him. A group of pre-teen girls giggled to each other as they stared at Cole. A few pulled out their phones to take his picture. He seemed oblivious to the attention. Analisa figured he'd learned to tune it out.

He wrapped his arm around her waist and pulled her closer. "Having fun?"

"I'm glad we came."

"Stick with me, kid, and I'll show you a good time," he said in a Humphrey Bogart voice.

A laugh escaped her. Several others on the tour turned to frown at them.

After the tour, they walked over the O'Callaghan-Tillman Bridge to the Arizona side, stopping midway to admire the bluish-green Colorado River churning almost one-thousand feet below. Unlike the Colorado, its wild nature controlled, she worried she couldn't harness her growing feelings for Cole.

She would count this day as one of the best of her life. Cole gave a vibrancy to everything around them. No matter what happened later, they'd always have Hoover Dam. She smiled, thinking of Bogart, Ingrid Bergman, and Casablanca.

"What are you smiling about?" Cole asked.

"Nothing. Just enjoying the warm weather and sunshine."

"And the company, I hope."

"Maybe the company," she teased.

"I'll pretend you didn't say that. You hungry?"

"Starving."

"There's a little place in Boulder City where we can get a burger and a beer."

"Let's go."

They had thick burgers, washed down with glasses of stout ale from a quirky little restaurant called Hoover Dam Brewing Company.

Their meal over, Cole said, "We need to walk off that food. Do you want to check out the antique shops?"

"I'm not so much into antiquing as I am into thrift stores."

He took her hand as they left the restaurant, and she didn't draw away. She would imagine Cole was a regular guy, and her for-real husband. She looked up at him as they strolled. His strong profile and firm chin showed a man confident and at peace with himself. His big hand in hers felt protective, not that she needed protection, but she liked knowing someone had her back. Cole had caused her to lose her job, just as Brad did, she reminded herself. Unlike Brad, Cole always treated her with respect and kindness.

They walked in and out of the many antique shops spread through the small town of Boulder City. At one shop that specialized in hats, Cole plucked a straw bonnet off a counter and plopped it on Analisa's head.

He tilted his head and studied her, a glimmer in his blue eyes. "I'd say you'd make a pretty little woman for my next Western."

She curtsied. "Why, thank you, sir. Your John Wayne imitation needs work."

"You really know how to hurt a guy."

Laughing, they left the shop and entered one more elegant than the others. The antiques were of a higher value, with cases stocked with estate jewelry.

Cole drew her to one of the cases displaying rings. "Which one do you like?"

Analisa shook her head. "You don't have to buy me anything."

"I'll pick one for you." He studied the rings while she hung back.

She didn't want to have anything that would remind her of him. A special gift from him would make their parting much harder.

"Can I see that amethyst, please?" he said to the clerk.

The young woman pulled out a ring with a pear-shaped gem surrounded by diamonds. Analisa gasped at the beauty of the amethyst that had to be two carets.

Cole presented it to her. "Try it on, please, Analisa."

The sincerity and pleading in his eyes were her undoing. She held out her right hand and he slipped the ring on her third finger. It fit perfectly. She turned her hand, admiring the clarity of the purple stone and the way the fading sunlight illuminated the facets of the jewel.

"It's exquisite, Cole. Amethyst is my birthstone."

"I know."

"How?"

"You put your birthdate on the marriage license." He turned back to the clerk. "I'll take it."

"No, you can't do that," Analisa said.

Cole touched her chin with his fingers until their gazes met.

"Let me do this one thing for you. It will make me happy."

Unable to speak, she nodded. Maybe Cody hadn't been an act, but the real Cole.

<><><>

On the drive home, Cole glanced over at Analisa seated next to him in the car. She rested her head on the back of the seat, her eyes closed. Today had been one of the most memorable of his life. He'd forgotten how it felt to be with a "real" person and not one of the phony Hollywood types he'd gotten used to.

His attention on the road, contentment stole over him. He'd been to Hoover Dam a half-dozen times, and had filmed a movie there once. Yet, today, touring the monument with Analisa, made everything bright, new, and exciting.

At the thought he might be falling in love with her, a small kernel of fear opened in him. He'd been in love once, with his high school sweetheart, but he'd been young and full of himself, focused on making his way to Hollywood and the movies. He'd broken that woman's heart, and while things worked out for her, he still carried guilt. He'd felt something close to love with Jennifer Brady, and when she'd cheated on him, she'd wounded his ego more than his heart. He wasn't good at love.

He didn't want to break another woman's heart and he didn't want to have his own broken. He liked Analisa a lot and hoped they could become friends. When they divorced, he wanted them each to walk away with no regrets and no hard feelings.

He slid a quick glance Analisa's way. The more time he spent with her, the more his feelings for her grew.

That could be dangerous for them both.

CHAPTER THIRTEEN

Analisa walked out of the college building with a spring to her step. She stopped to breathe in the early May air scented with flowers from the greenery surrounding the building. Exhaust fumes from the nearby highway mixed with the perfume of the flowers, but she didn't care. Nothing could destroy her carefree mood tonight. The school year was over, and in the fall, she'd begin classes full-time. Next year she'd graduate and hopefully find a job teaching.

At times she missed her bartending job, missed the customers, and most of all her friends at the Augustus. That job and that life were in the past, but her friends would always be there for her.

It had been two weeks since the day she spent with Cole at Hoover Dam. The day after, he'd gone back to L.A., then Prague. He called her whenever he had a break in filming. He didn't know yet when he'd come home. Her mind cautioned her to be careful. Resolved she would not fall in love with Cole, she would be content with the time they spent together as friends.

Home, Analisa changed into yoga pants and a top, appreciating the quietness of the house, with Rosa and Bennett each in their rooms. She sat at the kitchen island, a cup of hot tea in front of her, and turned on the TV. Using the remote, she flipped through channels. When she saw Cole's picture come up, she stopped and turned up the volume. *The Tattle*, a gossip show, filled the screen with a shot of Cole laughing with Lois Flynn. The sexy actress had her hand on Cole's arm.

Like a movie in slow motion, time seemed to crawl. Analisa took a comforting sip of the tea, drew a deep breath, and stared at the TV. The show's host, with a hint of snark in her voice, said, "Lois Flynn and Cole Lassiter sharing an intimate moment in Prague, where they're shooting a movie. Wonder what their spouses have to say about this."

Analisa's life had become fodder for the rumor mills. She stared straight ahead, her breath catching, her mind whirling with jumbled thoughts that provoked a headache.

Cole had told her he and Flynn were friends. Maybe he'd lied. He was a skilled performer. His "I'm an ordinary guy from Ohio" could be an act to suck Analisa into his orbit. She too played a part, that of a loving wife, in this real-life drama, she reminded herself. She closed her eyes and rubbed her forehead. They might have a contract marriage, but she would not allow Cole to disrespect her in front of the world.

But this was a show devoted to gossip. It lived on lies. She would not believe it of Cole. She would give him the benefit of the doubt. The more she knew him, the more she recognized his genuineness, like the heroes he played in the movies.

Analisa understood a little more of what Cole must go through constantly, with others trying to bring him down, to undermine him. A private person, she'd hate to live that way for long.

She hit the remote and turned off the TV.

<><><>

"I want to live here. This place is like a five-star hotel," Patti said. She sat on the upholstered sofa in the media room, a glass of white wine in one hand, and the other hand dipping into one of the bowls of popcorn set on the teak wood coffee table in front of them.

A few days after seeing the disturbing segment about Cole and Lois Flynn on the gossip show, Analisa had invited her friends over to celebrate the end of her school year. She also needed them to take her mind off Cole, how much she missed him, and how deeply the gossip had upset her.

After touring the sprawling house, and ohhing and ahhing over everything, the group enjoyed a meal of Rosa's chicken empanadas. Now, the women, including Rosa, sat in front of the large-screen TV to watch two of Cole's movies. It had been Analisa's friends' idea to watch them.

She didn't want to miss Cole, but she did, and she feared seeing him on screen would make her miss him more. She hadn't heard from him since seeing the gossip show and was glad. If they talked on the phone, her voice might give away her anger and concern.

"Let me live here and I'll cook for you," Patti said. "You don't even have to pay me."

"I can clean for you. You won't have to pay me either," Laney said between sips of wine.

"Ohh, and I'll do the laundry," Amanda chimed in.

Analisa laughed and waved a hand to silence them. "I'd love to have you all live here, but we've got the cleaning and laundry covered. Bennett is a trained chef, although Mom prefers to do the cooking."

"Darn right," Rosa said. "That stuffy Englishman doesn't make real food."

"Mom, let it go. Bennett is an excellent cook, as are you."

"Excuse me," Patti said in a bad imitation of an upper crust accent. "We didn't realize you already have staff."

Analisa stuck her tongue out at Patti, provoking a laugh from her. "I don't mean it that way," Analisa said with a chuckle. "Let's watch the movies."

The second show ended to silence in the room. The women dabbed tears from their eyes, their reaction to the movie, a spy thriller with a poignant love story. The fast-paced story had showcased Cole's talents, and also his looks. Analisa understood his frustration with his roles. As much as she enjoyed looking at Cole's impressive chest, parts of the script were contrived to find ways to get him out of his shirts.

"Cole is hugely talented," Laney said. "Sure, he's gorgeous, but he has such presence, you almost don't notice his looks. He becomes whatever character he's playing."

"Gotta love looking at that bod, though," Amanda said. "Analisa's a lucky woman."

Analisa stared at the now-black TV screen. She'd seen Cole's movies before but hadn't fully appreciated his skill. She wondered again how much of his seeming to care about her was real and how much was an act.

The house phone rang and she heard Bennett answer.

A few seconds later, he came into the media room. "Mrs. Lassiter, that was the guardhouse calling. We have visitors."

Before Analisa could ask who the visitors were, the doorbell rang and Bennett went to answer.

"You expecting anyone?" Laney asked.

Analisa frowned. "No." She heard voices, then the voices got louder and headed their way.

Bennett came into the room, followed by a middle-aged couple and a young blonde woman.

"Analisa! You're more beautiful than your pictures," the older woman said. Her arms outstretched, she headed straight for Analisa.

When Analisa stood, the woman enveloped her in a bear hug.

Analisa met Bennett's eyes. He shrugged.

The woman pulled away. Her blue eyes sparkled. "I'm delighted to meet the woman who's made my son so happy."

CHAPTER FOURTEEN

"You're—you're Cole's parents?" Analisa said in a thin voice.

"We're sorry to barge in on you like this," the man said. "My wife and daughter insisted." Smiling, he shook his head. "They are a force together."

He walked over and took one of Analisa's hands in both of his. "I'm Charlie, this is Cathy." He tilted his head toward the older woman. "This is our daughter Caroline." He nodded toward the beautiful tall blonde with Cole's blue eyes.

Caroline hugged Analisa. "I hope we didn't put you out too much. We had to meet you."

Struggling to keep her voice calm, Analisa said, "Uh-no. You're not putting me out. I'm glad you decided to visit. Cole's told me so much about you."

"Cole asked us to wait until summer when Charlie and I take our annual trip to Malibu," his mother said. "Caroline is a university professor. She's on break so we thought we'd take a quick trip out here."

Cathy's warm smile helped dissolve some of Analisa's anxiety. "I'm happy you did." Despite the fact Cole's family seemed like lovely people, a vise squeezed Analisa's chest. Her marriage to Cole wouldn't last. She didn't want to know and like his family.

"I've never heard Cole sound as happy as when he called to tell us he'd gotten married," Cathy said. "He sounded even more excited than when he got his first big part."

Her words made Analisa widen her eyes. Cole happy he'd married her? He was a better actor than she thought.

Analisa introduced her friends and Rosa to Cole's family.

"You must be tired and hungry," Analisa said, pushing aside her anxieties for the time. "We have some empanadas left and we'll make a salad."

"Thank you. We'd love something to eat," Caroline said.

"Let's go to the kitchen." Analisa turned to head out of the room

Bennett's voice stopped her.

"Mrs. Lassiter," Bennett said. "I'll put their bags in the extra upstairs bedrooms."

"That's fine." Thank God Cole wasn't here. The upstairs held only three bedrooms. With her in the master suite and Cole's family in the other two, she and Cole would have had to share a room.

They entered the kitchen when the sound of the front door opening made everyone stop.

"Who could that be?" Analisa asked. Anxiety fluttered in her stomach. She knew.

Cole came into the room, holding a duffel bag and a bouquet of wildflowers. He dropped the duffel and stared at the group.

"I thought you were still in Prague," Analisa said. Things had gotten more complicated.

Cole rubbed a hand down his face, and she noticed the fatigue that softened his features and the dark circles under his eyes. "We wrapped up early. I've been flying for twenty-four hours. It's good to be home."

He strode to her and handed her the flowers. "I've missed you." He snaked an arm around her waist and pulled her to him. His lips, firm and hot, slanted over hers.

He tasted like coffee and mint. His stubble rubbed against her face, the roughness enhancing his masculinity, making him even harder to resist. She felt everyone's eyes boring into them. She wanted to sink into the floor. She wanted to go on kissing Cole.

Finally, he released her and focused on his family. "What are you guys doing here?"

His mother and sister ran over to Cole and hugged him. His dad shook his hand.

"We couldn't wait to meet Analisa," his mom said. "She's everything you said she is and more."

Cole glanced over at Analisa, his eyes questioning. She smiled, trying to assure him, and herself, she could handle the unexpected visit from his family.

"We're going to call for our ride now," Laney said. "Let you spend time with your new family."

After seeing her friends off, Analisa strode back into the kitchen to find Rosa warming up the empanadas while Bennett made a salad. Cole and his family sat at the table talking and sharing a bottle of wine. She stood in the doorway and soaked in the homey scene as yearning washed over her. Most of her life, it had been just her and her mother. She'd always longed for siblings and a big, close family. If she and Cole were married for real and in love, his family would be hers. Analisa pushed aside the thought. It did no good to dream of what could never be.

After everyone had eaten and the kitchen cleaned up, the others retired to their rooms, leaving Cole and Analisa alone. She gave the already-clean stovetop one last swipe with a paper towel.

Cole leaned on the counter. "We need to address the four-hundred pound gorilla in the room."

She threw the paper towel in the wastebasket and turned to him. "That is?"

"I have to sleep in the master suite with you while my family's here." His eyes crinkled at the corners when he smiled. "I won't worry you. I'll sleep on the sofa in the sitting area."

She put a hand on her hip. "Of course that's where you'll sleep. I need to talk to you about something else."

He frowned and sank down onto one of the stools. "Something tells me I'd better sit for this."

Analisa pressed her palms on the counter and met his gaze. "I caught *The Tattle* on TV the other night."

He frowned. "This isn't going to be good."

"They showed a picture of you and Lois Flynn laughing together, and speculated the two of you were having an affair while in Prague."

Cole jumped up from his stool. "Sons of bitches. They love to make life miserable for others. You can't believe half of what they report."

"I know that, but please explain the picture to me."

He came around to her and gripped her shoulders to turn her to face him. "I hope you have more faith in me than to believe what you heard."

"I do. You told me you and Lois Flynn are friends and I've chosen to believe you."

His features softened, and he blew out a breath. "Thank you for that. In the picture, were we sitting at a table, and were there champagne flutes and water goblets on it?"

"Yes."

He stepped back and ran a hand over his hair. "That picture was taken a week ago. Lois's husband is sitting to her left. He'd said something funny and we were laughing. Her husband has been in Prague the whole time we've been filming. The show cropped his picture out. Lois and her husband have been happily married for years. They recently announced they're expecting their first child."

Analisa blinked back tears of frustration. "Thanks for clearing that up. I understand more of what you go through, but I don't like being made a fool of."

He gathered her into his arms. "I'm sorry, baby. With us being separated like this, it gives the tabloids and the gossip shows ammo. If you and Rosa come to Malibu for the summer, it will quiet them."

"My life is here, what's left of it anyway. I don't want this celebrity. I never did. If I hadn't lost my job, none of this would have happened."

He pulled away to stare down at her with concern in his blue eyes. "I know, and I feel guilt every day. You've been a real trouper. Let's make the most of our arrangement now, please. I'm being considered for a directing job for an important film. I don't need any scandals now, and you need to be treated with respect by everyone. Once the year's up and we divorce, the story will be in the papers and on the shows for a while, then forgotten as new stories take over. I'll hopefully be on my way to a directing career, and you'll have your degree."

He cradled her face. "You'll have your life back. I promise."

"Your parents and sister are nice people. I don't like hurting them or my mom. They'll be crushed when we divorce."

"We'll make our split as easy on them as we can."

"I wouldn't want them to ever know about our deceit."

"Don't make it sound like that."

"What else would you call it?"

He twisted strands of her hair around his finger. "An arrangement between two people who like each other and who are becoming friends."

CHAPTER FIFTEEN

Analisa came out of the master bath to find Cole waiting, clad only in boxers. Her nipples hardened at the raw desire in his eyes. Aware her short silk nightgown revealed more of her body than was safe, she resisted the urge to fold her arms across her breasts.

Cole smiled. "Don't worry. I promise to be a gentleman." His hot gaze scanned her. "You don't make it easy, wearing a filmy thing like that."

She flared her nostrils. "If I had a long flannel nightgown, I'd wear it."

"You'd be sexy in that too."

When she held him with what she hoped was a stern look, he backed away. "I won't give in to my baser instincts," he said.

While Cole used the bathroom, she slid between the cool, clean sheets on the king-size bed. Cole had made up the sofa with a sheet, blankets, and pillow. She felt guilty letting him sleep on the sofa after the long, exhausting trip he'd made from Prague.

An image of his muscled torso, slim hips, and long legs intruded into her thoughts. She pulled the covers to her neck, scant protection from her need for him.

She tossed and turned for what seemed like hours as sleep eluded her, her bed lonelier than ever, knowing Cole slept a few feet away, his even breathing the only sound in the room. If she went to him, he'd gladly give her what she craved, a night in his arms. One night with Cole would never be enough. Maybe if she hadn't begun to care for him, she could make love with him and walk away. With her growing feelings, she risked her heart by giving herself to Cole.

"Analisa?" His whispered word floated to her, pulling her from her half-sleep state.

"Cole? I thought you were asleep."

"I was but now I'm wide awake. I'm still on Prague time. I heard you moving around and figured you couldn't sleep either."

"I can't."

"Can I come over?"

Her heart pounded so loud she was sure he could hear it in the quiet room. "Not a good idea."

"To talk."

"I guess." The words slipped out.

Soft footsteps signaled his approach. He slid into the bed on the other side. Pale moonlight peeked through the curtains, gilding his tousled hair, making him look younger and more appealing if that were possible. He rested his shoulders against the headboard and yanked the covers up to his chest

Analisa sat up and pulled the covers with her, tightening them around her, then turned to him. "What do you want to talk about?"

"You," he said softly.

"Me? Why?"

"You intrigue me."

She laughed. "I'm hardly intriguing."

"You are to me. I know your father walked out on you and your mother. I can't imagine not growing up without my dad."

She settled more comfortably against the bed. "When I was growing up, I wanted a father and siblings, the whole white picket fence deal. As I got older, that dream faded. My mom is the best. She's always been there for me, and she tried hard to be both father and mother. We struggled financially, but Mom always had enough food for us, and she made sure my clothes were clean and that I was safe. She put me first, before her own needs."

"Rosa is a terrific woman, but that must have been rough, for both of you."

Analisa shrugged. "You handle life with what you're given.

My mom gave me a loving childhood. It wasn't like yours, but it's mine and I was happy."

"Have you ever been in love?"

"Too personal."

"You don't have to answer."

She chewed her lip. Brad was a long time ago, and her feelings for him died the day he trampled on her heart. "I was in love once."

"What happened?"

She turned to face Cole. "He wasn't who I thought he was."

Cole winced. "I deserve that."

"It ended badly."

"Want to talk about it?"

"Nope." She settled the covers around her. "Have you ever been in love?"

"Once."

"With Jennifer Brady?"

"Way before that. Her name was Norma, and we'd been together since freshman year in high school. Everyone, including us, thought we'd marry. We went to college together. Then I broke her heart."

"How?"

"I took drama at Northwestern. I wanted to act, but I wanted more. I wanted Hollywood, the whole star thing." He chuckled. "I sure got that, but they say to be careful what you wish for."

"What happened to Norma?"

"After graduation from college, I planned to head to Hollywood. I asked Norma to come with me, but she'd gotten accepted into grad school and didn't want to mess that up. I couldn't wait to get started on my career. We figured once she got her degree, she'd come out to Hollywood and we'd be together."

He slid closer to Analisa. In the dim light, his eyes held sadness that triggered a mix of empathy and curiosity in her.

"I missed Norma at first, but the excitement of Hollywood overtook any regrets I had that I'd left her behind. Truthfully, I hadn't really wanted her to come with me. I was anxious to strike out on my own, to be free. I've always felt guilty about that. Norma and I were supposed to marry, but my career meant more to me. I started to snag bigger and better parts, and I called her less and less. She got the hint I was drifting away."

"What happened then?"

"She came out to see me but we'd both changed. I used the excuse I was filming and couldn't spend much time with her, but Norma saw through the charade. I came home one day and found a letter from her. She was letting me go. She guessed I no longer loved her and she wanted to be free to find someone who would."

"Smart lady."

"She is. We've talked since then, and I've seen her a few times when I've gone home to visit my family. Norma's happily married to a doctor. They have two children. I'm glad things worked out for her, but I'll always have a little guilt that I fell out of love with her."

At the pain in his voice, Analisa skimmed fingers down his face.

He reached for her hand. "No matter what happens between us, I'll never hurt you, not intentionally," he said. "I've hurt one woman, and I vowed never to do that to another. I'll always play fair with you. I wasn't honest with you when I met you, but I will never lie to you again. Do you believe me?"

"I believe you, Cole."

"Analisa." His voice raw with emotion, he pulled her to him and kissed her, a kiss filled with yearning, desire, and tenderness.

She returned his kiss, reveling in his heat and his closeness. A little voice of reason broke through the sensual cloud covering them. She placed her hands on his chest and pushed away.

"We can't, Cole. We have to stick to our agreement."

"I know." He kissed her gently. "Get some sleep. We both need it. I'll go back to the couch."

"No. Stay here. It's more comfortable and you need the rest."

"You're sure?"

"Yes."

He gave her a long searching look. "'Night, Analisa."

<><><>

Analisa woke with a start. Something was different. She lay on her side as her sleep-blurred mind registered that something warm and heavy held her down. Cole! His arm rested across her middle, and his even breathing close to her ear told her he slept. Gray fingers of dawn bathed the room in shadowy light. She stayed still for long minutes, warmed by the heat of Cole's body. Careful not to wake him, she slipped from his arm and slid to the edge of the bed.

Turning, she faced him. In slumber, with dawn's light on his face, she could glimpse the little boy he'd been. She put a hand out, ready to caress his high cheekbones and full lips, then withdrew. If she woke him and he pulled her to him, she wouldn't be able to resist.

She flipped on her back. When they'd talked hours ago, she'd seen another side of Cole, saw traces of Cody. That he felt comfortable enough with her to share his story had touched her soul. Cole and Cody weren't so different after all, two sides of the same coin.

The thought comforted her. Closing her eyes, she relaxed and drifted back to sleep.

<> <> <>

Cole leaned over a sleeping Analisa. Her long, thick black lashes brushed her creamy skin. Her midnight hair fanned out over the pillow. She looked innocent and vulnerable. And desirable.

Like a punch to the face, guilt smacked him. She'd taken a chance on him. He didn't want her hurt, by him, or by vapid and mean-spirited gossip. He wanted to make her life better, hoped she'd remember him with fondness when they split. Surprised at the regret that pulled him at the thought of never seeing her again, he swallowed.

He settled onto the mattress and stared at the ceiling. He pictured himself with Analisa in his hometown, high school and college sweethearts. Would he have been as eager to leave her behind as he'd been Norma? He would never know, and it didn't matter. All that mattered now was that he treat Analisa right, make sure she didn't get hurt.

When she stirred beside him, he leaned over her again. She opened her incredible eyes, cloudy with sleep.

"Morning, beautiful," he whispered.

She gripped her covers closer around her, protection from him or herself, he wondered.

"Cole? What are you doing?"

"Watching you sleep. You're so beautiful."

She blinked. "Don't get any ideas, mister."

He laughed. "I've got plenty of ideas. Want to hear them?"

"No! The only reason we're in the same bed now is because there was no other room for you to sleep in. Once your parents leave, you're out of here."

"You're harsh, woman." Chuckling, he lay back down. "I need to go to L.A. tonight anyway. I won't be bothering you for a while."

He looked over at her and wondered if he'd imagined the sadness in her eyes when he said he'd be leaving. Deciding it was wishful thinking on his part, he slid out of bed.

"Up and at 'em, sleepy," he said in a teasing voice. "Unless you'd rather we spend the day in bed."

She waved a hand. "I'm getting up. You go put on more clothes."

"I'll be in the bathroom. If you change your mind about staying in bed all day, I'll make it worth your while."

She grabbed a pillow and threw it at his retreating back.

"Missed, but I like a woman with spunk."

CHAPTER SIXTEEN

"**O**h, my, this looks like the botanical garden at the Bellagio," Rosa exclaimed one week later, as their limo drove through the iron gates to Cole's Malibu Beach home. Cole had asked Analisa to come to Malibu now, as a favor to him. Filming on his current movie would wrap up soon, and the premiere of his latest release was scheduled for a week from now. He wanted her to go with him. He said they could put aside any rumors about him and Lois Flynn if he and Analisa presented a picture of a couple in love.

Fearful of going to his Malibu home and becoming closer to him, Analisa had relented, for her mom's sake, but also because she had a part to play in their marriage script—that of the loving new wife. The thought of walking the red carpet spiked her adrenaline with a combo of excitement and unease. She twisted the amethyst ring around her finger and tried to concentrate on the splendor of Cole's house and gardens.

Dense flowering shrubbery, like a festive blanket of bright colors, lined the brick-paved driveway that led to a landscaped courtyard with a stone fountain in the center. Bronze sculptures of playful fish spewed water into the fountain.

Their driver pulled up before the Spanish-style mansion, white stucco with a terracotta roof, and alighted from the car. He opened the back door and helped Rosa out. Her mouth open, she stood and stared at the house situated on a small bluff overlooking the ocean, like a castle of old.

Analisa grabbed the cat carrier holding Killer and slid to the open car door. Their driver took her elbow and helped her out.

The beating of Analisa's heart competed with the rhythm of the ocean far below. The main part of the house looked to be two stories tall, with wide windows and decks on all levels. The scent of roses and gardenias wafted over them from the beds surrounding the fountain. It had to take a team of gardeners to keep a property looking this good.

The double doors opened and Bennett stood there. He'd taken a flight earlier. Rosa and Analisa had wanted to drive there, to see something of the scenery. With little money and working long hours, both women had rarely left Las Vegas.

"Welcome," Bennett said. "I trust you had an easy trip." He spoke to both women, but his eyes were on Rosa.

Analisa looked over her shoulder toward her mother. Rosa's face had turned a pretty shade of pink. Surprise and confusion hit Analisa like one of the waves below. She had never seen her no-nonsense mother blush.

"We had an uneventful trip," Analisa said, turning back to Bennett.

He stood aside to let them enter and held out his hand to take the cat carrier.

Analisa stood in the middle of the two-story entry hall and stared up at the magnificent crystal chandelier that had to cost more than she made in one year bartending. Tiles made to look like pale wood covered the floor, and a sweeping staircase led to the upper level.

"This place is something else," Rosa breathed.

"Your rooms are ready if you want to freshen up," Bennett said. "I've prepared a light meal."

Analisa smiled at him. "Thanks, Bennett. You think of everything."

<><><>

That evening while her mom watched TV in her suite, Analisa sat at the small kitchen table and sipped a cup of hot mint tea. Rosa and Bennett each had suites on the first level. Analisa occupied the master suite on the second floor, where there were four more bedrooms.

She glanced around. The cat had staked out one of the sofas in the sitting area off the kitchen, where she now slept soundly.

The galley-style kitchen wasn't as spacious as the one in Vegas, but it had a homey feel with its ivory colored cabinets and stainless appliances. In other parts of the house, overstuffed sofas made the living and media rooms comfortable looking, and every room had a view of the ocean.

Analisa smiled, remembering the happiness on her mother's face when she saw her suite. Guilt over her contract marriage washed away her smile like a drenching of cold ocean water. She hoped Rosa wouldn't be too upset when Analisa and Cole divorced.

After their divorce, she'd have her teaching degree and her mother would be healthy again thanks to the physical therapists Cole had hired. Mary told her they'd hired another therapist to help while the women were in Malibu. She and her mom would have the house in Las Vegas too. Cole may have cost her a job she enjoyed, and their marriage might be a sham, but their contract would make life easier for her and her mom, especially her mom.

The front door opened and closed, then she heard voices. Analisa jumped up and faced the kitchen doorway. When she heard Cole's laugh, her pulse soared and she drew shallow breaths.

Followed by Bennett, Cole came into the room and stopped when he saw Analisa. His smoldering gaze trailed over her. Then he smiled, and the sun rose on her world.

Fighting her attraction to him, she remained rooted. Cole advanced toward her until they were inches apart. He brushed hair back from her face with a gentle touch.

"Hello, sweetheart. I hope you and Rosa are settled in. I see the cat's found her spot. What did you name her?"

She swallowed, finding her voice. "Killer."

Cole's laugh diffused some of Analisa's tension. "Told you it was a perfect name."

"Mom and I love this house," she said.

Her thirsty gaze drank him in. His hair had gone back to its natural dark blond and had grown, touching the collar of his blue button-down shirt. His distressed denim jeans hugged impossibly long legs. Cole Lassiter, actor and heartthrob, the stuff of many millions of women's dreams, was her husband.

She reminded herself she had a business deal with the man standing before her, a celebrated actor who could make people believe anything he wanted. He could even make her believe she was falling in love with him.

"Bennett's making me an omelet," Cole said. "Have some. I could use your company."

His smile stole her breath and she could only nod and follow him to the counter where Bennett had set two places. After a meal of southwest omelet, hash browns, and toast, Analisa relaxed and nursed her fresh cup of hot tea.

"Bennett is a true gem," she said when the other man left the room. "He seems to know what we want before we do. He's a talented cook." She grinned. "Don't tell Mom that."

"Bennett trained under the celebrity chef to the late, legendary Ada Romanoff. She was demanding, as I understand." His eyes gleamed with a conspiratorial light. "Rosa is a formidable cook, too. I'd hate to see her and Bennett in a cook-off."

"They've already started. I fear there will be blood."

Cole threw back his head and laughed. "I needed that. You always make me feel better."

Feeling lighthearted from their banter, she said, "We could pitch them as a reality show. *Kitchen Wars with Rosa and Bennett.*"

He laughed again. "Hollywood is rubbing off on you already."

Smiling, she shrugged. "When in Rome…"

Looking less tired and more relaxed, Cole reminded her of his alter ego, Cody, fun to be around. Before she could dwell on that potentially dangerous thought, her mom walked into the room.

"Cole!" Rosa said. "When did you get here?"

"A little while ago, Mama Rosa." He stood and hugged her.

Mama Rosa? Since when had Cole started using the nickname her friends had given her mother? Rosa clearly adored Cole. Divorcing Cole would be harder than Analisa thought.

"Sit, Rosa," he said, as he took his seat again.

"I'm fine standing." She stared down at their empty plates. "Why didn't you call me? I would have fixed you something."

"Bennett made us an omelet," Analisa said.

"An omelet?" Rosa waved a hand in a dismissive gesture, eliciting a "harrumph" from Bennett, who'd come back in and was now wiping the countertops.

Analisa suppressed a laugh at the narrowed-eyed looks her mom and Bennett exchanged.

"You look tired, Cole," Rosa said, turning her back on Bennett. "You should get to bed."

"Soon. I hope your rooms are okay. If you need anything, tell Bennett or Mary."

Rosa hugged herself. "I love my suite." She smiled slyly. "Analisa showed me around your suite. It looks like something out of a fantasy, a good place for making babies."

"Mom!" Analisa's face burned at her mother's heavy-handed hint at grandchildren. Cole glanced away and Bennett wiped the counter with renewed vigor.

"I guess I'll be going back to my rooms," Rosa said. "See you both in the morning." Scowling, she looked over at Bennett. "*I* will cook breakfast."

She strode out.

"Rosa has a point," Cole said. "I'm heading to bed."

"I'm tired myself," Analisa said, standing.

They said goodnight to Bennett and walked up the back stairs to the second floor. Outside the master suite, Analisa faced Cole.

"This is your room. I'll be glad to sleep somewhere else in the house."

"This is your bedroom for the time you're here. I've got four other bedrooms on this floor, plus the two suites on the ground floor, and the guest cottage. We have enough room for everyone."

"I didn't know about the cottage. I haven't seen the grounds yet."

"I'll take you on a tour tomorrow." He twisted the doorknob to the master suite, then stood back and gestured for Analisa to enter. "After you."

She folded her arms across her chest. "Oh, no, we are not sleeping together."

His eyes glinted and his full lips tilted in a teasing grin. "Relax. Have you really checked out this room?"

"What do you mean?"

"Come in." He took her hand and led her inside.

The corner room with windows that let in sweeping views of the ocean had cream colored walls and a king-size bed covered with a white down comforter, giving it a calming ambiance. Scattered rugs in geometric prints provided pops of color. Sliding glass doors led from the small sitting area to a roomy deck.

The doors to the deck were open, and a breeze scented with flowers and the salt of the ocean floated into the room. The gentle lullaby of the surf filtered through.

Breathing in the ocean air, Analisa turned to Cole. "This is an extraordinary room, but I haven't settled in yet. I'll be glad to move."

"How much did you explore?"

She pointed to double doors opposite the bed. "The bathroom, although it's more like a spa, and the doors next to it lead into a closet which is bigger than our whole downstairs in the townhouse where Mom and I lived."

Cole pulled a key out of his pocket and strode to a single door next to the desk. With the key, he unlocked the door and gestured for her to come over.

Analisa peeked into the room Cole had unlocked. Widening her eyes, she turned to him. "Another bedroom?"

"It was a nursery before I bought the house. Which is why there's this door between the rooms. This is where I'll sleep. Come in."

Analisa stepped into the room. Smaller than the master bedroom, the room had the same cream-colored walls, a queen-size bed with a white comforter, and pale wood floors covered by modern woven rugs. Sliding glass doors led to a small balcony. A door next to the bed was opened, revealing a walk-in closet. She glimpsed Cole's clothes in the closet.

She whirled on him. "I wondered why there was nothing of yours in the closet in the master suite."

"I had Bennett move my clothes here."

"He can't know we're not sharing a room."

"I told you before he's discreet. This room has a separate entrance from the hall so I won't have to bother you. Your mom won't know we're not sharing a bed."

"We will keep this connecting door locked, right?"

"Scout's honor." He leaned into her. "Unless you decide you'd like to keep it unlocked."

"Dream on."

Cupping her shoulders, he looked intently into her eyes, all humor gone. "Any chance I can make you change your mind?"

"You don't give up, do you?"

"Nope."

So what if they kept the door unlocked? She trusted him. He'd never do anything she didn't want. Maybe she needed the key to protect herself from her growing feelings for him. She held out her hand. "I think you should give me the key."

"You drive a hard bargain." He dropped the key into her hand.

"'Night, Cole." Analisa stepped into her room and shut the connecting door. She locked it, then jiggled the knob, making sure the door was secured.

She'd done the right thing. Why did she feel so...lonely?

CHAPTER SEVENTEEN

"It's so beautiful and peaceful here," Analisa said as she and Cole walked along the brick trail, bordered by gnarled trees, which wound along the side of the house through the gardens. True to his word, after breakfast the next morning, she and Cole were on a tour of the extensive Malibu property. Analisa stopped to admire the small marble fountain with a cherub spouting water from its mouth. Next to it stood a stone bench shaded by trees, a welcoming oasis waiting for her to sit and read or just contemplate.

"I love that fountain and that bench," she said. "I need to bring a book here and take in the beauty."

"These gardens are my solace from the rat race that's my life," he said. "Sometimes I sit out here and try to clear my mind of everything except the trees and flowers and the sound of the ocean."

Analisa sniffed. "What's that magnificent scent?"

"Probably freesias and a mixture of wildflowers."

One of the gardeners, wearing a floppy hat and white gloves and pushing a wheelbarrow, walked by. Analisa could see others working in a wildflower garden.

The gardener smiled and tipped his hat. "Good morning, Mr. and Mrs. Lassiter."

Mr. and Mrs. Lassiter. That shouldn't sound so right, but it did.

"Let's stop for a while." Cole took her hand and led her to the stone bench.

Analisa sat, her gaze drinking in the peaceful beauty of the outdoors. Across from them a shallow pond filled with various sizes of rocks beckoned her to take off her shoes and dip her toes in the water. The rhythm of the surf formed a background melody that lulled her into a euphoric state.

"This is how I picture heaven," she said, closing her eyes.

Cole chuckled. "I understand. I grew up landlocked, and I'm still amazed now to have the ocean so close."

"As a desert dweller, I can relate." She opened her eyes and twisted to face him. "Tell me about your journey from Ohio to movie star. You took drama at Northwestern. Did you always want to act?" Part of her warned against getting too close to Cole, but another part wanted to know all about him.

He gazed out toward the pond and the wildflower garden beyond. "I got the acting bug in grade school when I played Joseph in a Christmas pageant."

She laughed. "You played Joseph? With your blond hair and blue eyes?"

His eyes twinkled when he turned to her. "What can I say? My teacher recognized talent. I owned that role!"

"So playing a saint started you, huh?"

"You could say that. I acted in high school and college plays. Two days after graduation from Northwestern, I packed up my old car and headed west. I've never regretted it."

A shadow came over his eyes.

"But you left Norma."

He nodded. "I sometimes wonder how things would have been if she'd come out here with me and we married. I was young, cocky, and obsessed with my career. I suspect if I'd married anyone then, it wouldn't have worked out."

"How do you feel now, about marriage? A *real* marriage, I mean." The words slipped out, and she wished she could bite them back.

His gaze held her, his blue eyes darkening. "I'd like a *real* marriage to the right woman."

Could she be the right woman for him? She knew instinctively he wasn't playing a part. They stared at each other. The squawk of seabirds and the buzz of bees, mingled with the rhythmic clipping of hedge trimmers, faded. Cole's gaze drifted to her mouth and back again. The molten sapphire of his eyes sparked an answering heat that started in her chest and wound lower.

In the deep recesses of her heart, she wanted to be the woman for Cole. Before she did something crazy, like throw herself in his arms, she blinked and broke the contact, then stood. "I want to see the rest of the grounds."

He frowned, as if ready to say something, but he stood and took her hand in his. "Let's go."

The brick walkway circled to the back of the house and the Olympic-sized swimming pool, its blue-green water shimmering in the sunlight. A glass-topped table with orange and white striped umbrellas shading the sun, and surrounded by comfortable looking chairs with orange cushions, invited them to sit.

Analisa stopped and faced Cole. "Do you entertain here? The place is big enough to host wedding receptions."

He laughed. "We've never had a wedding reception here, but I have had some parties. I've been so busy lately with one movie after another that I haven't had time to go to any parties, let alone host one. Not that I'm complaining. I'm glad to have the work."

"If you stop acting, you could hire this place out. You're sitting on a gold mine." She gave him what she hoped was a saucy smile.

Humor flickered in his eyes. "The community would kick me out, but I'll keep that in mind for hard times."

He stepped closer. "The pool's heated, but the weather is still a little cool. You can swim whenever you want. Consider your stay here a vacation. I want you to enjoy yourself, Analisa. You deserve it. Don't worry about anything. You're doing me a huge favor, and I hope I can make your life easier in return."

He bent and planted a tender kiss on her lips. Wanting more, she pressed against him and wound her arms around his neck. When his lips firmed over hers, her body hummed with need.

Several passion-filled minutes later, Cole pulled away and rested his forehead on hers. "I shouldn't have done that," he rasped. "I want you, but I'll honor our agreement. I need you here with me, and I don't want to scare you off."

Her face flamed. Being so close to Cole, kissing him, made

all thoughts of their contract fly away in the salt-tanged breeze. She wanted more than a vacation.

"I guess we should go back in," she said, turning to head into the house, leaving him standing there alone.

CHAPTER EIGHTEEN

As they rode in the limo to the opening of his latest movie, Cole placed his hand over Analisa's. The day after their kiss on the deck, he'd left for a series of publicity appearances in Los Angeles and San Francisco to promote the movie that premiered tonight. She'd heard him come in early this morning, and he'd slept most of the day. His absence had allowed her to come to grips with *the kiss*, as she called it. He'd been right to end it. They were becoming friends, but anything more would make their divorce harder on them both. Much as she tried to convince herself Cole had been right, disappointment lay heavy in her chest. She'd wanted him that night, she wanted him now.

"You're so quiet," he said, breaking into her thoughts. "I understand why you're nervous. Everyone is their first time on the red carpet. When you stroll the gauntlet, take a deep breath, smile for the cameras and the onlookers, and walk slowly."

His gaze took a leisurely sweep of her body. The gleam in his eyes incited her to a different kind of nervousness.

"With you looking like that," he said. "No one will be looking at me."

"Thanks, but if that's supposed to reassure me, it doesn't. I've never been so scared in my life." Forcing a smile, she said, "Your female fans won't be watching me."

His lips quirked. "But now my male fans will have someone to drool over."

She tapped him lightly on his tuxedoed arm. Cole was in his element. "Thanks for trying to make me feel better." She might miss regular guy Cody Lamont, but she had to admit Cole Lassiter had shown himself to be a damn thoughtful man too.

They pulled up in front of the TCL Chinese Theater on Hollywood Boulevard. Their driver stopped, then got out of the car and went around to Analisa's door, opening it, and holding out his hand to her. Cole squeezed her hand. Following his advice, she took a deep breath before allowing the driver to help her out of the car.

The red silk of her slim column dress swished against her ankles as she moved. She felt like a glamorous model on the cover of *Vogue*. Too bad she had to send the dress back to the online shop that rented couture gowns. Nothing in her wardrobe came close to being red-carpet appropriate, and she hadn't wanted to use Cole's money. Praying she wouldn't trip in the sky-high silver sandals, she held on to the driver as Cole slid out of the car.

He took her arm and threaded it through his. "Smile," he whispered. Cole gave a smile and a wave to the cheering crowd.

Analisa smiled until her face hurt. The flash of cameras exploded around them. She felt like King Kong as flashbulbs propelled the poor beast to escape his chains and flee. She'd like to flee back to the house, where she would change into her nightgown, eat popcorn, and watch TV.

Anxious as she was, having Cole next to her comforted her. They entered the theater, and she released her breath, but continued to cling to Cole's arm.

He patted her hand. "You did great. You're a natural."

A nervous laugh bubbled from her. "I'm hardly a natural, but thanks for saying it."

<><><>

"I loved that movie. You're a terrific actor," Analisa said two hours later as she and Cole rode in the limo to the restaurant in Los Angeles and the party Cole's studio was giving for the cast.

"Thanks," he said. "I love what I do, although I'd rather direct."

"I hope you do that."

"I will soon. My old friend Jake Falco wants me to direct his next film."

She grabbed Cole's hand and squeezed. "That's great. I've

seen Falco's movies. He's good."

"He is. We were starving actors together." Cole smiled down at her. "He's also happily married with baby number two on the way."

Averting her gaze, she studied her amethyst ring, forever a reminder of Cole. Tonight, she didn't want to think about happy couples, and of her own business agreement with Cole.

"Now that you and I are together, there are no more awkward dates with women I don't know," Cole said, drawing her attention. "I can put my energies into learning all I can about directing." He shook his head. "What a relief to be behind the camera and not in front. I think in some way, I'll feel I've gotten my life back."

"What life would that be?"

He chuckled. "A private life without the paparazzi stalking my every move."

"Hate to break it to you, but I don't think you'll ever get away from stalking reporters and photographers."

"Bite your tongue, woman." His voice teased.

They walked into the restaurant to a standing ovation. Hoorays and congratulations were shouted. Cole acknowledged the kudos as he and Analisa walked to their table. Curious glances followed them, but Cole's hand in hers gave her the courage to walk with her head up, ignoring the looks.

They sat with Cole's female co-star and her husband, along with the director, the producer, and their wives. The others were cordial, but a little standoffish. If they knew the truth about her marriage to Cole, she feared she and Cole would be mocked mercilessly in the press.

The long night over, they entered his quiet house. Past one o'clock in the morning, she assumed her mom and Bennett had gotten home hours ago. Cole had secured tickets to the premiere for the other two, but the studio paid for the limo and insisted only Cole and Analisa ride in it. Rosa and Bennett had ordered a car from one of the services to drive them to the theater and back. Rosa had complained about having to spend the evening with Bennett, but when Analisa saw them in the back of the theater, Rosa was laughing at something Bennett had said. Analisa hoped the kitchen wars would finally end.

She and Cole walked through the living room with its comfortable sofa and chairs. As with the other rooms, glass doors led to a deck overlooking the ocean. The stone fireplace with its Spanish style grate stood dark. Analisa had images of sitting before a roaring fire, cozy, while a storm raged outside. She wondered if she'd be with Cole long enough to experience that. A spark of sadness zapped her at the thought of not being with him.

"I'm starving," he said. "How about something to eat?"

Her stomach rumbled. "I guess that's my answer." They'd been so busy talking to the well-wishers who'd come to their table at the restaurant that they'd eaten little.

Laughing, Cole cupped her elbow and led her through the living room and into the kitchen. "Could you pour us some wine and I'll make sandwiches."

"Sure. White?"

"That'll go with my famous ham and cheese sandwich."

"Famous, huh?"

"Just you wait."

Analisa pulled two wine goblets from the rack above the counter, then grabbed a bottle from the wine refrigerator. After pouring them each a glass, she sat at the counter while Cole assembled the sandwiches.

He'd taken off his tuxedo jacket, loosened his tie, and rolled up his sleeves. Fine golden hairs covered his tanned arms. The muscles of his arms flexed as he worked. Watching a hunky guy cook had to be one of the sexiest images in the world.

Gripping her wine goblet, Analisa took a huge gulp of the cold liquid. It slid down her throat, but didn't drown her rising libido.

"Voila!" he said, spreading his arms over the two sandwiches like a magician who'd just performed an amazing trick.

"Wow!" she said. "Those are some sandwiches."

Ham, cheese, tomatoes, and pickles were piled high between slices of crusty bread. On each plate, Cole had put some of Bennett's broccoli slaw.

"Wait until you taste them," Cole said, beaming.

He picked up both plates, two forks, and a few napkins. "Let's go sit on the deck. The moon is full and the ocean is calling us."

Carrying the glasses of wine, Analisa followed him to the deck off the kitchen. Cole set the plates, forks, and napkins on the tiled table, then pulled out a chair for Analisa. The cool ocean breeze made her shiver.

He pressed his hand on her shoulder, eliciting a ripple of heat through her. "You're cold," he said. "I'll get you something."

He went into the house and came back with his jacket and settled it on her shoulders. His scent, the faint lemon of his cologne combined with the freshness of his soap, enveloped her. She bit into her sandwich to distract from her desire for him.

She chewed, then glanced over to find Cole watching her.

"This is delicious," she said, wiping her mouth with her napkin. "The mustard enhances the sandwich, creating a culinary feast."

He grinned. "Told you I make a mean sandwich."

"Don't get too full of yourself," she said, grinning. "Anything would taste good as hungry as I am."

Rolling his eyes, he looked heavenward. "What am I going to do with this sassy woman?"

She laughed and looked out over the ocean, the ebb and flow of the tides eternal and mysterious. The moonlight gilded the water and stole over the deck, a mystical force that touched her heart with promise. The glistening sand provoked visions of walking along the beach, arm-in-arm with Cole.

Analisa felt his stare and turned to lock gazes with him. His eyes, dark and soft, studied her.

"A penny for them," he said, his voice husky.

"My thoughts are boring." If only he knew the flight of fancy her imagination had taken.

"I find everything about you interesting." He stared at her for long seconds. "I'm not ready to go in yet. How about you?"

"It's too beautiful out here and I'm still wound up from tonight. Thanks for taking me to the premiere. It was exciting to walk the red carpet." She looked down at the table, then back to him. "I can see how being a celebrity with people clamoring for you, photographing you, hanging on your every word, can be addictive. It's an addiction I'll resist, but I hate to admit I liked the attention tonight."

"Tell me about it. My first taste of fame was heady, better

than any addiction. I've seen the underbelly of celebrity and the toll notoriety takes on a person's soul. I fight to stay grounded, and I don't always win. I enjoy being famous, which is something I don't like to admit. When I disguise my identity, I like the freedom of being unrecognized, but I also miss the adulation."

He glanced away before focusing on her again. "One of the reasons I liked you from the beginning, and still like you, is you're real. I don't think you'll change."

The power of his words, and his honesty, touched her soul. "Thanks."

They sat in comfortable silence and finished the wine. Analisa figured she'd have one hell of a hangover, but sitting out here with Cole, surrounded by Nature's beauty, made it all worthwhile.

"It really is extraordinary here." She smoothed a finger along the colorful tabletop and inhaled the salt-infused scent of the ocean. The moonlight, the beauty of their surroundings, and the man with her gave her the courage to ask something that had been on her mind for a while. "Cole, what if it comes out we have a contract marriage? Won't that hurt your career?"

"We'll worry about that if it happens. I don't think it will hurt me much, and I sure hope it won't hurt you."

"Is there anyone in this city who might dig a little deeper into our relationship? We married so suddenly."

"I have enemies. Most of us do in this cutthroat town. There's always someone who wants to bring me down for their own gain. I try to live my life and not worry about it."

She shivered as a draft, like a premonition, rolled over her. "I hope what we've done won't hurt either of us. Or our families."

"That's a worry for another day," he said, standing. He held his hand out to her. "Let's go in. You're cold and it'll be dawn soon."

"Let's bring in the dishes and glasses," she said.

"Leave them. You're tired."

They walked up the short flight of stairs to the second floor. When they reached the landing, Analisa slipped off her shoes. She didn't want to make noise on the Italian marble floor.

At her door, she turned to Cole. "It was a fun night, once I got over my nervousness."

The cobalt intensity of his eyes made her insides tremble. He reached out, and his warm, long fingers caressed her cheekbones and trailed down her face.

With a tortured moan, he gripped her shoulders and drew her to him.

His lips, hot and urgent, found hers. At first, she stiffened, but the slant of his lips over hers ignited a fire within her. She dropped her shoes. They clattered to the floor. She wrapped her arms around his neck and molded herself to his firm body.

She opened to him, inviting him, wanting him. He tasted like wine and ocean breezes. Their tongues sparred in an erotic timeless ritual.

He cupped the back of her head, eliciting groans from her. His hard erection pressed against her. She wanted to melt into him.

When he pulled away, his ragged breathing matched hers.

"We'd better stop before we do something you'll regret," he whispered.

Embarrassment heated her face and she slid away from him. She reached down and grabbed her shoes, then opened her bedroom door.

"Good night," she mumbled before slipping into the room and shutting the door behind her.

She leaned against the door and gulped shallow breaths. Cole was wrong. She knew in the deep recesses of her heart she'd never regret making love with him.

She rubbed a trembling hand down her face.

She was falling in love with her husband.

CHAPTER NINETEEN

Analisa rolled over, not wanting to face the day and the memory of earlier that morning, on the deck with Cole. And that kiss.

A headache pulsed behind her left temple and her stomach churned. She'd had too much wine. Intoxicated with her red carpet experience, the alcohol, and the moonlit night, her imagination had soared, making her believe she was falling for Cole.

Shading her eyes against the sunshine streaming in through the windows, she sat up, then sank back down as a wave of dizziness hit her. She covered her ears against the swell of the ocean on the shore, the swishing sound throbbing in her head.

Not able to help herself, she ran a finger over her lips. She could still feel Cole's mouth on hers, could feel the urgency of his kiss, his hunger as their bodies melded together.

"Crap!" She could not, would not, fall in love with him. Heartache waited if she did. She had her agenda. Falling in love was not on her to-do list.

Cole would one day be a pleasant memory of a desperate time when she grabbed the only lifeline she could. At the thought of him as merely a memory, melancholy rolled through her like ocean waves, further agitating her stomach.

She gingerly got out of bed and walked on unsteady feet to the bathroom. A warm shower would help. A little breakfast, too. She glanced back at the bedside clock. Noon! Crap! Half the day was gone. She never slept this late.

Analisa leaned against the bathroom doorframe, fighting another wave of dizziness. She glanced around the room, larger than her living room in her old townhome. To her left and her right were gray and white marble countertops, each with a sink. The Jacuzzi soaking tub in marble and with a clear view of the ocean welcomed her to take a long bubble bath. Another time, she promised herself. On the opposite side stood the shower with frameless glass doors. The stall could comfortably hold two people. A vision of being here naked with Cole popped into her mind and sent heat to her lower body. She needed a cold shower.

<><><>

Later, feeling somewhat more human, Analisa headed down the back stairs. Half of her hoped Cole would be in the kitchen. The other half hoped he wouldn't. She wasn't sure she wanted to face him yet. She frowned at the raised voices coming from the kitchen.

She entered to find a tense stand-off between her mother and Bennett. Rosa stood toe-to-toe with the elegant Bennett.

"This is my kitchen," Bennett said. "I do the cooking."

"You call what you do cooking? Bah!" Rosa said. "Bland white-bread stuff." She poked her finger into her chest. "What I do is real cooking."

"You were happy enough to be in my company last night," Bennett said quietly.

"That was then. This is now."

"You've forgotten that quickly, Rosa?"

Her mom and Bennett? The pain in Analisa's head had gotten worse. The three aspirins she'd taken hadn't kicked in yet. "What's this about cooking?" she said, approaching them. She wouldn't think beyond cooking when it came to her mother and Bennett.

Rosa waved a hand at him. "I want to make enchiladas for dinner tonight and he wants to make steak. Said that's what Cole wants. My enchiladas are better than anything he can cook."

"Everyone calm down," Analisa said, a mother talking to misbehaving toddlers. "I need coffee."

With a huff and a scowl for Rosa, Bennett said, "Sit, Analisa, and I'll bring you some."

"Thanks." Analisa smiled at him. She didn't want any

problems between her and Bennett. Gripping her coffee mug, she took a long sip of the strong brew. "I needed that." She set down her mug and turned to the others, standing stiffly watching her.

"What's this about the cooking?" Analisa asked.

They pointed at each other and started talking. Analisa kneaded her forehead. "Please, one at a time."

Rosa folded her arms across her chest and glared at Bennett. "I'm a better cook than he is. I told him to buttle or whatever butlers do and leave the cooking to me."

Bennett straightened his shoulders, very much the proper British servant. "I am not a butler. I am a trained chef, and I've always cooked for Cole. This is my kitchen and I give the orders."

Analisa forced a smile. She didn't relish being the kitchen referee. "You're both excellent cooks. You just make different things. We can work out a compromise. I'm sure Cole would want that."

"It's my kitchen," Bennett said. "You have the place in Vegas. Rosa can cook there."

Rosa flared her nostrils. "I will cook both places."

Give me strength. Only she and Cole knew that when the year for their marriage ended, the fight for kitchen dominance would be a moot point. Until then, she needed to establish peace.

Analisa drank more coffee, needing the sustenance. "Is Cole at the studio now?" she asked Bennett. "He wants steak tonight, right?"

At his nod, she said, "If Cole wants steak, we should give him that." Rosa opened her mouth to protest, and Analisa put up a hand to quiet her. "Bennett makes a mean omelet. He can cook breakfast. Mom, you make lunch. Then, you take turns for dinner. Tonight Bennett cooks. Tomorrow Mom cooks. And so on."

Smiling, she swung her attention between the two, careful not to move her head too fast. "What do you say?"

Rosa narrowed her eyes. Bennett's mouth tightened.

He broke down first. Taking a more relaxed stance, he said, "Fine."

Eyebrow raised, Analisa turned to her mother. "Mom?"

Rosa's shoulders slumped. "Okay. Now, I make you lunch,

Analisa."

"Uh, how about Bennett makes me breakfast? I need something light."

With a self-satisfied smile, Bennett strode to the refrigerator and began pulling out ingredients for an omelet.

Rosa watched Bennett, her lips tilted in a semblance of a snarl, then she ignored him and grabbed two newspapers from the counter and slapped them in front of Analisa. "The premiere was fun." She slid a glance at Bennett. "I would have had more fun if I'd been alone."

"Harrumph," was Bennett's only answer.

"Looks like you and Cole had fun last night," Rosa said. With a sly smile, she added, "You are a beautiful couple and you'll make beautiful babies."

Trepidation made Analisa want to ignore the papers. She hated her picture being out there for the world to see and judge. Her curiosity won out. She picked up the first paper, a trade paper for the film industry. Dominating the page was a picture of Cole and her, arm-in-arm, walking into the Chinese Theater. Her eyes wide, she looked like a deer caught in the headlights. Sheesh. She needed to learn how to put on a game face while with Cole. The next paper, a tabloid, showed her getting out of the limo and reaching for Cole's hand outside the restaurant. In that picture, her attention focused on Cole. The dreamy expression on her face showed a woman in love.

She was a better actor than she thought. She hoped her actor husband thought she merited an award.

CHAPTER TWENTY

The gentle breeze caressed Analisa's shoulders through the light sweater she wore. She sat on the deck enjoying a delicious steak dinner with her mom and Cole. She'd never eaten steak so tender and flavorful. In the interest of keeping the fragile kitchen truce, she'd compliment Bennett later.

Below them, the surf flirted with the shore, the gentle swooshing sound soothing Analisa's anxieties. Seated across from her, Rosa laughed at something Cole said. Analisa pulled herself from her musings and raised her gaze to find Cole watching her. The blue fire in his eyes made her wonder if he was thinking about their kiss last night.

Since he'd gotten home from the studio an hour ago, she'd tried to avoid looking directly at him or talking to him. She'd tried to stop thinking about that kiss, too, but it replayed in her mind like a video on a continuous loop. She needed to get over her growing obsession with Cole Lassiter.

"By the way," he said. "My parents are coming in a few days for a visit."

Analisa picked up her wine goblet and took a huge sip. She had enough trouble trying to act like a woman in love in front of her own mother and the world. Now, she'd have to pretend to Cole's parents.

"I can't wait to see your parents again," Rosa said. "There are certainly enough bedrooms in this house."

"My parents always stay in the guest cottage when they visit so it shouldn't upset anything much here."

"I like your parents," Analisa said. Thank God they wouldn't be in the house with her all the time and she could relax her guard.

Rosa pushed her empty plate away. "The steak was juicy, but Bennett can't make Mexican like I can."

Analisa ignored Rosa's statement about Mexican food. "Mom, you should tell Bennett how much you enjoyed the steak."

"I won't make his head any bigger than it is."

Analisa and Cole exchanged a look. Analisa cut the last of her meat and shoved it into her mouth, trying to suppress a grin.

Rosa stood and began clearing the empty plates.

Bennett hurried out to the deck. "I'll clean the table," he said.

With a "harrumph," Rosa glared at him. "I'm going to my room to watch my soaps I DVR'd. Good night, Analisa and Cole."

Rosa's failure to include Bennett in her "good-nights" made Analisa smile.

"Coffee and apple crisp, Analisa, Cole?" Bennett asked.

"Maybe later. I'm full," Analisa said. "I could use some coffee though."

"Coffee for me, too," Cole said. "I'll have some of that apple crisp later."

The wine, the dinner, and the ocean had helped Analisa relax. Now here with Cole, she could almost believe he was Cody Lamont, the guy she'd begun to fall in love with. If only he were.

She scanned the spacious deck overlooking the pool and ocean. The table inlaid with colorful Navajo-styled tiles, the polished wood floors, and the low white iron railing cried money and prestige. She didn't need all this. Having the love of a faithful man, a man who would stand by her in life, was all she needed to be happy.

"A penny for them," Cole said, drawing her attention.

"I told you before, my thoughts aren't worth that much."

He leaned forward. "Let's talk about what's bothering you."

A slow burn began at her neck and spread to her face. "There's nothing bothering me."

"You know exactly what I mean. That kiss." He leaned back, waiting.

Her lips tingled. "It was a very nice kiss, but it can't happen again."

He jerked his head back. "'*A very nice kiss*?' It was an amazing kiss, unless you didn't like it." His eyes wandered to her mouth. "I think you liked it more than you want to admit."

"Whether I liked it or not isn't the point. Our marriage is in name only, and I intend to keep it that way." God, she sounded like some self-righteous schoolmarm in an old Western.

"Analisa." His voice had softened. "I've been attracted to you from the first moment I saw you at the Capri. I won't hide the fact I want you, but I would never do anything you didn't want."

Frustration flashed across his face. "My self-indulgence got us both into this mess. I've uprooted your life more than mine. I would never hurt you."

They grew quiet as Bennett came out carrying a tray with two mugs and cream and sugar. When he'd left them alone again, Analisa poured cream into her coffee and took a sip before lifting her gaze to Cole.

"You've been generous with the terms of our, uh, contract," she said. The comforting whoosh of the ocean grabbed her attention, and she glanced out to the water, silvery in the moonlight, before turning back to him.

"I could have fallen for Cody Lamont." The confession slipped out. Eyes wide with embarrassment, she drank more coffee.

The surprise flitting across Cole's chiseled features matched her own astonishment.

He reached across the table and placed his hand over hers. "If you could fall for Cody, why not Cole?"

She freed her hand. "Being with Cody Lamont is so much easier than being with Cole Lassiter. I don't believe I could live life as the wife of a movie star for long. And I'm not sure I'd want to." Waving a hand, she said, "This is beautiful, a fantasy. I understand why they call Hollywood *La La Land*. None of this is real."

"Sure, much of what's around us is a fantasy, but I'm real. I'm still that guy from Ohio with five siblings and upright, loving parents. Let's give our relationship a real chance and see where it goes. Take a gamble on me, ordinary Cole Lassiter from Ohio."

Analisa stood slowly and stared down at him, at his eyes glinting in the light, at his sculpted cheekbones, his gilded hair, made paler in the moonlight. He'd be so easy to love.

"You'll never be ordinary, Cole."

She whirled around and strode into the house, away from him, away from temptation.

CHAPTER TWENTY-ONE

The next morning, after a light breakfast of toasted English muffin with strawberry jam and several cups of coffee, Analisa went in search of Rosa, and found her and the cat in the workout room with the physical therapist Cole had hired. This was Bennett's day off, and Analisa looked forward to a cease-fire in the kitchen. She didn't see Cole and assumed he'd had an early call at the studio.

Rosa was using bands to strengthen her shoulders, under the direction of Shawn, the therapist. Killer sat on the yoga mat washing herself.

"Looking good, Mom," Analisa said, coming into the room. She glanced at Shawn. "How's it coming?"

"I wish all my clients were like Rosa. She's almost back to new. She'll be ready to party shortly."

"Partying, here I come," Rosa huffed. "I'll be better than before. I've even lost weight."

Analisa laughed. "Party? Mom, you've never partied in your life."

Finished with her exercises, Rosa dropped the bands. "In my younger days, I partied all the time. Life was good..." She let her voice trail off.

From the sadness that flickered in her mom's brown eyes, Analisa guessed Rosa remembered the time before her husband abandoned her. Cole may have uprooted their lives, but his generosity would make things better for Rosa. Analisa resolved to appreciate him more while guarding her heart.

As the women said goodbye to Shawn, Killer walked over to Analisa and wound around her ankles. She picked up the purring cat and held her close. "Don't you have an appointment at the vet's today to have Killer spayed, Mom?"

Rosa nodded. "I'd better get ready. I've signed up to volunteer at the vet's clinic a few days a week now that I'm better."

"Mom, you have to relax and take care of yourself."

"I have to keep busy." Rosa studied her. "What about you? You like sitting around all day? That's not like you."

Her mother's words made Analisa jerk her head up. She'd been restless. Her inactivity led her to focus too much on Cole. Since she was sixteen, she'd held down a job. Marriage to a multi-millionaire celebrity shouldn't keep her from doing meaningful work.

"You're right, Mom. I need to keep busy and do something worthwhile. Once school starts in the fall, I'll be plenty busy."

"You still plan to go back to Vegas for school?" Rosa turned off the overhead light and gathered her towel from the rack.

"Why wouldn't I go back to Vegas?" Analisa asked. "Our home is there."

"Your home is with your husband."

Analisa slid her gaze from her mother's. "I can live both places. Lots of people do."

"I suppose. I need to change out of these clothes before I leave for the vet's."

Analisa scanned her mother. Rosa wore stylish workout clothes she'd recently bought. She'd lost a little weight. A few weeks ago, with Analisa's help, Rosa had found a talented hairdresser who styled her curly hair to a becoming length. The springy curls that framed Rosa's pretty face with its high cheekbones and wide-set brown eyes made her look years younger than fifty. She had a glow about her that Analisa had never seen before.

"Mom, I love your hair like that."

Rosa patted her curls. "I like it too."

"How are you getting to the vet's? With Bennett off today, he can't drive you."

Rosa lifted a shoulder. "I called for a car. No way I'd ask that stuffy Englishman. Glad he's not here today."

Analisa suppressed a grin. Rosa didn't sound at all glad Bennett wasn't there.

"I'm going to take a walk on the beach and think about what I can do to keep busy," Analisa said.

"Be careful."

"I will." Relieved Rosa didn't question her further about why she planned to move back to Las Vegas, Analisa went to her room to fetch a jacket. The ocean breezes could be cool. Dressed in denim Capri pants, a white T-shirt, khaki jacket, and rubber flip-flops, Analisa headed to the beach. She needed to think, to chart a new course. While married to Cole, she needed to do something she could be proud of.

Because they lived in a secure compound, the paparazzi didn't bother them here. Although Cole said he'd occasionally find photographers with long-lens cameras perched up in the hills, their cameras aimed at the beach.

The salt-scented gentle wind ruffled her hair and brought the lure of foreign lands on the other side of the ocean. She'd always wanted to travel and see the world but never had the money. Maybe when her year with Cole ended, she and Rosa would travel.

She went down the steps to the beach and stopped to take off her sandals. Breathing deeply of the fresh air, she wiggled her toes in the soft sand. Having grown up in Las Vegas, she'd been to the ocean only a few times, when she and her mom took a rare vacation. With little money, they'd driven to California, found cheap motels, and enjoyed the seaside for a few days. Maybe while here now, they could drive up to Big Sur. She'd always wanted to see it.

Leaving her sandals on the steps, Analisa strolled along the water's edge. The tranquil waves pushed seafoam onto her feet, then receded, then teased her feet again. She smiled at others walking, jogging, or playing Frisbee with their dogs. She could get used to the laid-back beach life, even if the multi-million dollar mansions she passed didn't scream "laid-back."

She had to remember the reason she'd taken this walk, to open her mind, to come up with something she could do that would be useful. Rosa had taught her to work hard. The spoiled wife of a movie star wasn't her style.

She sauntered, her mind jumbled, until a thought came to her. She could ask Cole for suggestions. He'd probably tell her she didn't need to do any sort of work, but to enjoy her leisure. She'd insist. That settled, she turned back.

Cole's Spanish-style house appeared, a fantasy mirage. Her heart leapt at the sight. What an exquisite, yet comfortable place. It reflected Cole's attitude—easy, without pretense. She had to admit he still had a lot of Ohio in him.

<><><>

When Cole came home from the studio that evening, Analisa met him at the door. His grin when he saw her galvanized her pulse to new heights. She could lose herself in that smile. She wouldn't. Of course, she wouldn't.

"To what do I owe this?" he asked, closing the door behind him. "If I'd known you'd be here to welcome me home, I would have left the studio sooner."

"I wanted to discuss something with you."

"That sounds ominous."

"It's not," she said with a laugh.

"I need a glass of wine after the day I've had. Let's have a drink and sit outside."

Seated on the deck off the kitchen, a glass of white wine each, the setting sun painted a panorama of gold, purple, and pink over the ocean.

Cole sipped wine, then leaned closer. "What did you want to talk about?"

She circled the rim of her glass with her finger. "I'm used to staying busy. This place is a dream, like an extended vacation. I need something worthwhile to do. Mom is volunteering at the pet clinic. Can you help me figure out something I can do?"

"I want you to consider this a vacation, but I know you like to keep busy. Let me think." He looked out over the ocean. The sun's rays reflected on his golden stubble and the burnished gold of his hair. Cole Lassiter really was extraordinarily great-looking, but the more she knew him, the more she saw his innate decency, his humbleness.

"I know," he said, his attention on her again. "One of my best friends here is Pete Carrillo."

Analisa widened her eyes. "The action movie hero? Mom and

I are huge fans."

Cole laughed. "I hope you're my fans too."

"Of course we are."

He took a mock bow from the waist up. "Thank you. Right answer."

"What does Pete Carrillo have to do with my wanting to keep busy?"

"His wife Emmaline does a lot of charity work. She's always looking for volunteers. She's genuine. I'll give you her number and you can call her."

"Charity work? I like that. Thanks."

"That's settled. How about a walk on the beach before dinner?"

"I had a walk earlier."

"Not with me. I assure you I give the best walks."

She laughed. Cole had a way of making her feel light-hearted. "Let's go."

When they got to the bottom step leading to the beach, they toed off their shoes. Cole took her hand in his. She didn't resist.

Walking with Cole, Analisa could almost believe they were a real couple in love. Several people passed them and smiled. A group of teenage girls stared at Cole and giggled as they walked by.

"Your fans?" Analisa said, grinning up at him.

"What can I say? Teenage girls love me."

"You say that in jest but it's true. My friends, Mom, and I love your movies. You're a talented actor."

He stopped and stared down at her. "Thank you."

"Are you sure you want to give up acting to direct?"

"I'll continue to act, but I like being behind the camera. I like the control but I also want some privacy from photographers." He grinned. "And freedom from crazy publicists."

He squeezed her hand, and they started walking again.

"Are you saying your publicist is crazy?" Analisa asked.

"You've met Teresa. What do you think?"

"I think you're right. Why do you keep her on?"

"She's the best in the business."

They walked in silence before turning back. Dusk had descended, but the moon hadn't risen yet, giving the ocean an inky-black sheen. Lights from the houses spilled over the beach, a magical place where time didn't exist. Only she and the man next to her lived in this world.

Approaching the house, they heard arguing. Analisa and Cole frowned at each other.

"Bennett and Mom are fighting again," she said. "I thought Bennett had the day off."

"I guess he ended his day early. I've never known anyone to ruffle Bennett's feathers like your mother."

"Mom is usually the soul of calmness. Those two seem to rub each other the wrong way."

They entered the kitchen to find Bennett and Rosa facing each other in a standoff.

"Dinner is mine tonight," Rosa was saying. "This is your day off, so what are you doing here?"

"Maybe I missed you, Rosa." Bennett's voice had taken on an unmistakable huskiness.

Rosa's face pinked. Analisa put out a hand to Cole, holding him in place so as not to disturb the other couple.

"Don't try to flatter me," Rosa said to Bennett. Her voice sounded breathy.

"I don't flatter. I tell the truth."

Silence from Rosa.

"I'll make the salad," Bennett said.

Cole and Analisa walked into the room.

Cole smiled at Rosa. "Bennett knows how I like my salad. It's great you guys can share the kitchen."

Rosa lifted her chin. "His salad won't go with my chicken mole enchiladas. But I'll let him make it because you like it."

"You'll love my salad," Bennett said. He went to the cabinet and pulled out a large salad bowl.

Despite the rising tension between Rosa and Bennett, sexual energy crackled through the room.

Shaking her head, Analisa met Cole's surprised gaze. Her mom and Bennett?

CHAPTER TWENTY-TWO

Analisa took her driver's hand and stepped out of the limo. Since she left her Kia in Las Vegas, Cole had insisted she use a hired car and driver to get around L.A. Smoothing a hand down her turquoise linen sheath, she walked toward the restaurant as the car pulled away.

She'd bought the dress at a small boutique in Malibu, planning to wear it to her graduation next year. A zipper went up almost the entire back of the dress, and it fit her perfectly, hugging her curves. She hoped she was dressed appropriately to meet Emmaline and the other women on the planning committee for the annual charity ball for needy children. Clutching her beige leather purse close, she held her head high as flashbulbs went off from the cameras held by paparazzi who hung out at the Japanese restaurant, one of the city's best, frequented by celebrities and the cream of Los Angeles society.

She'd talked to Emmaline Carrillo on the phone a few times in the past week since Cole suggested she call the woman. Analisa liked the other woman's breezy attitude. This would be her first meeting with Emmaline and the others. She wanted to make a good impression.

"I'm meeting Emmaline Carrillo," Analisa told the maître d'.

"Of course, madam. This way," he said with a smile.

Curious eyes watched her, and whispers came from tables, as she followed the maître d' through the elegant restaurant with its dark wood floors and white-clothed tables. Located in the city, the restaurant's windows overlooked lush greenery, making it seem as if the building stood on a tropical island. Analisa tucked strands of hair behind her ear. She wondered if those watching knew she didn't belong there. Leading a double life could be exhausting.

The maître d' led her to a round table situated at the back of the room in a location that allowed for watching and being watched. Butterflies threatened to take over Analisa's stomach. She smiled at the three women around the table and sat in the velvet-covered chair the maître d' held for her.

One of the women, a friendly-looking blonde, held out a manicured hand to Analisa. "Hi, I'm Emmaline. So nice to meet you."

Analisa shook hands with Emmaline and relaxed a little. Emmaline seemed as nice in person as she had been on the phone.

"Let me introduce you to the others," Emmaline said. "Girls, this is Analisa Lassiter. She's the lucky woman who snagged Cole."

Emmaline nodded toward a woman with platinum blonde hair and hard turquoise eyes.

"This is Meredith Hightower, wife of the director John Hightower."

Meredith nodded but didn't say anything. Warning bells went off in Analisa's head. She'd be careful of this one.

The other woman, another blonde named Tiffany Trumball, married to a producer, gave Analisa a sincere smile when they were introduced. Tiffany looked to be no more than twenty-five years old. Her producer husband, a power broker in Hollywood, had to be much older. Trophy wife or not, Tiffany seemed approachable.

"I explained over the phone that the charity gala is in six weeks," Emmaline said. "One of our group, Paige, left to go on location with her husband. She and Tiffany were working together to secure donations from merchants for our silent auction. You'll work with Tiffany. She can fill you in."

Analisa smiled at Tiffany. "I look forward to working with you, Tiffany."

"Me, too."

"I think what you're doing for the kids is wonderful," Analisa said, impressed with the women's desire to support the charity. These wealthy women were willing to give their time and money to help others less fortunate.

Emmaline smiled. "Kids House does so much for disadvantaged children. It gives us pleasure to make things a little easier for them."

The others nodded.

Details for the charity affair were hammered out between cups of sake and various fish entrees during the long lunch. Meredith ignored Analisa, but the friendliness from Emmaline and Tiffany made up for the other woman's snub.

Lunch over, and a little unsteady after so much sake, Analisa went to the ladies room. She'd already called the limo driver to pick her up. Before going back into the restaurant, Analisa stood before one of the gilt-framed mirrors to reapply her lipstick.

The door opened and Meredith Hightower entered. Analisa suppressed a groan. She did not want to be alone with the unfriendly woman she'd begun to think of as a barracuda. She pasted on a smile, hoping to hide her distaste.

The woman scanned Analisa with cold eyes. "Is it true you were a bartender when you and Cole met?"

"Yes."

"You married awfully fast."

"Sometimes people fall in love immediately."

"Or is it something else?" She stared at Analisa's midsection. "You don't look pregnant." With a smirk on her pretty, cosmetically enhanced face, Meredith continued. "Let me give you some advice. This place will eat you up. You don't look like you can handle the gossip and the mean-spiritedness. Those looks of yours won't last. You'd better go back to Vegas where you belong."

"Excuse me." Analisa pushed past Meredith to open the door and exit. The less time she spent around Meredith Hightower the better.

CHAPTER TWENTY-THREE

That night, after dinner and some TV with her mom, Analisa went to her room to read. Her face washed, her teeth brushed, and dressed in a pair of comfortable yoga pants and a T-shirt, she sat on an upholstered chaise. The doors to the deck were closed against the cool ocean breeze. Reclining, an open book on her lap, she couldn't concentrate. She found herself listening for Cole's steps on the stairs.

She hadn't seen Cole since their walk on the beach a week ago. His film was shooting into the wee hours. Some mornings before dawn, she heard his bedroom door open and close. He'd called her from the set whenever he had time, sounding exhausted. She'd never realized how chaotic filming could be.

Not wanting to bother Bennett, Analisa had made a sandwich for Cole each night and left it in the refrigerator so he'd have something to eat when he came home. Anxiety and disappointment warred inside her. She wished she could offer more, but knew the less she saw him, the better for her heart.

Her gaze wandered the comfortable, elegant suite. A beautiful modern seascape from an artist she hadn't heard of hung on the wall over the bed. She'd done an internet search on the artist and learned he was an up-and-coming local who was rapidly establishing a national following. If Cole had chosen that painting, he had a good eye. She was learning more and more about her husband.

She picked up her book, only half paying attention to the cozy mystery by an author she loved. Her restlessness threatened to overcome her. Close to midnight, when she found herself dozing off, she decided to try to sleep. She set the book on the table next to her when a soft knock sounded at her door.

She jumped up and crossed the room to open the door to a haggard-looking Cole.

"Hey!" he said.

He slipped inside and she shut the door.

"What's wrong?" she asked.

He raked fingers through his hair. "Nothing's wrong. It's been a long day, but I wanted to see you."

She studied the fine lines around his eyes and mouth, the paleness under his tan. His longish hair was ruffled. "You look tired."

"Yeah." He moved to the sitting area and sat on the small sofa. "Filming didn't go well today. Lots of takes. One of the actors is a young woman, only eighteen, and she kept flubbing her lines." He blew out a breath. "Her mother is the actress Gloria Harper, a powerhouse here, and although the director wanted another woman, a talented actor, for the part, the studio forced him to take their star's daughter."

Analisa chuckled. "I guess favoritism happens everywhere. I left a sandwich for you in the refrigerator."

"I finished it. Thank you for making it and the others this past week. That meant a lot to me."

At his softly-spoken words, satisfaction swelled her heart and she smiled.

He patted the sofa. "Sit, and let's talk for a while."

His eyes darkened as they traveled over her. She resisted the urge to cross her arms over her chest, knowing her nipples had hardened under his gaze. She sat gingerly on the edge of the seat and twisted to face him.

"I missed you today," he said, his voice thick. "It was a hell of a day on set and all I could think about was you, coming home to you." He studied her. "I like the idea of having you here waiting for me."

Trying to make light of his words despite the fluttering in her chest, she said, "I wasn't exactly waiting for you every night."

His wide grin made him look boyish and charming. "I like to flatter myself that you're walking the floors, anxious for me to be home, like the wives of seafarers centuries ago."

"You should be a screenwriter with that imagination."

He put a hand over his heart. "Way to hurt a guy." Settling back, he said, "How did your lunch go today?"

She relaxed her shoulders. "It went well. Most of the planning has been done. The gala is for a good cause and I'm excited to be part of it. I like Emmaline and Tiffany Trumball. I'll be working with Tiffany." Analisa scrunched up her nose, remembering Meredith.

"I hear a 'but' in there," he said. "What's wrong?"

Analisa fingered the edges of her shirt before raising her gaze to meet his again. "How well do you know Meredith Hightower?"

He stiffened. "Why?"

"She was cool to me and she suggested I must be pregnant because how else could I have gotten you to marry me. She also said I couldn't handle Hollywood and I should go back to Vegas." At the anger that flicked over Cole's face, Analisa waved a hand. "What she said doesn't bother me, but I can't figure out why she dislikes me so."

He leaned forward and took one of Analisa's hands in his. "I think I know. Meredith came on to me after I'd been in Hollywood a while. I was up for my first big role. Before that, I'd had bit parts in TV and a few indies. She told me if I became her lover, she'd guarantee her husband, who was directing the movie, would cast me. I refused her, and she's never forgiven me."

"And she still holds that against you?"

"She has a long memory, and she wields a lot of influence in the industry. She takes young guys as lovers all the time and isn't used to being turned down. I got the part, without her *help*."

"Good for you."

"Stay away from her and her husband, as much as possible. They're bad news. If I'd known she was part of the group, I wouldn't have suggested you contact Emmaline. Meredith's husband is well-respected for his directing abilities, and I have a good working relationship with him, but I don't socialize with the Hightowers. Meredith is much younger than her husband, and I believe she was his second wife, a trophy wife." He laughed, a short, bitter sound. "I guess she's getting too old for him. He's rumored to have at least two young 'girlfriends,'" he said with finger quotes.

Analisa shuddered.

Cole stood and reached for her hand to pull her gently up. "Be careful."

Analisa watched the play of emotions on his face—the anger and the concern for her. She thought again how easy it would have been to fall in love with medical supplies salesman Cody Lamont. Cole Lassiter had more edge, but his decency showed through in what he said, and in the way he treated her and Rosa.

She didn't want to be a Hollywood wife like the ones on that TV show, or like Meredith. She didn't want to deal with spiteful women, didn't want all the pretense.

"What?" he said. "You're staring at me like I've done something wrong."

"I'm tired."

He skimmed a finger down her face, prompting a tingle along her nerve endings.

"Good night, Analisa." He slipped out and closed the door quietly behind him.

CHAPTER TWENTY-FOUR

"Analisa, I know we've recently met, but I consider you a friend," Tiffany said. She and Analisa sat at a table in Cole's study going over plans for the silent auction for the Kids House charity gala. Since the lunch ten days ago, the women had met twice at Cole's.

Smiling at the sincerity in the young woman's hazel eyes, Analisa said, "That's so nice of you. I consider you a friend, too." And she did. For all her glamorous looks, the younger woman retained a wholesomeness that spoke of her Iowa upbringing. She'd told Analisa she'd come from a small town there to Hollywood when she was eighteen, eager to make it as an actress. That hadn't worked out for her.

Tiffany took sips of her iced tea as Analisa gathered their papers into a folder. Analisa had the feeling the other woman wanted to say more, and she lingered over the papers, giving Tiffany time.

"I think we've been very productive," Analisa finally said when the papers were all stacked.

"We have," Tiffany said. "I couldn't work as well with Emmaline and Meredith. They ignore me, especially Meredith. I guess they resent my age and my marrying a man so much older."

"That's your business, and I wouldn't worry about the others."

Tiffany swallowed and met Analisa's gaze. "Can I confide something in you?"

"Of course."

"I told you I'd come to Hollywood when I was eighteen, but I couldn't find work in the industry."

At Analisa's nod, Tiffany continued. "I didn't tell you I became an escort for old, wealthy men." She looked down at the table, then back to Analisa. "I'm not proud of that, but I needed the money."

Analisa touched the other woman's arm. "I'm not judging you."

"That's where I met Stan," Tiffany said. "He paid for my new boobs, diction lessons, and a new wardrobe. He made me into his doll, someone to look good on his arm."

Tiffany picked up her glass with a shaking hand and sipped. Analisa gave her an encouraging smile.

"I grew up poor," Tiffany said. "Stan showed me a different life. When he asked me to marry him, I said yes. He offered security." Sadness reflected in her eyes. "I liked the houses, the clothes, the fancy cars more than I liked him."

"You were very young. Many women would be seduced by all that."

"I was twenty. I'm twenty-five now, and I'm miserable. Stan cheats on me all the time. He ignores me except when he wants sex or wants to prance around with me on his arm to show off to his rich male friends, like I'm some sort of prize dog. When he's not ignoring me, he tells me I'm stupid and I'm nothing without him."

"Tiffany, I'm so sorry." Analisa closed her eyes. She didn't want to hear any of this, but the other woman was hurting, and she needed someone to talk to. Analisa opened her eyes to find tears streaming down Tiffany's face.

"You're a good person," Analisa said, reaching out to squeeze Tiffany's hand. "Don't let your husband or any man disrespect you."

"If I divorce him, I get almost nothing, according to our pre-nup," Tiffany said. "How can I give up all I have?"

"I can't tell you what to do, but sometimes a person's self-respect is the most important thing she owns."

"Thanks, Analisa. You're a true friend." Tiffany swiped at her tears and stood. "I need to get home. Stan is having some business associates over for dinner and he'll expect me to look sexy and keep my mouth shut."

"Remember, I'm here to talk anytime you need me."

Her heart heavy for Tiffany, Analisa waved to the young woman as she got into her limo. Being a trophy wife took hard work. You always had to look good and lived in fear your husband would trade you in for a newer model. Tiffany had entered into a form of contract marriage, too. The other woman had given up her self-respect for money and all the trappings of celebrity.

Analisa hadn't given up her dignity for Cole, and she knew he wouldn't want that of her. He made few demands on her and always treated her with respect.

With a wry smile, she slipped into the house and shut the door. Cole treated her with respect except when he'd lied about being Cody and she'd lost her job because of him.

Cole still worked late filming, but came home at a decent hour whenever possible. She'd taken to waiting for him and keeping him company while he ate a sandwich or an omelet she'd prepared. He didn't expect her to wait up, but truth be told, she liked talking with him. During those times, they shared a comfortable intimacy even while keeping up mundane conversations about each other's day. Cole's movie should wrap up tonight, and tomorrow they'd attend a party for the cast and crew. Cole told her not all his movies ended with a party, but this one had been particularly grueling, and everyone associated with it needed to let off steam.

She looked at the entry hall clock and quickened her pace. Cole's parents were arriving today for their lengthy stay. They should be here soon. Cole sent a car to pick them up at the airport. For the past few days, the cleaning crew had been working to prepare the guest house for his parents. Analisa loved the little cottage with its cozy living room with a fireplace, a tiny, but upscale kitchen, and large bedroom. She could be comfortable there. She still hadn't gotten used to the main house, a mansion really.

<> <> <>

After Cole's parents, Cathy and Charlie, had settled into the guest cottage, they sat with Rosa and Analisa in the living room having before-dinner drinks while Bennett prepared the meal.

Analisa scrunched into a corner of the L-shaped sectional. Cathy and Rosa sat near the other end, with Charlie in one of the side chairs, covered in the same white fabric as the sofa. Pillows in bright blue and white arranged over the sofa and chairs gave the elegant room a fresh vibe, mirroring the ocean outside. A glass-topped coffee table rested on a white area rug. Golden hardwood floors covered the entire room. Doors to the deck were opened to the gentle salt-laced breeze.

"I'm always relaxed here," Cathy said.

"Coming from Las Vegas and the desert, being so close to the ocean is a real treat," Analisa said.

"The house is comfortable too," Rosa said. "I like how Cole decorated it. He's a great guy. He treats us well."

Charlie sipped his whiskey before setting the glass down. "Of course he treats you well. Cathy and I tried to instill good values in all our children."

"You've done a great job," Analisa said. Cole, for all his astonishing looks, talent, and money, showed his decency in the respectful way he treated her and Rosa, always looking out for them. "I love it here, but I miss Las Vegas too."

"Your house there is beautiful," Cathy said.

"Cole's next movie will be shot in Italy," Analisa said. "When he leaves for Rome, Mom and I may go back to Vegas for a while."

Charlie frowned. "You're not going to Rome with him?"

Analisa almost choked on the wine she'd sipped. She jerked her head up to stare at Charlie. "Uh, Rome? Cole and I never discussed my going with him." She waved a hand. "He's on set long hours. We wouldn't see each other anyway."

"Nonsense," Cathy said. "You're newlyweds. You'll find ways to spend time together."

A smile wreathed Rosa's face. "Ana, you must go to Rome. I've always wanted to see it."

"You can go with Analisa and Cole," Cathy said.

Rosa waved in a dismissive gesture. "Oh, no, the newlyweds need time alone. They haven't had a honeymoon yet."

Bennett came into the room, stopping further conversation.

"Dinner is ready," he said.

He glanced at Rosa, and Analisa could swear he blushed. Interesting. She'd rather focus on whatever was going on between her mom and Bennett and not on the idea of going to Rome with Cole.

Cole walked into the media room later that evening, where the others had gathered to watch TV. He stopped in the doorway and drank in the cozy scene before him. He could have been on the set of a warm-hearted movie about a close-knit family gathered for the holidays.

Analisa, Rosa, and his parents were laughing and talking, a group who enjoyed being together. He didn't need stardom and wealth. The tableau before him was the real deal.

His mother noticed him first.

"Cole!" She jumped up and ran to embrace him.

Over his mom's shoulder, his gaze connected with Analisa's. His world spun a little out of control as he stared at the woman who'd become so important to him in such a short time.

His mother released him, and he strode toward his wife, attention focused on her like a laser. "Hello, sweetheart." He pulled Analisa gently from her chair and kissed her soft, inviting lips. She pressed closer and returned his kiss. For an insane minute, he wondered if she meant the kiss or if she played to the camera, acting the part of a woman in love.

"How was your day?" he asked when he'd ended the kiss.

"My meeting with Tiffany was productive, and I've been having a nice visit with your parents." He wondered if he imagined the slight tremor in her voice, and hoped his kiss had done that.

"Omelet or sandwich, Cole?" she said, then turned to his parents. "Cathy and Charlie, would you like something to eat?"

"No, thanks, I'm full from dinner," his mom said.

"I'd like an omelet," his dad said.

His mom stood and glared at her husband. "You don't need to eat anything more. Let's go to bed and leave the lovebirds alone."

Rosa stood, too, and made a show of yawning. "Time for bed."

<><><>

Cole sat at the kitchen counter after the others had gone to their rooms. Analisa poured him a glass of wine.

"You put on an Oscar-worthy performance when you came in," she said. "A man in love with his wife."

"Maybe I wasn't acting," he said.

Her face turned a delicate shade of pink. She went to the refrigerator to take out the omelet ingredients. At times like this, just the two of them, comfortable, relaxed, he could almost believe they'd married for love and didn't have a contract that would soon end. He wished they were in a true marriage. The thought hit him with the force of a thunderbolt.

"How was your day?" she asked, setting the ingredients on the counter.

"Last day of filming, and it was the smoothest one yet. I'm glad not every movie is as much trouble as this one. I hope today didn't stress you too much, with Tiffany coming over, then my parents."

"Me? Hardly. I used to tend bar, remember?"

He laughed.

As she prepared the food, he said, "I leave for Rome in one week."

"I remembered."

"I could be gone a month or more."

"Uh-huh." She put sliced mushrooms, diced green peppers, and chopped onions in a pan and began sautéing them.

"Analisa?"

She broke an egg into a bowl and reached for another before turning to him with a frown.

"Why don't you meet me in Rome when we have a break in filming?" he asked.

She almost dropped the egg she held. "Were you talking to your mom?"

"No. Why?"

"Your mom said that same thing earlier today."

"She has nothing to do with this. You've got your passport now, and I mentioned before about having you come with me on location. I wanted it to be the right place, and Rome is perfect. You'll love it there." It suddenly became important he talk her into joining him in Rome. Away from the manufactured fantasy of Hollywood, maybe they could get to know each other better.

Without answering, she turned back to her omelet and broke two more eggs, whisked them, then poured them into the pan over the sautéed vegetables.

His sipped some wine, his stress level rising like the heat on the stove. He prepared an argument to use if she said no to Rome.

The omelet finished, Analisa slid it onto a plate, buttered the bread she'd toasted, and placed everything in front of him. She leaned on the counter. "Cole, I can't go to Rome. I'm involved with the charity event."

He swallowed some omelet, took a sip of wine, then shrugged as relief settled over him. She hadn't said no. "Don't worry about that. The women are married to men in the business. They understand there are times you need to travel with your husband. The event is in five-six weeks?"

"Five."

"The first two weeks in Rome will be crazy, but things should settle down, and we'll take a break in filming. You'll have two weeks to work on the gala before you join me in Rome. You'll only be gone a few days. I may not be back in time to escort you to the gala, but if there's any way I can manage it, I will."

She stared at him with her incredible brown-gold eyes. "I think that could work out."

He wanted to raise his fist in the air in triumph. Instead, he smiled. "We'll have fun."

CHAPTER TWENTY-FIVE

The setting sun cast a rosy glow over the Roman Coliseum, not far from Analisa's hotel window. As it had for two thousand years, the iconic monument stood as a testimony to man's greatness and his brutality.

Amazed to be in Rome, she hugged herself and blinked, expecting to wake up and find the past months with Cole, and now a visit to the Eternal City, were all a dream. She breathed in the perfumed air of the room, still not quite believing the magic. Analisa wanted to see it all—the Coliseum, the Ancient Roman Forum, the catacombs, the Vatican, the Sistine Chapel.

Her heels clicking on the marble floor, she walked to the desk and grabbed the travel brochures, then sank onto one of the velvet chairs to thumb through them. A few days in Rome wouldn't be enough time to sample all its charms.

Cole had promised to share Rome with her. A few days with Cole would leave her wanting more of him. She wouldn't think of that now.

Her cell phone rang, and she hurried to the night table where she'd left it. When she saw Cole's picture come up, her heart stuttered for a beat.

"Hey, Cole."

"Analisa."

The way he said her name, husky and soft, made her insides quiver. She sat on the edge of the bed.

"How's the room?" he asked.

"Awesome." She glanced around at the elegant penthouse

suite in one of Rome's best hotels. Richly colored Oriental rugs were scattered over the marble floors. Exquisite artwork hung on the walls, complementing the heavy wood furnishings and the table tops decorated with hand-worked inlays.

There was only one bed, a king, but Cole had told her he'd sleep on the pullout sofa in the living room. Because the cast and some of the crew were staying at the hotel, Cole thought putting Analisa in a different room would cause gossip they didn't want. She'd agreed, yet the thought of spending nights so close to him stirred her stomach with a brew of anticipation and anxiety.

"I feel like I'm in Cinderella's castle," she said.

He chuckled. "You're more beautiful than Cinderella, but I'm no prince."

He was becoming a prince in her mind, but she'd never tell him.

"I apologize again that I couldn't be at the airport to meet you today," he said. "We're almost done shooting for the day, and I have the next three off so you and I can explore Rome."

Excitement made her smile. "There's so much I want to see, Cole."

"I can't wait to show it to you. I felt the same way my first time here, and the feeling never goes away."

A voice called loudly in the background.

"They want me back on set," he said. "I should be at the hotel in about two hours. We'll go out to dinner."

"See you then."

After they hung up, she pressed the phone to her chest. The more time she spent with Cole, the more she fell under his spell. She suspected Rome would soon have her under its spell.

True to his word, Cole got back to the hotel two hours later. While he showered, Analisa sat by the window in the living room and tried to read from her Kindle. But her attention kept drifting to the Coliseum, now aglow with lights. She'd always been a history buff, especially ancient history, Rome in particular. No matter what happened to the rest of her life, she'd always have these days in Rome with Cole. Rather than stir up more anxiety, the thought comforted.

"Ready?" Cole's softly spoken word made her jump.

"I didn't mean to startle you," he said.

"You didn't. I was daydreaming." She set down her Kindle and stood, smoothing her hands down the sides of her beige Capris. She'd paired the pants with a bright yellow tank and matching sweater, and wore yellow wedge-heeled Espadrilles on her feet.

"You look sexy as hell." His appreciative gaze roamed over her.

Her knees weakened with the insane urge to grab him and kiss him and never let him go. "Thanks. I'll get my purse." She hurried out of the room before he could notice her blush.

They strolled through the teeming, narrow Roman streets. Cole held Analisa's elbow, helping her negotiate the ancient cobblestones. When they came to the Piazza della Rotonda and the Pantheon, she stopped and gasped.

"The Pantheon. It's beautiful." She sounded like a country bumpkin in her awe, but she didn't care. She'd dreamed of one day seeing the ancient temple, now a Catholic church.

Cole chuckled. "It is. It's closed now, but we'll tour it another time. Let's eat. I hope we can find a table at my favorite restaurant here on the piazza."

He led her to a group of white-clothed tables at an outdoor patio. As they walked, others stopped and stared, whispering and snapping pictures with their phones. Analisa tuned them out. Tonight belonged to her and Cole, and she wouldn't think of the future or the past, or Cole's fans who appeared to be all over the piazza.

A man wearing a tuxedo hurried over to them as they entered the patio. "*Signor* Lassiter, you honor us with your presence."

"Thanks, Camillo. Do you have a table for us?"

"For you, always." The man turned to Analisa with a toothy smile. "This is your lovely wife? I read about your marriage in the papers. Tonight, dinner is on me, my wedding gift."

"You're a good friend, Camillo. Thank you. This is Analisa." Cole turned to her. "Camillo's restaurant is the best in Rome."

Camillo took her hand and brought it to his mouth to brush a kiss on her knuckles. "*Signora* Lassiter, you are lovelier than your pictures. *Signor* Lassiter is a lucky man."

"Thank you, Camillo."

He put them at a table that fronted the Piazza della Rotonda, then clapped to summon a waiter who brought over a bottle of red wine and two glasses. Camillo poured them each a glass, then went inside to put in their food orders.

"Is this table all right with you?" Cole asked Analisa. "We're already attracting a crowd. We can go inside the restaurant if you want."

"I'm getting used to the attention, and I'm learning to tune it out," she lied. She doubted she'd ever get used to celebrity, but Cole worked hard and clearly relished this break and the attention. She wouldn't make it harder on him.

"Camillo is your friend, but he's also a businessman," she said. "Having Cole Lassiter sitting in such a prominent place at his restaurant is good for business."

"Thanks for understanding." He smiled. "You're a quick learner."

She held up her wine glass. "Cole, thank you for bringing me to Rome."

After their exquisite dinner of antipasto with fresh vegetables, cheeses, and meats, and gnocchi with fresh-shaved truffles, Analisa and Cole relaxed over homemade gelato and steaming cups of espresso.

"This is the best meal I've ever eaten," she said. "I will never eat gnocchi again because nothing can compare with Camillo's."

Cole laughed. "He'll be happy to hear that. Next time you have a craving for gnocchi, we'll have to come back here."

Averting her eyes, she finished off her gelato and picked up her cup of espresso. If she ever came back to Rome, it wouldn't be with Cole. Pushing aside her sadness at the thought, she met his gaze. "Our contract will be over before we can come back here."

"We won't think of that now." His expression serious, he studied her. "I've wanted to ask you something. You don't have to answer, but I need to ask."

Frowning, she set down her cup. "What is it?"

"You're not only beautiful, but you're smart, interesting, and warm. I can't imagine any man not wanting to be with you. You told me you were in love once. Ready to tell me about it?"

She chewed her lip and held his gaze, resting her arms on the table. Cole had become her friend, and Brad was a long time ago. Her mind made up, she said, "His name was Brad. I met him eight years ago when I was twenty-three. It was a bad time in my life. I'd had to drop out of college because I had no money. He came into the dive bar where I worked. The bar was nothing like the Capri. Brad lived in Phoenix but came to Vegas on a regular basis for business. We got involved quickly. I thought I loved him. He said he loved me and wanted to marry me."

"What happened?" Cole asked.

"He got married, but not to me."

"What?"

"Brad was engaged the whole time he was with me. His fiancée lived in Phoenix. After we'd been together six months, I had a few days off work, and decided to drive to Phoenix to surprise him. When I got there, I tried calling him but he didn't answer. I went to his workplace. Imagine my surprise and humiliation when I found out he was on his honeymoon." She swallowed as remembered pain hit her in the gut. "Some of his co-workers looked at me with sympathy, but others laughed at me. I left there feeling like a dog with my tail between my legs."

Anger glinted in Cole's eyes. "That son of a bitch."

"Tell me about it. I confided in a woman I thought was my friend at work and she spread the word. Soon my own co-workers were whispering and snickering about me."

"They were small people, not good enough for you."

"Thanks. There's more. Rat bastard Brad had the nerve to come into my bar a few weeks later, ready to take up where we'd left off. He knew I'd found out he'd gotten married, but he shrugged it away and said he figured he'd keep me as his Vegas girlfriend. I punched him in the nose."

Cole laughed. "You punched him? Good for you. If I ever meet him, I'll punch him too, for good measure."

She gave him a wry smile. "I got pleasure out of seeing him bleed, but I got fired from my job because I hit him. They frowned on employees beating up their customers."

Cole grabbed her hand across the table. "God, Analisa."

Tears welled behind her eyelids at the sudden release of the hurt she'd held for so long. "Men seem to have a way of getting me fired. I'm not sorry I hit him."

"I'm sorry I got you fired."

She pulled free of Cole when a waiter came over and replaced their cups of espresso with fresh ones.

"I was ready to leave that bar anyway," she said. "Through a friend, I got the gig at the Capri. Things worked out after all."

Cole leaned over the table to kiss her cheek. "If you hadn't been at the Capri you and I might never have met. I'll always regret the pain I've caused you, but I'm glad we met, and I hope you never have your heart broken again."

It was probably too late. Analisa feared her heart would shatter when she and Cole separated.

Over the next three days, they saw all the Roman sights they could fit in. They threw their obligatory three coins each into Trevi Fountain. Analisa wished for business success, to return to Rome, and most of all, for the love of a good, hard-working man. When Cole teased her to find out what she'd wished for, she wouldn't tell him. He could make some of her wishes come true.

Her last night there, they strolled through the Ancient Roman Forum in the moonlight. She hooked her arm through his, the most natural thing in the world now.

"It's magical here, isn't it?" she asked, looking up at him. "To think that two thousand years ago, Romans walked over these same cobblestones and looked at these same buildings. I wish I could go back in time and see these buildings intact, clean, and colorful."

He stopped and pulled her closer. "I'd like to go back in time with you."

The huskiness in his voice sent hope curling through her.

"I wish I could take you to the Amalfi Coast," he said. "Vesuvius is something everyone should see. The whole coast is gorgeous and romantic, a place made for lovers." He skimmed a finger over her lips. "I thought of taking you there for my break, but I'd be in violation of my contract."

"Violation? How?"

"The best way to drive the Amalfi Coast is in a fast car that hugs the winding curves. My contract prevents me from taking unneeded chances while I'm filming."

Tenderness shining from his eyes, he wrapped strands of her hair around his finger. "I'll take you there someday." His gaze held hers. "I think we would have been lovers if we'd been together in another time," he said softly.

"Why do you say that?" she asked in a quivering voice.

"I would have wanted to be with you then. I want to be with you now. Do you believe in reincarnation?"

"I'm open to the possibility."

He gathered her to him and crushed her against his chest. "The first time I saw you behind the bar at the Capri, I felt as if I've always known you."

His heart beat steady against her cheek, filling her with peace. They stood that way for minutes, ancient pillars strewn around them, silent sentinels to all the others who'd come before.

He shifted her gently away and took her hand in his. "I guess we'd better head back to the hotel. I have an early call tomorrow and you have a flight to catch."

At the thought of leaving Rome and Cole, unhappiness, like the shadows on the ancient relics, covered Analisa.

When they got to their room, they stopped inside the door and stared at each other. In the dim light coming in through the windows, the smoldering intensity of Cole's sapphire eyes held her as surely as if she were in his arms.

"Analisa," he said, his voice raw with need.

She dropped her purse and went into his embrace.

Like a ravenous man, his mouth descended on hers, devouring and feasting. She slid her palms up his arms to wound around his neck. His lips slanted over hers again and again, seducing and cajoling.

She wanted what his mouth and body promised. His lips traced the seam of hers, and she opened to him, giving herself fully. She wouldn't think about the past or the future, only about this night with this man.

He kissed his way down her chin to her neck and behind her ear, eliciting small whimpers from her. She leaned into him, wanting to meld her body with his. Heat, like molten lava from Vesuvius, flowed through her veins.

Burning, restless, her breasts tight, her body needed Cole. Her soul craved him.

His hands circled her waist, and he pulled away to stare down at her. "I want to make love to you," he whispered.

She could only nod.

Taking her hand, he led her to the bedroom.

CHAPTER TWENTY-SIX

Cole backed her up against the large beckoning bed. His eyes glazed with need and want, he said, "You're sure?"

Swallowing around her dust-dry throat, she squeaked out, "Yes."

He closed his eyes for several seconds. Then, he released her and dug into the pocket of his jeans to pull out a foil-wrapped packet and set it on the nightstand.

"You carry that around with you?" she asked.

"Only when I'm with you." He placed his finger over her mouth. "No more talking."

As if she were a delicate work of art, he reverently slipped off her silk top, then reached behind her to unhook her bra. When she started to put her arms over her breasts, he stopped her, grabbing her hands and kissing the palms.

She kicked off her sandals, and he helped her peel off her jeans.

He yanked the comforter down, and she slipped onto the bed. Undressing, he stood before her, gloriously naked. Hungry for him, she scanned his taut, well-toned chest muscles, the golden hairs gleaming in the dim lamplight. His slim hips led to long, muscled legs. His throbbing erection told her how much he wanted her.

"You're magnificent," she whispered.

The intensity of his deep blue eyes burned her flesh as surely as his touch. He settled onto the bed, leaning over her with his weight on his forearms.

"I've wanted you since the first moment I saw you," he whispered. "I want to make love to you all night."

She caressed his cheek. "I've wanted you for a long time, too."

When he took one of her pebbled nipples into his mouth, she moaned low in her throat. He worshipped her breasts until she squirmed, an ache only he could satisfy building in her. He slipped off her lace panties, then sat back on his knees as his eyes, wicked and sizzling, wandered over her. "You are the most beautiful woman I've ever seen."

She held out her arms and he gathered her to him. Their naked bodies pressed together, fitting in all the right places, as she'd known they would.

He kissed her waiting lips, then trailed kisses down her throat to her breasts. She skimmed her fingers along the warm, sculpted flesh of his back, reveling in his heat and strength. His fingers followed where his lips had been, leaving a trail of fire in their wake.

Taunting and teasing her breasts, he drove her into pleasure-filled tremors until she came in a rush. She finally stilled, spent, unable to move.

"Wow!" she managed to say.

Bracing himself over her, he looked at her with eyes filled with desire, and something else that made her breathing shallow. His lips curved into a slow, sexy smile. "I'm not finished with you."

Kissing his way down to her stomach, he twirled his tongue in her navel before blazing a path down her thighs. He placed tender kisses on the inside of her thighs, then worked his way back up her body to feast on her breasts again. Scorching heat consumed her, and she clutched his hair.

"I want you inside me," she whispered.

"We have all night."

"Now. I need to feel you."

He sat up and grabbed the foil-wrapped packet he'd taken out earlier and pulled on protection. When he braced himself over her again, she opened her legs, welcoming him. He entered her smoothly, filling her. Moving slowly back and forth, he whispered her name.

She wrapped her legs around his ankles and pulled him closer. He drove harder into her. Gripping the firm muscles of his back, she bucked up to meet his thrusts. His skin stretched over his high cheekbones, and his passion-glazed eyes locked with hers.

Analisa tunneled her fingers through the thickness of his hair, moving her hips to his erotic rhythm. Consumed by an unquenchable fire, she willingly gave her body and her soul to Cole.

He kissed her again, a deep drugging kiss, claiming her, taking all she offered. His tongue explored her mouth as he took her on a wild ride she never wanted to end. Desire rippled through her into a swelling of need, until she couldn't think, could only feel, only want.

She came alive in his arms, in ways she'd never experienced. Bolts of excitement rocked her as her orgasm ripped through her. Crying out his name, she clung to him.

Cole's body tightened. With a ragged growl, he shuddered with his own climax. He nuzzled her neck and held her, his body heavy, until they'd both settled down.

He rolled the condom off and slid out of bed. He yanked the covers over her before heading to the bathroom. In the bed again, he settled her into the crook of his arm, pulled her close, and kissed the top of her head, his movements tender.

Analisa lay quietly as her body came down from her ecstatic high. She filled her lungs with the subtle scent of his lemony aftershave mingled with the musk of their lovemaking. She snuggled closer, wanting his heat, wanting the man she loved.

She loved her husband.

CHAPTER TWENTY-SEVEN

Analisa tuned out Emmaline's voice droning on about the charity gala plans. A week after Rome and Cole, Analisa had trouble concentrating on anything but him, his lovemaking, and her love for him.

"Analisa, did you hear me?" Emmaline's strident voice cut through Analisa's thoughts.

Analisa's face heated, and she looked up. "Sorry. What did you say?"

"Do you and Tiffany have your report?"

Analisa shuffled the papers in front of her. "Right here." She gave Tiffany a reassuring smile. The other women intimidated Tiffany.

After Analisa gave her report, Meredith and Emmaline gave theirs, then the group had lunch by the pool at Emmaline's expansive house in the Hollywood Hills. Over a meal of steamed lobster tails, salad, and crisp white wine, Emmaline and Meredith gossiped. Tiffany added a few biting comments about some of the actors they knew, but the other women ignored her. Glad she'd never liked to gossip, Analisa tried to enjoy her lunch and ignore the talk swirling around her.

When the conversation quieted, Meredith looked at Analisa. "How are you enjoying life as a Hollywood wife, *Mrs.* Lassiter?" she asked.

"I'm enjoying being Cole's wife," Analisa said.

Meredith swept her cold gaze over Analisa. "This town will suck the life out of you. I'm not sure you have the balls it takes to survive here."

"Leave her alone, Meredith," Emmaline said.

Analisa smiled at Emmaline. "It's okay. I'm plenty strong enough to survive here or anywhere. I always consider the source when anyone speaks."

Tiffany giggled. Emmaline suppressed a grin.

Meredith's face reddened and her eyes narrowed. She grabbed her wine glass and chugged the rest of what was left. Emmaline's butler, who'd been standing at the side, rushed over and refilled the glass.

Much as she disliked Meredith, the other woman's words stoked insecurity in Analisa. She wanted to run, screaming, out of there. If she were to stay with Cole, would she become like Meredith, sniping at others, putting others down? She shivered at the thought.

The lunch ended soon after, to Analisa's relief. She and Tiffany walked out together to their waiting cars and drivers.

"That Meredith is a witch," Tiffany said. "Don't let her get to you."

"I don't."

"You're strong, Analisa. I admire that."

"You're stronger than you know, Tiffany."

The other woman shrugged. "I don't think so, but thanks for saying it." She smiled. "I can't wait to pick up our dresses tomorrow. It will be fun."

"I'm looking forward to it, too." Analisa had let Tiffany talk her into shopping for a dress for the gala at a boutique on Rodeo Drive. Analisa had tried to rent a gown for the gala but the sites she'd visited didn't have anything in her size. Cole insisted she use the credit card he'd opened in her name. She'd broken down and used it for the beautiful silk dress in shades of purple she'd found at the boutique. It might take a while, but she would pay Cole back. Tiffany had found one at the same shop. Both dresses had needed alterations, and they'd pick them up tomorrow.

Home in Malibu, Analisa trudged slowly inside, her mind churning with Meredith's snarky comments, and her own disgust with the woman. As she started for the stairs and her room, she heard voices coming from the kitchen. Thinking Cole's parents, who were still staying in the guest house, were in the other room, she headed there to say hello. The picture that greeted her stopped her in her tracks.

Rosa and Bennett stood next to the stove, but they weren't cooking. Close to each other, they stared into each other's eyes. Bennett reached out and brushed hair away from Rosa's face. Analisa suppressed a gasp and stepped back.

Her tiny mom lifted her face to the tall Bennett, then skimmed fingers over his lips.

"What am I going to do about you, Rosa?" Bennett asked, his voice thick.

"Whatever you would do with a woman you're attracted to."

The flirty sound of her mom's voice made Analisa clamp a hand over her mouth to keep her from crying out, "No! You're Mom. You're not supposed to do those things."

Bennett bent down and gathered Rosa in his arms. "My room is close."

"Let's go."

Hand-in-hand, they rushed out. Analisa sank against the wall. *Oh. My. God.* She'd suspected her mom and Bennett were a tad sweet on each other. But sex? Her mom having sex? She wouldn't let her mind go there.

Analisa beat a hasty retreat to her bedroom.

At dinner on the deck with Rosa and Cole's parents, Analisa's mind jumbled with the image of her mom and Bennett this afternoon in the kitchen. She should be happy for her mom. Rosa had worked hard her whole life after her husband walked out. When Analisa was growing up, Rosa never had a boyfriend. She deserved to be in love.

"You're so quiet tonight, Analisa," Cathy said. "You miss Cole, don't you?"

"I do." She did miss him, but worry over her mother kept her quiet, too. Things had gotten complicated. What would happen to her mom and Bennett when she and Cole divorced? She didn't want her mom hurt.

After dinner, Analisa begged a headache and went to her room. She sat on her deck overlooking the ocean. The gentle sound of the waves sweeping the shore didn't soothe her as usual.

A soft tap on her bedroom door made her start. "Come in,"

she called.

The door opened, and Rosa slipped in.

"Mom? What's up? Are you okay?" Analisa gestured for Rosa to join her on the deck.

Rosa took a seat next to her and settled her gaze on the ocean. "It's so peaceful here. Vegas is my home and I love the house Cole bought us there, but I wouldn't mind staying here forever." Rosa turned to Analisa with dreamy eyes. "There may be something that will keep me here."

"It is beautiful, but I miss Vegas." Analisa braced herself for a discussion she dreaded. "What would keep you here?"

"We need to talk," Rosa said.

Analisa felt she was the mother and Rosa her teenage daughter with boy troubles.

Rosa's smile brightened her face like the California sun. "I'm in love for the first time in my life."

"I saw you with Bennett this afternoon in the kitchen."

"Oh, my." Rosa touched her cheeks. "What did you see?"

"You went to his room, Mom." Analisa's head felt ready to explode at the accusing tone of her voice. This was Mom, the woman who'd always been there for her.

"I'm old enough to go to a man's room if I want," Rosa said.

"Mom, I'm sorry. I'm happy for you, I really am. You've never even dated all these years."

"I worked too hard to have time for a man. Not working these few months, even though I was injured, made me realize there's a life out there waiting for me. Seeing you and Cole so in love showed me the time's come for me to think about myself and grab for my share of happiness."

Guilt over her selfishness quieted Analisa. Gathering her thoughts, she stared out at the dark ocean, then turned back to her mom. "You deserve all the happiness in the world. I'm a little shocked." Her face burned. "You're my mother. I guess I'm jealous of Bennett. It's always been the two of us. I don't want to lose you, Mom."

"Baby, I'll always be your mother and I'll always be there for you, no matter what. Be happy for me."

Analisa got up from her chaise to embrace her mother. "I like Bennett. I hope he makes you happy." Blinking away tears, she straightened and stepped back.

"He makes me very happy," Rosa said. "Bennett is so handsome, so tall, so powerful. I love his British accent. He comes from royalty, you know, but his family lost their title and all their money. I don't care. I love him."

The time had come for Analisa to tell her mom the truth about her and Cole. "I have water in the small refrigerator in my room. I'll get us some. I have something to tell you."

CHAPTER TWENTY-EIGHT

Analisa, in halting sentences, told Rosa about her contract with Cole. When she finished, Rosa, bottle of water halfway to her mouth, froze and stared silently at Analisa, then slowly set down the water.

"Say something," Analisa said.

"I thought it strange you two married in a rush, but once I saw you together, I knew you were in love." Rosa shrugged. "Sometimes people know right away when they meet *the one*."

Analisa blew out a breath. "I've fallen in love with Cole. I'm afraid to tell him because I don't know how he feels. Everything he does gives me hope he loves me, but he's an actor. I don't want my heart broken again."

"He's a skilled actor, but I've seen how he looks at you. He's not acting."

Since she and Cole had made love, Analisa had come to a decision. As much as she wanted him, they couldn't make love again. She loved him too much. Her heart had begun to break into little pieces when she thought about splitting up with him. She had to protect what was left of her heart. She needed to know he loved her.

"So what happens now?" Rosa put a hand to her throat. "If you and Cole divorce, do you plan to go back to Vegas? What will happen to Bennett and me?"

"I don't know, Mom. That complicates things, but we'll work it out." Analisa frowned. "You can't tell Bennett the truth about our marriage. Please. If word gets out, it'll unleash a torrent of bad publicity. We could look like fools. It might even keep Cole from getting a director's job, something he really wants."

"Couples in love don't keep secrets from each other."

"Has Bennett said he loves you?" A fierce protectiveness rose in Analisa. If Bennett was playing Rosa, he'd be sorry.

Rosa straightened. "Of course he loves me. You don't think I'd go to bed with a guy who didn't? I'm not that kind of woman."

Analisa turned away, fighting more guilt. She'd made love with Cole, who'd never said he loved her.

"Mom, please keep this under wraps. Let's see what happens. Promise you won't tell Bennett?"

"I'll keep quiet. For now."

<><><>

"You'll be the most beautiful woman at the gala," Tiffany said as she and Analisa left the boutique on Rodeo Drive where they'd picked up their altered gowns.

Analisa shifted the garment bag holding her gown over one arm as she slipped on her sunglasses against the harsh sunlight. She smiled at the other woman. "Thanks. You'll look amazing too. I wouldn't have this gown if it weren't for your help." She chuckled. "I felt like Julia Roberts in *Pretty Woman* the first time I walked into that shop. As soon as the sales people realized I was with you, they were all over me."

Tiffany rolled her eyes before sliding on her large black designer sunglasses. "That's how they treated me the first time I went in there. Their attitude changed real quick when I started spending huge sums of money."

"Girls, over here. Let's have nice smiles."

The shouted words made Analisa jump. Photographers aimed cameras at her and Tiffany.

"What the hell?" Analisa said.

"Ignore them," Tiffany said. "Come on, I'll buy you a cup of coffee. I have a secret I want to share."

Annoyance and anger propelled Analisa across the street as the photographers followed her and Tiffany. She fought the urge to scream at them to leave her alone. A video of her losing control would be all over the internet within minutes.

The women found a table at the upscale coffee shop and bakery. The manager shooed the photographers away and hung up the women's gowns in the shop's closet.

After they put in their orders for cappuccino, Analisa removed her sunglasses and looked outside to where the paparazzi waited. "How do you stand having those cameras around?"

"I've gotten used to it," Tiffany said, pulling off her sunglasses. "At first, I liked feeling special. Now, I pretty much ignore them."

"They don't make me feel special. I don't like a lot of attention drawn to me. Haven't since high school when the mean girls mocked me because I didn't wear the latest designer styles."

"We have the Hollywood version of mean girls here," Tiffany said. "You got that kind of treatment at school in Las Vegas?"

The women were quiet as the waitress set steaming cups of cappuccino in front of them.

Analisa sipped hers, then turned her attention back to Tiffany. "If I'd gone to my local high school where most of the kids didn't have much money, I doubt I'd have stood out. I got a scholarship to an all-girl private school where the kids' parents were wealthy. The other girls picked on me for four years. My mother was so proud I'd gotten the scholarship, I never told her."

"I'm sorry," Tiffany said.

"It was a long time ago and it made me a stronger person, but I don't like being the center of attention."

Tiffany laughed. "You're beautiful and you're married to one of the hottest guys in the world, so get used to it."

"I doubt I ever will." Once she and Cole divorced, she could go back to her quiet life, or so she hoped. Her future might be private but it would be lonely without Cole. She sipped her coffee in a futile attempt to wash away her sadness.

Tiffany leaned close, her expression serious. "I've made a decision."

Analisa set down her cup. "About what?"

"I'm leaving Stan," Tiffany said.

Analisa squeezed Tiffany's hand across the table. "Tiff, I know that had to be a hard decision for you. I think you'll be happier for it. Let me know if you need anything. I'm here to help. If you need a place to stay, my home is always open."

Tears filled the other woman's eyes. "You're a true friend. Thanks for the offer, but I have a place. Stan was away last week, and I moved most of my clothes out. He only comes to my room when he wants sex, but he has a new girlfriend so he hasn't bothered me in a long time. He won't notice my closet is emptier."

"Good for you that you found a place."

Tiffany drank coffee as she glanced around the small shop. Setting down her cup, she looked at Analisa and chewed her lip.

"I didn't tell you everything before," Tiffany said. "I'm in love. His name is Jack and we've been lovers for a year now. Jack's close to my age, and he's a talented writer. Two of his screenplays have been optioned. I know he'll make it big someday. Right now, he tends bar at one of the places on Rodeo. That's how I met him."

Analisa sipped her drink and watched Tiffany over the rim of her cup. Tiffany's eyes lit up when she spoke of Jack. Finished with her coffee, Analisa pushed aside the empty cup. "Tiff, you're my friend and I don't want you hurt. Are you sure about Jack? Maybe you need time alone before you jump into another relationship."

"I know it might look like I'm afraid to be on my own, but I'm not. I truly love Jack. I've offered to show his scripts to Stan, but he won't let me. He wants to make it on his talent. He's been after me to leave Stan and move in with him. He says he can support us on his bartending salary and tips until he hits it big. I plan to get a job. I won't be dependent on any man again."

Tiffany smiled and touched Analisa's hand. "You gave me the courage to leave Stan. You made me realize I need to get back the self-respect I lost. I see how much you love Cole. Your whole face lights up when you say his name. You're strong and you didn't give up who you are when you married him. I want what you have, and I think I'll get that with Jack."

Apparently Analisa wasn't as good an actor as she thought if Tiffany could tell she loved Cole. "When will you tell Stan?"

"The day after the gala. He won't care now that he's found another blonde younger than me. According to the terms of our pre-nup, if I leave him, I can take only my clothes and a few select pieces of jewelry. I'm okay with that."

Gladness and anxiety for her friend clogged Analisa's throat. "I'm proud of you, and I wish you all the joy in the world. But I worry about you, too."

"Don't worry about me. It'll all work out." Tiffany signaled the waitress for another round of coffee. When it came, she held up her cup in salute. "To Analisa, my best friend, who gave me back my self-respect."

CHAPTER TWENTY-NINE

Two nights before the charity gala, Rosa, Cole's parents, and Analisa sat on the sectional in the media room watching an action movie, bowls of chips and salsa on the table in front of them. Her nerves on overdrive to rival the car chases in the movie, Analisa had trouble concentrating. She wished Cole could be home to escort her to the gala. She didn't relish the thought of going alone into the den of vipers that was Hollywood's elites.

Bennett came in and out of the room refreshing their drinks and snacks. Whenever he did, his gaze met Rosa's. Rosa blushed prettily, and Analisa noticed Bennett found excuses to touch her hand. Cathy and Charlie, engrossed in the film, didn't seem to notice.

The movie's credits were rolling when Analisa heard the front door open. Frowning, she looked at the others.

A weary-looking Cole came into the room, a golden stubble on his jaw, his hair ruffled, and his clothes wrinkled. His T-shirt was tucked messily into his jeans. He was beautiful.

Analisa ran to him. He scooped her up in his arms, holding her close. His deep kiss claimed her and inflamed every cell in her body. She forgot about the others. All she knew and felt was the man in her arms.

Chuckling and the sound of someone clearing his throat broke through Analisa's sensual fog. Heat spread from her neck to her face. She pulled away and turned to see the others, including

Bennett, watching with knowing looks. Rosa nodded and gave Analisa a sly smile.

After hugs for his family and Rosa, Cole reached for Analisa again and held her against his side. At his closeness, images of making love with him, of feeling him deep inside her, made treacherous heat unfurl in her.

"I thought you couldn't get away for another week," Analisa said.

"I asked to film my scenes out of order. I worked practically around the clock, but I had to come home. I couldn't let you go to the gala alone."

The power of his words and the tenderness in his voice shot yearning and hope through her. Everything around her faded as they stared at each other.

"You look tired, son," Charlie said, breaking the mood.

Scrubbing a hand over his face, Cole said, "I'm exhausted. I want a sandwich, a beer, and bed, in that order."

"I'll make you something to eat," Bennett said, heading to the kitchen.

Rosa followed Bennett out of the room.

<><><>

Seated at the large kitchen table, Cole enjoyed the sandwich and cold beer, and kept up a conversation with the others with half a mind. He couldn't think straight with Analisa sitting so close. Her perfume, a light scent with hints of jasmine, teased his senses. He'd been anxious to leave Rome. He had to see Analisa, to hold her again, make love to her. She'd dominated his waking hours and his dreams. He'd missed his wife, missed her smile, her laugh, her warmth.

He glanced over at her now. She was saying something to his mother. The smooth column of Analisa's neck invited him to kiss her and nibble at her sweet flesh. Her elegant long fingers, the nails colored a soft pink, drummed on the tabletop. Her thick black hair tumbled down her back, begging him to run his fingers through its silkiness.

She must have sensed him staring because she turned to him. Her expressive eyes, chocolate flecked with gold, sparked fire as they met his. If the others weren't there, he'd give in to his fantasy and throw Analisa onto the table to make wild love to her. His erection strained against his jeans.

"Would there be anything else, sir?" Bennett asked, interrupting Cole's erotic musings.

"No, thanks, Bennett. I need to turn in." With a glance at his lap, Cole picked up his bottle of beer. "After I finish this."

His parents stood. "We'd better head to bed, too," his mom said. "Tomorrow we want to hear all about Rome and your new movie."

"Deal," Cole said.

Murmuring their "good-nights," his parents left.

Rosa strode over to where Bennett was cleaning up. "I'll help Bennett before I go to bed."

When she'd walked away, Cole whispered to Analisa, "I picked up vibes between Bennett and Rosa. I knew they were attracted to each other, but something's different."

"You're observant," Analisa said. "They're in love."

"Wow! I go away for a while and see what happens."

She laughed, a light tinkling sound that stirred his heart. He placed his hand over hers. "I've missed you. I can't stop thinking about you. I want to make love to you all night, Analisa."

She blushed a pretty shade of pink and withdrew her hand from his. "I thought you were exhausted."

"I'll never be too tired to make love to you."

Emotions played on her exquisite face—desire, tenderness, then anxiety.

"What's wrong?" he asked.

She fingered the hem of her T-shirt and glanced toward Rosa and Bennett, then turned back to Cole. "Not here."

"We can talk in the bedroom."

"No, on the deck."

He shrugged and followed her outside.

They stood at the railing looking out over the beach below, the white foam of the waves in stark contrast to the darkness.

He took one of her hands and turned her to face him. "Talk to me, Analisa."

"We can't do that anymore, Cole."

"Do what?" The sense of despair filling him told him the answer.

"We can't make love again," she whispered.

"Why? We want each other. What happened in Rome proved that. We're legally married."

She shook her head, making her silky curls float around her face. He wanted to scoop her up and carry her off to bed, to allay her fears, to prove to her they were good together.

"Our marriage is a contract for our mutual benefit," she said. "I've thought about this, and I want to go along with the original agreement, a marriage in name only."

"It stopped being a marriage in name only that night in Rome," he said softly. "I would never use you or hurt you. I believe we have real feelings for each other. We owe it to ourselves to explore those feelings."

She broke free of him. "I can't, Cole. This is for the best." Head high, she walked away, her swaying hips luring him. He resisted the urge to go after her.

Cole gazed out at the inky ocean. The back and forth movement normally calmed and grounded him. No matter how successful or rich he became, the ocean always reminded him he was no more than an insignificant grain of sand. Tonight, he couldn't find calmness.

Analisa had feelings for him. He knew it. The more time he spent with her, the more he wanted her in his life. Tomorrow he would start his plan to seduce his wife and convince her she belonged with him.

CHAPTER THIRTY

Sunlight pierced Analisa's eyes, forcing her to open them. She glanced at the bedside clock. Nine. She'd gotten to sleep around three that morning. The beginnings of a headache, brought on by lack of sleep and stress, throbbed.

An hour later, dressed in jeans, a pink tank top, and tan sandals, Analisa headed down to the kitchen. She heard voices as she approached, then was greeted with the vision of Cole, her mom, and Cole's parents seated at the table finishing breakfast.

"Here she is now," Cathy said, looking toward Analisa.

Cole jumped up and went to her. Taking her hand, he kissed her cheek, every bit the doting husband. How dare he look fresh and well-rested when she felt like crap? She suppressed the urge to growl at him. Never a morning person, she avoided those who were perky so early, especially husbands who didn't seem to mind her rejection the night before.

"Sit, sweetheart." Cole led her to the table and held out a chair for her.

"I'll have your eggs in a minute," Bennett called from the stove.

"Coffee?" Cole said, holding up the pot.

"Can I have it intravenously?" Analisa asked.

Cole laughed and poured her a cup. "Don't like mornings, I see."

She glared at him before taking a life-saving sip. Setting the cup down, she forced herself to smile at the others. "'Morning, everyone."

After a chorus of "good mornings," Rosa said, "You look tired, Ana. Didn't you sleep well?"

Analisa felt Cole's stare. She wouldn't give him the satisfaction of knowing she'd been kept awake by thoughts of him. "I slept fine."

Bennett brought over fluffy scrambled eggs, crisp bacon, and sourdough toast, along with a plate of fresh fruit. She dug in.

"Cole is taking us all to the Getty Center today," Cathy said.

Analisa swallowed her egg too fast and coughed. "He is?" Cole, the devoted husband and the caring son. He made it hard to resist him.

"We'll leave as soon as you're done breakfast," Cole said. "I'll take the SUV and drive. I don't want to call for a car. It'll just be us on a family outing."

Family outing. The words filled Analisa with a bittersweet craving. For the hundredth time, she wished Cole weren't a famous movie star. They'd do family things together without the annoying paparazzi who dogged their steps whenever she was with him. She didn't want strangers fixated on her every movement. She wanted a nice, private life, something she'd never have with Cole.

After they'd eaten and freshened up, Analisa and the others waited at the front door for Cole. He drove up in a black Escalade, pulled to a stop, and jumped out.

He wore his hipster "disguise" of a ball cap low over his face, aviator style sunglasses, ripped jeans, a black T-shirt, and black Converse high-tops.

"Nice disguise," she said, as he walked around to open the passenger doors. He helped her into the front seat, and she whispered, "Why didn't you dye your hair black and wear nerd glasses? Sure fooled me with that one."

"You gonna ever forgive me for that?" he asked.

"Nope." She got into the car and reached for the seatbelt, ignoring his frown.

At the first view of the Getty Center, a spectacular white building sitting atop a hill overlooking the highway, Analisa's bad mood diminished. Maybe her own confusion about their relationship, her anxiety, had made Cole's jaunty attitude put her in a foul mood earlier.

They'd had Rome. She'd succumbed to the romanticism of the Eternal City and her own desires. She shouldn't have expected Cole to be heartbroken because she refused to continue a physical relationship with him. Yet, part of her wanted Cole to pursue her, to be bothered by her rejection. She didn't know what the hell she wanted.

They entered the elegant modern museum, and Cole took Analisa's hand. When she started to pull away, he drew her closer and bent to whisper in her ear. "We have to put on a show for the public and our parents."

The group agreed to split up and meet for lunch later at the museum's restaurant, where Cole had made reservations. The others took off together to explore, leaving Analisa with Cole. Museum-goers stared at him, and some even snapped his picture. Analisa assumed his disguise didn't fool everyone, but no one approached them.

Glad to be left alone by the paparazzi and Cole's fans, and as excited as a wine lover in a vineyard, Analisa vowed to forget her doubts and anxieties for a while and lose herself in the exhibits and the sweeping architecture. Every room contained sculptures and artwork that transported her back to other times and cultures. She stood in front of busts by Bernini and remembered Rome and making love with Cole. The memories warmed her like the sun streaming through the large windows.

"The exhibits change on a regular basis," Cole said. "I'll take you to the Getty Villa in Malibu. It's filled with Ancient Roman, Greek, and Etruscan artifacts. I know how much you love Ancient Rome."

She doubted she and Cole would be together long enough to come back here or go to the Getty Villa. She swallowed her regret. "I'd like that."

After lunch at the restaurant overlooking the Santa Monica Mountains, Analisa and Cole strolled the extensive gardens while the rest of their group toured more of the museum. The perfume of the flowers bordering the stream and waterfall, the lush greenery, and the intimacy of Cole's closeness cocooned Analisa in a fantasy world.

She could almost believe he was an ordinary guy, someone

who could be a father to her children, a man she could spend her life with.

They stayed until closing time, then headed home to a meal prepared by Bennett. For once, Rosa didn't argue she wanted to cook. After dinner, Rosa, Cathy, and Charlie begged tiredness after the long day and retired.

Analisa and Cole sat alone on the deck, drinking lattes. "I had fun today," Analisa said.

"I'm glad."

Her attention on the ocean below, she enjoyed her drink. Exhaustion set in, and she placed her empty cup on the table and stood. "I'm tired. I think I'll go to my room and watch TV before bed." She scooped up Killer when the cat walked past. "I'll take Killer with me."

"If you need me, you know where to find me," Cole said softly.

She buried her face in the cat's soft fur as she left the deck. The purring animal clutched to her chest wouldn't hurt her, but neither could it fill the empty places in her heart.

CHAPTER THIRTY-ONE

A nalisa leaned her head back and let the multiple spraying jets in the shower stall wash over her. She wished the warm water could clear away her nervousness. The charity gala was tonight. As one of the chairs, she had to be "on" all night. Thank God Cole would be with her.

His parents had left for Ohio that morning with the promise to visit again at the end of the summer, along with several of their kids and grandkids. Since this was Bennett's day off, he and Rosa had set out early to see some of the tourist sites.

Analisa stepped out of the shower and began toweling herself. At the light tapping on the connecting door between her room and Cole's, her pulse soared. She threw on a short robe and unlocked the door. Cole stood there, his longish blond hair ruffled, his blue eyes sleepy. His boyish appeal wrapped around her heart.

"I guess I'm still jet-lagged." He leaned against the doorjamb. "Probably should have stayed home yesterday rather than going to the Getty. My nap today lasted longer than I'd planned. When do we have to leave for the gala?"

"The driver is picking us up in ninety minutes."

Cole scanned her. "That gives us plenty of time."

"To get ready?" Excitement jolted her at the wicked gleam in his eyes.

He leaned closer. "To make love to you. My mind's conjured all kinds of fantasies seeing you standing there in nothing more than a robe with your hair wet and mussed."

"Down, boy," she said, putting her hand on his chest and pushing him away. "Get dressed."

Grinning, he shook his head. "I'll get dressed, but you know what you're missing."

She shut the door and locked it. Yes, she knew exactly what she was missing.

Her thoughts on Cole, Analisa dried her hair and used her curling iron. She kept her hair loose with gentle curls to tumble over her shoulders and down her back. Sitting at the vanity table in her room, she applied her makeup, using more eye shadow and mascara than usual. The other event chairwomen planned to have their hair and makeup professionally done, but Analisa wanted to look like herself, not some enhanced version that wasn't real. Tonight would be her introduction to Los Angeles society. She smiled at the irony. She'd enter society and leave it when her contract with Cole ended.

Her makeup finished, she slipped off her robe and put on a purple lace bra and matching panties. Standing in front of the full-length mirror, she ran her hands down her body, remembering Rome and Cole's kisses and caresses. Her body heated, and she moaned.

Determined to quit obsessing over him, she strode to the closet and pulled out her dress, holding the soft silk against her. Analisa had fallen in love with the shimmering gown in graduated shades of purple and lavender as soon as she saw it.

She slipped on the gown, zipped it up the back, then turned to the mirror. The wide-eyed woman staring back at her bore little resemblance to bartender Analisa Barbero in her working uniform of white shirt, black pants, and comfortable shoes.

She twirled slowly to study herself from all sides. Her pushup bra enhanced her cleavage in the strapless deep purple bodice. The dress skimmed her curves, the varying shades going from purple to lavender. The sensuous swish of silk around her ankles promised a night steeped in magic. Never in her life had she dreamed of owning a dress like this. She felt like a princess and a sexy siren enveloped in clouds of purple.

Chuckling, she shot her image a rueful smile. Midnight would come soon enough for this Cinderella when her contract with Cole expired. Then she'd be back to being plain Analisa Barbero from Las Vegas.

The car would be there in ten minutes. She pulled her silver stiletto sandals from the closet and sat on the bed to slip on the shoes, worlds apart from the flats she wore to work. Finished, she took one last look in the mirror, then plucked her silver beaded purse from the dresser. She strode to the door and opened it to a tuxedo-clad Cole, with his hand up, ready to knock.

His eyes widened. "Wow! You are gorgeous!"

The passion lighting his eyes made heat flow through her like fine, aged whiskey. Part of her wanted to grab him by the arm and haul him into the room to make love all night. Before she acted on that temptation, she stepped into the hall and shut the door firmly behind her.

"Thank you," she said. "Most men wear a tux well, but you bring it to a whole new level." The cut of the tuxedo enhanced his lean, muscled body. With his blond hair slicked back and his chiseled features, he had to be one of the most beautiful men in the world. His polished looks couldn't disguise his animal magnetism and raw sexuality. No wonder he came alive on the screen.

He grinned one of his sexy trademark smiles. "Thank you, ma'am." He held out his arm to her.

Heat flared out from her stomach to her lower parts. Forcing a smile against the desire that raged in her, she threaded her arm through his.

<><><>

They entered the ballroom arm-in-arm to a flood of flashbulbs from the photographers hired for the event. Analisa smiled for the cameras but didn't release her hold on Cole. She hoped she presented a picture of calm and cool on the outside. Inside, butterflies on steroids partied in her stomach.

Cole bent to whisper in her ear. "You're getting to be a pro at this. I'll be by your side all night. You have nothing to worry about."

She lifted her face to stare into his eyes, blue as a gentle sea. "Thank you," she whispered.

He kissed her tenderly on the lips, to another barrage of lights.

The ballroom had been transformed into a small version of

the Palace of Versailles, with gold-framed floor-to-ceiling mirrors along one wall, crystal chandeliers hanging from the gilded ceiling, and white-draped tables with gold flowers in the center of each.

"This is a fantasy," Analisa said, her voice breathy. "The decorators and party planners Emmaline hired have done an amazing job."

"You've seen one fantasy, you've seen them all," Cole said with a chuckle.

"Cynical, much?" she said, looking up at him.

His eyes gleamed. "Just a little."

"Analisa, you're here." Tiffany ran over to them. With her swept-up hairdo and elaborate, beaded, high-necked gown, she looked like a wealthy Victorian lady.

"Hey, Tiff," Analisa said.

Cole smiled a greeting to the other woman.

Tiffany nodded to Cole, than grabbed one of Analisa's hands. "Come see the table set up for the silent auction. It looks amazing."

Cole patted Analisa's hand, still held in the crook of his arm. "I'll be at the bar."

"Okay. I won't be long."

"You look beautiful, Tiff," Analisa said as they walked toward the tables displaying the items for the silent auction.

"Thanks. So do you. Told you that gown would be perfect for you."

When they reached the tables covered in gold satin, Analisa studied the expensive wares. "The display is beautiful and shows off the gifts perfectly." She turned to Tiffany. "You did a great job designing it. You're very talented."

"That's so nice of you to say."

Analisa touched the other woman's arm. "It's the truth."

"You're the best. Thanks. I hope the auction goes well."

"It will. Don't worry. I need to find my husband and have a drink." Analisa glanced around the room, filled with the cream of Hollywood and Los Angeles society. Like a James Bond movie set at a Monaco casino, beautiful women wore ball gowns in every color of the rainbow, though red dominated. She was glad she had decided on something other than red. Men, dressed in elegant bespoke tuxedos, their air of superiority and wealth evident in their self-satisfied, tanned faces, shouldered through the crowd or gathered to talk in small circles.

"Where's your husband, Tiffany?" she asked.

Tiffany pointed to a group of men standing next to a mirror across the room. "He's the one with the blonde glued to his side."

Analisa steeled her face against the surprise that slammed her. She'd known Tiffany's husband was much older, but this man, obese and bald, had to be at least seventy. A very young woman in a body-hugging gown clung to him. His hand was on the woman's butt.

"Tiff, how humiliating for you."

"He can't make me feel like less of a person, not any more. Thanks to you."

Analisa gave Tiffany a quick hug. "I'm going to find my husband now."

She headed to the bar and Cole. Other men watched her as she walked. Since she'd met Cole, she'd not looked at another man. Cole was all she needed.

"Hey, there," she said when she reached him.

"Hey, sweetheart," he said.

She took the flute of champagne he held out.

Her good mood shattered when she spotted Meredith Hightower headed their way. "Uh-oh. Look who's on her way over."

Dressed in a red gown that hugged her substantial curves, and enough diamonds dangling from her ears and around her neck to rival the chandeliers, Meredith grabbed a flute of champagne from a passing waiter before she reached them.

"Hello, Cole. Analisa," the other woman said, her attention focused fully on Cole. She put a hand on his arm. "You're looking good."

He stepped away and drew Analisa against him. "Hello, Meredith. Where's John?"

The other woman chugged her champagne and grabbed another from a waiter. "Last time I saw him he was trying to get into the pants of some young bimbo. What else is new?"

"Analisa and I need to mingle. See you around, Meredith."

Cole put his hand on the small of Analisa's back and

propelled her away from Meredith.

"Thank you, Cole. She's not a happy person. Why does Emmaline put up with her?"

They nodded hellos to others as they walked, then stopped near one of the tables loaded with seafood appetizers. Although she hadn't eaten since breakfast, Analisa was too nervous to sample the delicious-looking food.

Cole leaned closer. "Emmaline puts up with Meredith to stay on the right side of Meredith's husband, for her own husband's sake. Meredith has a lot of pull in this town, and Emmaline needs her on projects like this. And Pete needs parts. He doesn't want to make an enemy of Meredith's husband. I would never put you in that position. I'll stand or fall on my own."

"I like that about you," Analisa said.

"Let's forget them. I want to dance with my wife." He took her glass and set it on the table along with his. Taking her hand, he led her onto the dance floor.

When he took her into his arms, she laid her head on his solid chest and gave herself over to the wonder of Cole, his closeness and gentleness as they glided around the floor to the slow, romantic tune.

She inhaled the subtle scent of his aftershave with hints of citrus as peace stole over her. His heart beat steady and sure against her cheek. As they danced, Analisa forgot everything except the man who held her. Others stared, but she closed her eyes and tuned them out. She felt protected in his arms, a security edged with excitement. She let herself imagine she and Cole were in love, that they weren't corrupted by those around them, that they had a loving, faithful marriage.

Somewhere in her consciousness, she knew the music ended, yet she and Cole clung to each other, swaying to a tune only they could hear. The click of cameras brought her back to reality. She wondered if someone had taken their picture. They drew apart, and she opened her eyes to find Cole staring down at her with tenderness.

"Analisa," he whispered. The way he said her name, raw and needy, stirred her with longing.

"Cole, dude, glad you could make it." The deep masculine voice cut through the sensual net that surrounded Cole and

Analisa.

His arm around Analisa's waist, Cole turned to the man who'd spoken. "Hey, Jake."

The other man, tall and muscular, with chiseled, movie-star features, his black hair tied into a low ponytail, smiled. "Graceann and I just got here." He nodded toward the woman next to him, a very pregnant stunning brunette with sparkling green eyes.

The woman grinned and gave Cole a hug. "You're looking extraordinary, Cole, but then you always do." With a warm smile for Analisa, she held out her hand. "You must be Analisa. I'm Graceann Falco, and this big lug next to me is my husband Jake."

The women shook hands. Analisa immediately liked Graceann and Jake. Their friendliness and warmth seemed genuine, so different from some of the others she'd met since coming to Los Angeles.

"Let me see your ring," Graceann said, holding onto Analisa's hand to examine her amethyst ring. "Beautiful example of thirties workmanship. Did you get it at an estate sale?"

"Cole bought it at an antique shop."

Graceann smiled and dropped Analisa's hand. "He has exquisite taste. I'm a jewelry designer. I have a shop and workroom on our property in the Hollywood Hills. Have Cole bring you around soon. We'll have coffee and chat."

"I'd like that."

Someone called Jake's name, and he and Graceann said their goodbyes to Cole and Analisa.

She watched them walk away. "They seem like good people."

"They're the best," Cole said. "Jake and I got to Hollywood about the same time. He's done some acting, but mostly he's a producer and screenwriter, very successful."

"I've seen pictures of him, but he's better looking in person. They appear happy. I hope it's for real, and not like what I've seen with other couples." An ache for the kind of love that shone between the Falcos pulled at Analisa.

"Their happiness is real," Cole said. "They have an interesting backstory. Graceann and Jake went to the same high school in Pennsylvania. They met again years later when Graceann hired him to be her pretend fiancé."

"Pretend fiancé?"

Cole laughed. "Yup. They fell in love and their pretend engagement turned to a real marriage. You could say they had a contract engagement like we have a contract marriage." He leaned closer to whisper in her ear. "Sometimes people fall in love when they least expect it."

She shivered at the challenge that blazed in his eyes.

Swallowing her anxieties, she stepped back and met his gaze. "What if it comes out we have a contract? What will people say when they find out you bought me the house in Vegas and you're paying me $500,000 as part of the contract when we divorce?"

"They'll think the house and money are the divorce settlement. Don't worry about it."

Analisa felt someone nearby and turned to find a waiter hovering. When she stared at him, he scampered away.

CHAPTER THIRTY-TWO

A nalisa rested her head on Cole's shoulder as they rode home in the limo. He put his arm around her waist and drew her closer.

"Things went well, didn't they?" she said.

"It was a beautiful party. You and the others should be proud. Your hard work raised a lot of money for the kids."

"We did."

"You looked like a pro on that stage announcing the silent auction winners. Maybe I need to worry about acting competition from you."

She laughed. "Not hardly." While on stage announcing the winners to an enthusiastic crowd, Cole's reassuring smile had helped her fight her nervousness at being the center of attention.

She settled more comfortably against him, inhaling his comforting, familiar scent, and rested her hand on the velvet jewel case on her lap. "Thank you for buying me this beautiful necklace designed by Graceann Falco. You beat out a lot of bids. I love the necklace, but you didn't have to buy me anything."

"You worked hard and you deserve it. It makes me happy to buy you beautiful things."

With thoughts of Cole and of the evening, she let herself drift off to sleep.

"Wake up, sleepyhead," Cole said, kissing her temple.

Analisa sat up. They were in front of his house.

"Let's get you to bed," he said.

Arm-in-arm, they entered the quiet house and went up the

stairs to their bedrooms.

At the door to her room, Cole bent to brush his lips over hers in a gentle kiss. "Sweet dreams, Analisa."

She didn't want gentle. She wanted Cole. All night. Wrapping her arms around his waist, she pressed against him and kissed him deeply, opening to him, letting him know how much she wanted him.

With a groan, his tongue swept into her mouth, and he backed her up against the wall.

She pulled away and ran her fingers over his lips. "Stay with me tonight."

"You're sure?" he asked in a thick voice.

"Yes."

They stumbled inside the room together, and Cole shut the door with his foot.

Need and desire reflected in the depths of his eyes, and something else that filled her heart with hope. He turned her around and unzipped her gown. The slow slide of the silk along her bare legs scorched her flesh. He unhooked her bra and let it fall to the floor.

Gently pulling her to face him, he skimmed his long fingers down her face, his gentle touch forming a delicious knot of love in her. He kissed his way to her neck and the tender spot behind her ear. When he cupped her breasts, massaging and caressing, her skin caught fire, and she curled her fingers over his shoulders as a torrent of pleasure ripped through her. He bent to suckle one hard nipple, than the other. She threw her head back, her senses tuned to Cole and only him.

Moaning his name, her body tingled and trembled, and she felt herself losing control.

With a guttural murmur, he gathered her to him. "Analisa." The hunger in his voice shot heat through her veins.

He scooped her up in his arms and carried her to the bed. Holding her, he yanked the covers back and settled her on the mattress. He pulled off her sandals and her panties.

He undressed and lay next to her. She gripped his shoulders and rubbed her body against his.

"If you keep doing that, I won't last much longer," he rasped.

"I want you so much."

"I'll give you everything you want. And more."

He kissed a hot path down her body, his hands following where his lips touched. Heat built in her, twisting and consuming. She arched her hips, begging him to fill her.

He continued his onslaught, tormenting her with his tongue and hands until she couldn't think, could only feel. Cole was everything she'd always wanted, and all she hadn't known she'd wanted. She filled her lungs with him, his scent that was uniquely Cole, and dug her fingers into his shoulders. Aching for him, she parted her legs in invitation.

"Please, Cole," she whimpered.

Leaning over the bed, he reached into the night table drawer to draw out a packet. He ripped it open and pulled on protection.

He settled his hard-muscled body between her legs. "I have never wanted a woman more than I want you."

She skimmed the warm, firm flesh of his arms. "I'm yours." She bit her tongue and swallowed her words of love.

CHAPTER THIRTY-THREE

Analisa sliced through the water with long strokes, from one end of the pool to the other, kick turned, then swam back again. Since the night of the gala five days ago, she and Cole had made love more times and in more places than she could count. There were spaces in the house and in the gardens that made her blush, remembering their lovemaking. She rolled over to float on her back. As the water embraced her, a giggle bubbled up in her. She never imagined she could be this happy and this much in love.

He hadn't said the words, but she knew Cole loved her. She'd miss him the next few days. He'd left early yesterday on a publicity tour of the East Coast talk shows to promote his film, an action one, releasing in a week.

The gentle hug of the water couldn't dispel the anxiety that washed over her. She could finally admit to herself she wanted to stay with him after their contract ended, wanted a real marriage, one based on love, respect, and faithfulness, not a celebrity coupling.

"Ana?"

At her mom's voice, Analisa jerked upright and swam to the edge of the pool to squint up at Rosa standing there. At the concern on Rosa's face, Analisa pulled herself from the pool and grabbed a nearby towel to dry off.

"What's wrong, Mom?"

"You should come in now."

Her mother turned on her heel and hurried away before

Analisa could quiz her. Analisa threw on her swimsuit cover, then followed into the kitchen. Bennett, at the counter, a grimace on his face, held the TV remote. The TV was turned on to the gossip show, *The Tattle*.

"Why are you watching that?" Analisa asked.

"You'll see after the commercial," Rosa said. "Ana, I'm so sorry."

With dread pressing against her chest, Analisa stared at the screen. When the commercial ended, the host announced they had exclusive pictures of Cole Lassiter and his wife, and asked the question, "Is Analisa Barbero Lassiter a gold-digger?"

A video of Tiffany and her leaving the boutique with their glittery garment bags over their arms flashed on the screen. Analisa sank onto a stool, insides trembling.

The host, a smirk on her overly made-up face, continued. "Did hot tamale Las Vegas bartender Analisa Barbero blackmail Cole Lassiter into marrying her? What does she know he doesn't want revealed? *The Tattle* has learned Barbero and Lassiter have nothing more than a contract marriage. He bought Barbero a house in Vegas and is rumored to have agreed to pay her five-hundred thousand dollars when they split. Our investigation has revealed Barbero was fired from her job at the Augustus Hotel for inappropriate behavior days before she married Lassiter, and she was on the brink of bankruptcy. Barbero hit the jackpot when she married Lassiter. Come clean, Lassiter. What does Barbero have on you?"

More pictures flashed on the screen, of her and Cole kissing as they entered the ballroom for the charity gala, and again clinging to each other on the dance floor.

"Do these look like the pictures of a couple in love, or an actor and his equally talented wife playing their parts? You decide."

The host went onto another story, and Bennett switched off the TV.

Stunned, Analisa froze, all feeling gone. Rosa wrapped her arms around her and rocked her, as if Analisa were still her little girl.

"I'm sorry, baby," Rosa crooned as she stroked Analisa's hair.

"They think I'm a gold-digger," Analisa said when she found

her voice. "They investigated me." She drew away from her mother. She hated this whole celebrity thing. It was high school all over again—the vile names and mockery—but on a much bigger scale. As long as she stayed with Cole, the fishbowl life would never end. Her every movement would be monitored and dissected. Cole could be hurt by this, too. Some people would believe the vicious gossip that he had something to hide.

"Cole will set everything straight," Bennett said. "I've worked for him for years, and he's the real deal." His sympathetic gaze met Analisa's. "Rosa told me about your marriage contract. Your marriage might have started as a business agreement, but Cole loves you. I've seen how he looks at you."

Analisa blinked back tears. "Thanks, Bennett. I'm worried about Cole also. This could affect the roles he's offered and his directing dreams. I can't talk about any of this now." Her flight response kicked in, and she trembled with the need to escape. "I have to get out of here."

Rosa stroked her arm. "Where will you go?"

"Home, to Las Vegas."

"Shouldn't you wait for Cole?" Rosa asked.

Analisa stood. "I've had enough of Hollywood with its games and lies. I need to go away, to clear my mind."

<><><>

Analisa had hired a driver and car to take her and Rosa back to Las Vegas. Late that evening, with their luggage around them, along with Killer in her carrier, the women stood in the entry hall of the Las Vegas house Cole had bought them.

"I guess we're back," Rosa said.

Her throat thick with unshed tears, Analisa could only shake her head. Cole had called her repeatedly during the day and left numerous voicemails and texts, all of which she'd deleted without reading. Having him near or talking to him muddled her thoughts. She needed a clear head and time away from him to think.

After unpacking, Rosa and Analisa ate spaghetti with marinara sauce and drank red wine, neither speaking. Rosa pushed away her half-empty plate and met Analisa's gaze.

"You shouldn't have run away like that, Ana. You're a fighter. You should have stayed and fought for your man."

"They called me a gold-digger. They might be calling Cole worse."

"Who cares what those malicious gossipmongers say? They lie for ratings. I know, Cole knows, you know, you're not a gold-digger. You can't let others' words hurt you. I raised you to have pride."

"I do have pride, Mom, which is why I left. I love Cole, but I have to think of his career, and not only myself." She took a deep breath. "I believe he loves me, but I don't know if I can handle being married to a celebrity, always in the public eye."

She rubbed her forehead. "I hate being stalked by paparazzi, hate being called names. I'm sickened by some of the things I've seen in Hollywood—the gossip, the sniping, the lies, the rampant adultery. It's not the life I want, not the marriage I want."

Meeting her mother's gaze, she said, "I love this house, and I want you to be comfortable for the first time in your life. We may have to give it all up if I pull out of my contract with Cole."

Rosa squeezed her hand. "I'm not worried about this house. I'm only worried about you. I want you to be happy, my Ana. You love Cole, and your marriage has become real in every sense. You're afraid."

Analisa widened her eyes. "How did you...?"

"I wasn't born yesterday."

"We never said we love each other."

Rosa threw up her hands. "Stubborn people. What are you waiting for? I want to knock both your heads together."

"Mom, what will happen with you and Bennett?"

"Bennett is a good man. We'll figure something out. My place is with you now."

Analisa's phone rang. Cole's face came up, the face she loved.

Rosa raised an eyebrow when Analisa rejected the call. "Who else knew about your contract with Cole?" Rosa asked.

"No one."

"Someone found out."

Analisa snapped her fingers. "Of course. The gala. That waiter eavesdropping. The tabloids and gossip sites pay money for celebrity stories. I wonder if he sold our story."

"What?" Rosa said.

"It doesn't matter now." Analisa shook her head. "We've had

a long, exhausting day. I have to do a lot of soul-searching."

Rosa stood. "I'm going to bed. You coming?"

"Soon. You go ahead, Mom."

"If you want to talk, I'm here for you."

After Rosa left, Analisa made some mint tea, put on a sweater against the chilly desert night, and went out to the deck overlooking the pool. A glimmer of moonlight lit a faint trail across the still water. The calmness of the quiet desert instilled a modicum of peace in her.

Maybe she'd been too hasty in running away. She'd never felt at home in the often vicious, rarified enclaves of Hollywood. She loved Cole, but did she love him enough to go back into that den of vipers? She felt Cole loved her, but maybe she was wrong. He was a gifted actor.

She sipped her tea and stared out over the pool. Killer came on the deck and jumped onto her lap. Analisa held the purring cat close, rubbing her chin on its soft head.

"What should I do, Killer? Am I a coward for running?" The cat's purring echoed in the quiet. She sat cuddling the cat as images rolled through her mind like movie trailers. She and Cole laughing together, their day at Hoover Dam, him buying her the amethyst ring, talking on those nights when he came home late from the studio. Walking with him on the beach, holding his hand. Making love with him. Rome.

The comforting tea, the warm cat, the desert, all combined to open her heart and mind. She knew Cole. She would fight for him and for their life together. She'd talk to him and listen. Tell him her fears of living in the spotlight. She'd told Tiffany sometimes all you had was your self-respect. Analisa had to keep hers. She and Cole would work things out.

<><><>

After a fitful night, Analisa rose early. When Cole called today, she'd talk to him. Seated at the kitchen counter finishing off a light breakfast, the TV was set to a morning talk show out of New York, but she paid little attention.

When she heard Cole's name, she jerked her head up and grabbed the remote to increase the volume. The host announced Cole Lassiter as his guest. Analisa's gaze riveted on the screen as Cole came on and shook hands with the host, then took a seat.

Her heart jumped at the sight of Cole. Under his tan, the dark circles beneath his eyes telegraphed his stress and exhaustion. He brushed a hand over his hair, mussing it, making himself look more adorable. She wanted to jump through the screen and hug him to her.

The show's host made the introduction, then said Cole had something important to say to the world and to his wife. Analisa's hand froze with her coffee mug halfway to her mouth. She slowly set down the mug.

Cole stared into the camera. "Recently, an ugly story about my wife and my marriage was all over social media and on those shows that feed on hurting others. They've driven her out of Los Angeles, that woman who never hurt anyone."

He let out an audible sigh. "As to my marriage, yes, I do have a contract with Analisa. I did something stupid that caused her to lose her job. I felt guilty and I wanted to help her. And in my self-indulgent way, I figured marriage would help me too, by keeping me out of the tabloids and the whole Hollywood thing of dating women for publicity."

His sad smile arrowed straight to Analisa's heart. "All I want is to do what I love, act, and hopefully, to direct one day soon. I don't need all the other phony stuff that comes with Hollywood celebrity."

Shrugging, he said, "I guess staying under the radar of the gossipmongers didn't work out so well. Analisa is the kindest woman I've ever known. You can call me any names you want. Say whatever dirty lies you want about me. But I don't want my wife called gold-digger or worse. She's a wonderful person and deserves everyone's respect. She sure has mine."

He seemed to look directly at Analisa. "One thing I didn't plan on was falling in love with my wife. I love Analisa in a way I've never loved anyone. I fell in love with her the first time I saw her, but I was too much of an idiot to realize it. And I continued to be an idiot by not telling her how much she means to me. Analisa, if you're listening, I hope you'll forgive me and give me a chance to be a real husband."

Tears streamed down Analisa's face.

"Now, if you'll excuse me," he said to the show's host. "I have to catch a plane to Las Vegas and try to win back my wife."

CHAPTER THIRTY-FOUR

Analisa showered and took special care with her makeup and hair, even if she was dressed casually in a cotton top and capris. Nervous as a teen on her first date, she paced the living room, then the deck, then the media room, and now the pool area.

"Sit, Ana," Rosa said for the twentieth time. Rosa sat on one of the lounge chairs with Killer on her lap. "Cole will be here. Bennett said he hired a private plane." Rosa sighed. "I wish Bennett were coming, too. Bennett called Cole after we'd gone to tell him we'd left for Vegas."

Analisa stopped her pacing and faced her mother. "I figured Bennett told him. That's okay. Cole said he loves me, but I still don't know if I can handle a Hollywood marriage."

"You're strong. You can handle anything. Listen to Cole, tell him how you feel, and let your heart decide."

The rumble of a car engine cut through the quiet of the early evening. Silence, then the sound of a car door opening and closing. Anxiety rooted Analisa to the spot.

Rosa removed Killer from her lap and stood, then walked to the sliding doors that led to the patio. She passed Cole as he came out.

"Good luck, Cole," Rosa said.

"Thanks, Mama Rosa." He dropped a quick kiss on her cheek.

"I'll leave you two." Rosa patted his hand, then walked into the house.

Analisa stared at Cole, seeing the golden stubble on his chin, the sadness in his blue eyes, the dark circles under them. She steeled herself against her fierce desire to run to him, to hug him and comfort him. They needed to talk.

"I saw your interview this morning," she said.

"I'd hoped you would." He stayed where he was and made no move to come closer. "I was going to call you, but since you've ignored my other calls, I figured I'd head out here."

"I needed time to think."

His lips tilted in a sad smile. "I understand."

"I think I know who leaked our story," Analisa said. "A waiter was eavesdropping at the gala when you and I discussed our contract. I think he sold what he heard to the gossip sites."

"I'm not surprised. The wait staff at those events have to leave their cellphones behind, but not their ears. Right now, it's you I'm worried about."

He took a few steps closer and stopped. Analisa wondered if he feared she'd reject him if he got too close.

His eyes softened. "I'm sorry you were hurt, by me and by the vicious bloodsuckers who get pleasure from hurting others. When I came up with the idea of the contract, I wanted to help you, and also me. I never envisioned any of this. Can you forgive me?"

Mustering her thoughts, her attention wandered to the pool. The dying sun cast a golden track over the water, as if showing her a future rich in love and happiness if she'd let go of her fears and follow her heart.

Swiping a tear from her eye, she turned back to Cole. "I don't need to forgive you. You did nothing wrong. Except for getting me fired." She smiled, trying to lighten the mood. "I know you didn't want to hurt me. I don't want this to hurt your career."

His bright smile rivaled the sun, and he closed the distance between them. "I'll be fine. It's you, us, I'm concerned about now. I love you, Analisa. More than I thought possible to love anyone. Can you learn to love me?"

"Oh, Cole, I can't learn to love you because I already do. I loved Cody Lamont from the first day he walked into my bar, and I love Cole Lassiter even more."

When he held out his arms, she took a half-step back. "I have to talk to you about something first."

Disappointment and anxiety flashed over his face. "Okay."

She hugged herself, holding her need for him close. "I want a real marriage with you. But I'm afraid. I don't want to be a Hollywood Wife. I don't want the kinds of marriages I've seen there—the infidelity on both sides, the sneering, and jealousy. Old men with young trophy wives, married women taking young lovers. The ugly rumors and innuendos, the name calling. I don't know if I can handle all that, or if I want to. I want faithfulness, respect, and love."

He focused on her like a laser. "It's what I want, too. A good marriage is one both parties work hard at. I hate the unhappiness and nastiness I see with some couples. You've met my parents. You know where I come from. I want a strong relationship like theirs. My family keeps me grounded. *You* keep me grounded."

He cupped her shoulders and drew her to him. "We'll be strong for each other. Together, we'll make our marriage work. I can't promise life with me will be easy. But I can promise to always love you and honor you. I want a future with you, Analisa. You grew up in Las Vegas. You understand games of chance. Please gamble on me and take a chance on us."

She blinked back tears. "We'll have a real marriage?"

"Real in every sense." He reached into his jacket pocket and pulled out a jewel box. He opened it to reveal a large pear-shaped diamond ring. Holding one of her hands, he got onto one knee and held out the box. "Analisa Barbero Lassiter, will you marry me again?"

Blinded by the tears streaming down her face, she said, "Yes."

Grinning, he slipped the ring on her finger, gathered her into his arms and swung her around. Her laughter rang through the desert air, changing her hurt and anxiety to hope.

Cole set her down but held her in the circle of his arms. He kissed her, sealing their new contract, one made in love.

EPILOGUE

Six months later

Her wedding day. Again.

Sunlight spilled through the stained glass windows in the small church in Beverly Hills. Analisa and Rosa stood in the vestibule waiting to walk down the aisle. A guitarist played *Glasgow Love Theme* from the movie, *Love, Actually*. Patti, Analisa's maid of honor, walked slowly over the white carpet to the altar where the priest, along with Cole and his best man, his brother Clint, waited.

Afterwards, they'd have a reception at the Malibu house, on the deck, with the ocean below and the sun shimmering overhead. Happiness, like the perfume of the flowers in the church, filled Analisa.

"Don't be nervous," Rosa said, patting Analisa's arm.

"I'm not nervous." Holding her bouquet with one hand, Analisa ran her free hand down the ivory silk of her couture gown, a slim creation that skimmed her body. Rather than a veil, she wore a garland of miniature white roses.

"I'm relieved you and Cole decided to make this marriage legal," Rosa said, smiling.

"Mom, it was always legal, but now it will be blessed."

"Just in time, too," Rosa said with a pointed glance at Analisa's belly.

Smiling, Analisa pressed a palm to her stomach. Just six weeks pregnant, she hadn't started to show yet.

The guitarist began playing and singing his version of the Train song, *Marry Me*. Rosa threaded her arm through Analisa's as the women began their stroll to the altar.

The wedding guests stood and turned to watch them. In the front three pews, Cole's parents, Cathy and Charlie, sat with their children and grandchildren. Cole's sister, Caroline, gave Analisa a smile and a thumbs-up. Amanda and Laney were seated on the opposite side, with Tiffany and her Jack behind them. Bennett, Rosa's new husband, sat in the front pew on the bride's side.

Then Analisa had eyes only for her husband. Her heart pumped with love for him and for the joy he'd given her.

Dressed in a tuxedo, his blond hair slicked back from his chiseled features, his beauty took her breath. The love shining from his blue eyes claimed her soul.

When she reached Cole, Rosa slipped away to sit next to Bennett. Cole took Analisa's hand and squeezed it.

Leaning over, he said, "We gambled on love and we won."

"The best game of chance ever."

***

*Read Graceann and Jake's story in *A Groom for Christmas*, available in ebook and print.*

LOVE
BY
CHANCE

CARA MARSI

In Sin City, a couple, unlucky in love, gamble on each other. Win or lose?

Holidays have never brought Las Vegas hotel concierge Laney Sikora anything but bad luck in the romance department. The worst was her fiancé dumping her on Valentine's Day. Via text. She's determined to spend New Year's Eve alone with no romantic entanglements. But when her hunky new neighbor locks himself out of his apartment, she can't leave him standing in the hallway. What's a girl to do?

Las Vegas is just a pit stop for Chicago native and radio personality Chance Carlisle while he waits for his agent to land him something bigger in L.A. But in the meantime, he keeps bumping into—literally—his adorable, but accident-prone, neighbor. Their private New Year's Eve celebration leads to a plan: they'll become the Bad Luck Partners, dating only on holidays and special events, avoiding holiday heartbreaks and matchmaking mamas.

But Fate might have something else in mind for the klutzy cutie and the hotshot talk show host. Can their temporary partnership become a forever deal?

GAMBLING ON LOVE

CHAPTER ONE

"You can't sit home on New Year's Eve, Laney. You've got to come to the party."

Laney Sikora's best friend and co-worker, Amanda, pushed aside her empty coffee cup and rested her elbows on the table to lean closer, her eyes meeting Laney's.

Laney waved a hand. "Stop with the puppy dog eyes. It doesn't work on me. If I go to the party dateless, I'll be a drag on you and Ben. Go. Have fun. Don't worry about me. You know my luck on holidays. I won't tempt fate."

"It's just coincidence that all those things happened to you on holidays."

"Coincidence? *Au Contraire*. Let me get us more lattes, then I'll refresh your memory about my so-called coincidences." Scraping her chair back, Laney stood. And plowed into something hard. With a yelp, she jumped away.

"Whoa!" a male voice, very close, said. "Are you hurt?" he asked in a softer tone.

Raising her gaze, she connected with sapphire blue eyes. "I'm okay. I'm the one who bumped into you. Sorry. Are *you* hurt?"

He smiled, and Laney thought she might swoon. Not only did he have delectable, kissable lips, he had dimples. Dimples!

His muscled chest covered by a dark green T-shirt didn't hurt either. She slid her gaze to his tight-fitting jeans that molded to his muscular legs. Swoon-worthy for sure.

"I'm a big guy," he said. "It takes a lot more than a bump by a pretty woman to hurt me."

You sure are a big guy. And hot!

"I am sorry, though." Hoping he couldn't read minds, she smiled and scooted around him to head toward the counter to order the lattes. Taking her place in the long line, she glanced around the crowded coffee bar. Mr. Hunk had taken a seat at a table overlooking the Vegas Strip. Forcing her mind from the erotic lane it had been about to go down, she took in the other patrons. As usual, tourists mingled with the natives. After five years living in Las Vegas, Laney could pick out the tourists. They were the ones wearing shorts, T-shirts, and sandals at the end of December. She shivered. Today the high temperature registered fifty degrees. If Laney were back in her hometown of Philadelphia, she'd consider fifty comfortable. After years in the desert heat, she couldn't tolerate any temperatures under sixty.

Balancing the lattes in her hands, she went back to where Amanda waited. As employees of the nearby Augustus, a luxury hotel and casino, Laney and Amanda liked to come to this coffee shop on their breaks. The smirk on Amanda's face told Laney her friend found the accident with the blue-eyed hunk amusing.

Handing Amanda her latte, Laney sat. "Wipe that smirk off your face."

Amanda burst out laughing. Her laughing fit over, she grinned at Laney. "That guy's smokin'. We don't usually see the likes of him in these parts." With a gleam in her eyes, she said, "You realize you're a klutz around guys? Hot guys make you nervous."

Laney sipped her drink before answering. "Seriously? How could I be a klutz around hot guys when I hadn't even seen that one before I hit him?"

"Your hot-guy radar was up so you knew one was nearby."

When Laney started to protest, Amanda held up a hand, stopping her. "Enough about Mr. Hottie whom neither of us will ever see again. Please go to the New Year's Eve party with me and Ben. I know there will be eligible guys there."

"Now I get it." Wrapping her hands around her ceramic coffee cup, Laney gave Amanda a cutting look. "You're trying to fix me up with someone. No way. Especially not on a holiday. Hello? The Halloween party in October."

"Darren was the worst kind of jerk to make out with that

bimbo in the closet during the party. You're better off without him. Consider yourself lucky you hadn't dated him long. You found out his true colors before you invested more time in the relationship."

Laney sipped her coffee, as if the warm liquid could dissolve the knot in her chest. Setting down her cup, she said, "Maybe I didn't have a lot of time with Darren, but Chris was another matter. Valentine's Day the year before last. Ring a bell?"

Amanda reached across the table and put her hand over Laney's. "Honey, I'm sorry. Chris always seemed so nice. What kind of jerk calls off your engagement by text?"

"My fiancé, that's what kind of jerk. He didn't have enough respect for me or the guts to break up to my face. Then he eloped with that lawyer from his firm. On Memorial Day. Darren was a rebound relationship. I learned. No more relationships for me, not for a long time. And I'm definitely not starting anything with any man on a holiday."

CHAPTER TWO

Chance Carlisle sat at a table by the window and sipped his coffee, his attention on the sexy number who'd bumped into him. Good thing he'd had a top on his Styrofoam cup or they could have both been burned.

He'd been in Vegas one month now, and he'd seen a few beautiful women among the hordes of natives and tourists along the Strip, but none like the beauty who'd collided with him.

Maybe she wasn't supermodel beautiful, but her navy blue business suit couldn't hide her slim body with its lush curves. Her mahogany mass of softly curling hair trailing down her back and those black-lashed amber eyes had his libido revved up. She could run into him any time.

<><><>

Driving home from the bakery the following morning, Chance hummed along to a Beatles tune on his car radio. The sweet, delectable, smoky scents of glazed donuts and coffee made his stomach rumble. He normally made breakfast for himself, but had run out of coffee and eggs, which had sent him to the coffee bar yesterday for some much-needed caffeine on his way to work. With very little free time, he hadn't had a chance to go food shopping lately. Although his radio show started at two in the afternoon, he got to the station by eleven every morning to prepare. Tonight after work, he'd join some co-workers for dinner and gambling at one of the casinos. He didn't enjoy gambling, but this was Vegas.

Waving to the guard at the gate of his condo complex in

Henderson, Chance went through the opened gate to the parking lot. And nearly collided with a car backing out of a spot. He slammed on the brakes and hit his horn. The other car, a silver Honda Accord, stopped. Shaking his head, he passed the car, and did a double take. The driver, the same beautiful brunette from the coffee shop yesterday, put her hands up in apology.

Hot or not, the woman was an accident waiting to happen.

<><><>

Laney carefully pulled out of her parking spot. *Crap*. The guy in the black SUV she almost hit couldn't possibly be the gorgeous guy from the coffee bar yesterday. What were the chances? Must be someone who looked like him. Yet, there couldn't be two seriously smokin' guys around. This wasn't Hollywood.

She drove to the Strip and the Augustus where she worked as a concierge. Because tourists flocked into Vegas between Christmas and New Year's like birds flying to warmer climes, most of the hotel employees worked overtime during the holidays. Today Laney would work a double shift, until midnight. Tomorrow, New Year's Eve, she would work regular hours.

Although she loved handling inquiries and helping hotel guests get tickets to sought-after shows and reservations at popular restaurants, it proved exhausting at times. Her degree in hotel management hadn't prepared her for the variety of guests she dealt with at the Augustus. Some were easy to handle. Others not so much.

By eight that night, Laney's face hurt from smiling so much. The lines at the concierge counter had been steady all day. With a welcome lull in the activity, she glanced across the marble-floored lobby inlaid with mosaics to the large glass doors at the hotel entrance, offering a clear look outside. A majestic 65-foot LED Christmas tree stood in the grassy circle in front of the hotel. The thousands of tiny lights changed color in a dazzling show every evening during the holiday season. She felt herself relax as she enjoyed the show in progress.

With a sigh, she turned back to the counter as a customer approached. Smiling at him, a guy about her age, thirty-two, she gestured for him to come forward.

"What can I help you with?" she asked.

The guy smirked. "I need a date for tomorrow night. You doing anything?"

"Sir, no one here can find you a date. Unless you need tickets for a show or an exhibit, or restaurant reservations, please move on so I can assist the next person."

He leaned on the counter, invading her space. She smelled alcohol on his breath and took a step back.

"You're hot," he said, slurring his words. "I want a date with you."

Laney hit the button on the floor to call her manager. Stu, a fatherly middle-aged man who'd taken Laney under his wing, hurried over from his office across the lobby. "Everything okay, Laney?"

"Stu, this gentleman thinks I can get him a date for tomorrow."

"I don't want just any date," the man said, stumbling on unsteady feet. "I want her."

"Sir, please come with me." Stu gripped the man's upper arm.

Curling his lip, the guy broke free and bolted away.

Laney and Stu looked at each other and shook their heads.

When midnight finally arrived, Laney understood the term, "dog tired." She wanted to curl up like a dog and sleep for twenty-four hours. At least she had shorter hours tomorrow, and New Year's Day off.

She walked through the casino to the elevators that would take her to the parking garage. As usual, noisy crowds filled the casino. With no windows, it could have been noon or midnight. Bells on the slots went off constantly, groups of people watched blackjack games and roulette, sometimes cheering. Elderly women guarded several slot machines at once, the looks on their faces daring anyone to sit at one of the "their" machines. Laney coughed at the light scent of tobacco, glad the Augustus, one of the newer casinos, had a better ventilation system than the older ones.

A variety of people, some well-dressed, some not so much, of all ages and sizes, wove their way through the casino. A young woman teetering on sky-high sandals and wearing a red dress with a plunging neckline, brushed past Laney. Three college-age guys, wearing T-shirts with beer logos, and carrying huge mugs of beer, leered at the young woman as she passed.

Glad to be out of the noise, crowds, and smells of the casino, Laney entered the parking garage and nodded to the valet guys who congregated at the doorway. Although she'd parked her car at the far end, she didn't fear walking through the garage. Security cameras were everywhere, and people came and went at all hours here.

When she'd gotten halfway to her car and out of sight of the valets guys, rough hands seized her arms from behind and swung her around.

"You think you're too good for me?" a male voice growled.

She faced the guy from earlier in the evening. "Let me go!" She pulled, trying to free herself, but he gripped one of her arms and dug his fingers into her flesh. She looked around. The valet guys were too far away to hear, and no guests were nearby. The security cameras would pick it up, but it would take a while for the guards to get there.

Adrenaline rushed through her veins. She kicked her attacker in the shins.

"Bitch!" He tightened his hold on her arm.

She swung her purse and hit him in the head. When he reeled, she broke free and started to run back to the entrance. He grabbed her shoulders and yanked her toward him.

Laney dug her elbow into his chest and was rewarded with a grunt from him. "Let me go!"

"You heard the lady. Let her go." The deep male voice sounded vaguely familiar.

Laney's attacker freed her and pushed her away from him. He high-tailed it out.

"Thank you." Laney raised her gaze to her rescuer. "You! This is unbelievable."

The smokin' guy from the coffee shop and the condo parking lot widened his baby blues. "We meet again. Are you okay? Did he hurt you?"

"I'm fine. I may not have been if you hadn't come along. Thanks again."

"I'm glad I could be here to help. Good thing I let my co-workers talk me into going out tonight to this casino. Do you need to report this?"

She nodded. With a wry smile, she said, "There are cameras everywhere. I guess the security people are a little slow tonight."

Footsteps slapped the cement, and two security guards, along with one of the valet guys, ran toward them.

"What's going on?" one of the guards said with a glare at her rescuer. "Is this man bothering you?"

"I'm fine. Thanks to this man," Laney said. "He chased off the scum who tried to attack me."

"Thank God," the other guard said. "You need to fill out a report."

"On my way," she said.

The men turned back to the casino and she started to follow.

"I'll go with you," her rescuer said.

She stopped and faced him. "I'm okay now."

"I want to be sure you get out of here safely. I'll stay with you until you're in your car."

"Thank you." Great-looking and a gentleman. With dimples. A combination she hadn't seen much of lately, if ever. Maybe this signaled a change in her luck. Nope. She couldn't think that way. No men for her for a while.

With a glint in his eyes, he leaned closer. "Does trouble follow you around?"

Laney bristled. "Of course not."

"Considering how we keep bumping into each other, we should introduce ourselves." He held out his hand. "Chance Carlisle."

"Laney Sikora." She took his proffered hand. When they touched, warmth jolted up her arm, and she quickly released him. *Chance*. Win or lose?

CHAPTER THREE

"**E**bony, it's just you and me, girl. We'll ring in the New Year together." Ebony, Laney's fat black cat, opened one eye, yawned, and went back to sleep.

"Nice company you'll be." Laney chuckled. "At least I don't have to worry about you breaking up with me by text or making out with someone in the closet."

Dressed in yoga pants and a long-sleeved T-shirt, her hair in a loose knot on top of her head, Laney prepared to spend New Year's Eve watching her favorite movies and snacking on tortilla chips, salsa, guac, and wine. Lots of wine. At least she'd have no bad luck with any man this holiday.

As she set a bowl of chips next to the salsa and guac on her coffee table, her thoughts drifted to Chance Carlisle. Funny how she'd run into him all those times, and strange he'd been at her condo complex. Technically, she'd only run into him once, at the coffee bar. He'd been her superhero in the casino parking garage at midnight, saving her from who-knew-what. She shuddered about what might have happened if Chance hadn't come along.

She wondered where he would be spending New Year's Eve. Probably with some supermodel. A guy with his looks had to attract gorgeous women. A pang of regret knotted her stomach as loneliness swamped her. Truth be told, she wanted a man in her life, someone trustworthy who'd always be there for her.

Pushing aside the thought, she slid a DVD into her player and settled back on the sofa to watch one of her favorite rom-coms, *The More, the Merrier*, an old black and white from the forties.

Joel McCrea had been such a hunk. There weren't many men like him around anymore. Although Chance Carlisle came close.

As the opening credits started rolling, Laney heard loud cursing from the hall outside. Heart pounding, she paused the movie and padded to the door to look out the peephole.

She blinked. Chance Carlisle, wearing jeans, a T-shirt, and barefoot, his hands on his hips, stood in front of the door across from hers. She could be hallucinating, but she hadn't had one sip of wine yet. He released another loud curse and pushed against the door, as if trying to force it open.

Laney opened her door and peered out. "Chance?"

"Laney! What are you doing here?"

"I live here. What's going on?"

He smoothed a hand over his black hair, ruffling it, making him look adorably hotter. "I live here and I locked myself out when I went to check if my newspaper had been delivered. They missed me this morning and I had to call them." He blew out a breath. "No paper, and no key."

Shock propelled her to step back. "You live here? Across the hall?" She knew someone had moved in a month ago, but hadn't seen her new neighbor. That explained why Chance had been in the condo parking lot yesterday.

He reached her in two long strides. "I'm renting from the owner. You're my neighbor?"

"Afraid so."

He gave her one of his sexy grins that made her libido go into a frenzy.

"You're not planning to hurt me, are you?" he asked, a teasing gleam in his eyes.

"Of course not."

His grin got wider. "Just checking, after our last encounters."

Narrowing her eyes, she tilted her head toward him. "If you live across the hall, why haven't I seen you? There are only two units on this floor."

He shrugged. "I don't work normal nine-to-five hours. I usually leave for work around 10:30 in the morning and I don't get home until seven or eight at night."

"That explains it," she said. "I work nine-to-five most days."

He ran a hand over his hair again, frustration tightening his features. "I locked my phone in my place. Can I use yours to call a buddy who has a spare key?"

"Uh-sure. Come in."

A short time later, his face a mask of resignation, Chance handed Laney's phone back to her. "Guess my buddy's at a party and either can't hear the ring or turned his phone off."

"Once he gets your voicemail, I'm sure he'll call back," she said.

They stared at each other. His eyes held a questioning look. They were neighbors. She couldn't let him wait in the hall.

"Why don't you stay here until your friend calls? I've got plenty of food and wine."

"You're not expecting a guy?"

With a wry smile, she said, "Do I look like I'm expecting anyone?"

Blue fire sparked from his eyes as he scanned her.

Laney's nipples hardened under his scorching gaze. She should have worn a bra. Who knew a hunky guy would land on her doorstep? Should she curse fate or thank it?

"I think you look beautiful," he said softly.

His deep, smoky voice covered her like satin, warming every cell in her body. She felt awake in a way she hadn't in a very long time. Ignoring the tingling inside her, she held up a hand. "I'm doing the neighborly thing. Don't get any ideas."

"No problem." He grinned. "Do you believe in fate?" he asked, echoing her thoughts.

"Not particularly. Why?"

"Something's at work here between us. We keep meeting."

"Just coincidence." Of course it was coincidence. And yet...

He glanced around her place, his gaze landing on her Christmas tree in a corner of the dining area. "Pretty tree. Is it real?"

"Afraid not. I had a real one my first Christmas here. It's hard to keep a Christmas tree moist in this dry climate." She shook her head. "Ebony, my cat, was a kitten then. She climbed the tree and brought it down. I learned my lesson."

He laughed and turned toward the TV. "What are you watching?"

"A classic from the forties."

"I'm a film buff. What movie is it?"

"*The More the Merrier.*"

He grinned. "Jean Arthur and Joel McCrea. Definitely a classic."

A guy who knew an old black and white comedy, and even the actors? Maybe her imagination had conjured Chance up. That would be her kind of luck.

She held up the wine bottle. When he nodded, she said, "Make yourself comfortable. I'll get another glass."

She set the wine on the coffee table and headed for the kitchen. She hadn't gone far when she tripped on something soft and big. Her face met the carpet. Ebony, shaking her tail in indignation, ran away. How had she missed a fourteen-pound cat?

Strong arms pulled Laney up as embarrassment flamed in her. "I don't know what happened. I've never tripped over Ebony before."

Chance ran his hands over her shoulders. "Are you okay?"

"I'm fine. We seem to have this conversation a lot."

"I get the impression you're a tad accident prone." His lips quirked in a grin he clearly tried to suppress.

"I'm not accident prone. Things seem to happen around the holidays. Probably too much on my mind. I'll get that glass."

CHAPTER FOUR

"I always enjoy that movie," Chance said an hour and forty-five minutes later. "Arthur and McCrea had a chemistry and sensuality missing in a lot of current movies that have explicit sex."

"I agree." Laney had watched that movie at least twenty times, but viewing it with Chance made it feel new again. They'd laughed together at the antics of Charles Coburn as he played matchmaker to Arthur's and McCrea's characters. She'd sighed at the end and had been sure she'd heard Chance sigh too.

He reached for another chip and dipped it into the guac. They'd gone through a bag and a half of chips and most of the salsa and guac. And one bottle of wine.

"I've got another holiday movie, a newer one with Cameron Diaz and Kate Winslet."

He grinned, showing those dimples, and Laney's heart did a little dance.

"Bring it on," he said.

She stood. "Let's take a break. I'll get more food and wine. If we're going to drink wine, we need more than chips and salsa. I can cut up some cheese and open a box of crackers. I have a pizza in the freezer I can heat up. What do you think?"

"Sounds great. I'd better go with you to make sure you don't trip over anything on the way to the kitchen." His eyes sparkled. "I'll cut up the cheese. I'm not sure I trust you with a knife."

She glared at him.

Laughing, he picked up the empty bowls and followed her.

Laney pulled a bag of chips from the pantry cabinet. The bag refused to open and she pulled harder. It split open. Chips flew out and onto the floor. "Damn!"

Amanda had said hot guys made Laney flustered. No way. Chance might be scorching, but Laney barely knew him. She had too much on her mind and was easily distracted, which caused her the slight mishaps.

Chance's lips quirked as he set the bowls on the counter. "I'll clean the chips off the floor and throw them away." He gingerly took the bag of chips from her and poured them into a bowl. "Show me to the cheese."

"I'll get the salsa first." Forcing herself to act cool and in control when she felt anything but, Laney opened another cabinet and grabbed a jar of salsa. When she tried, and failed, to open it, Chance took it from her.

Heat, hotter than a bowl of habaneros, swept over her at the sight of Chance's biceps bulging as he twisted the jar lid open.

He caught her watching him and winked.

Ducking her head, she opened the refrigerator door and reached in, letting the cold air chill her burning face. She grabbed a block of cheddar and clutched it to her chest while she closed the refrigerator door.

Chance quirked an eyebrow. "You going to cling to that cheese or do you want me to cut it up?"

She handed him the cheese, careful not to touch him, afraid if she did, she'd spontaneously combust. "The knife is in the top drawer to the right and the crackers are in the cabinet above that. The cutting board is on the counter. I'll get you some plates."

He saluted. "Whatever you say, boss."

At his teasing, her muscles relaxed, and she smiled. "Do you like Perrier? I have a couple of bottles in the fridge. Maybe we should drink that and go slow on the wine. A little later, I'll put the pizza into the oven."

"Sounds like a plan."

While Chance prepared the food, Laney pulled out water goblets and two bottles of Perrier, and set everything on a serving tray. She plucked a bottle of red wine off the counter, opened it, and set it with the other items.

Working side-by-side with Chance relaxed her even more.

Surprising herself, she felt happy, with an overwhelming compulsion to hum Christmas tunes. Resisting that urge, and smiling at her fanciful thoughts, she carried her tray into the living room, followed by Chance with the food.

Once the food and drinks were set on the coffee table, they turned on the new movie. As they watched, Ebony stretched out between them on the sofa. Laney's usually shy cat seemed to have taken a liking to Chance. Animals were good judges of people. The cat had stayed away from Chris and Darren. Maybe Laney should start taking relationship advice from her cat.

Halfway through the movie, Laney baked the pizza, and they drank wine as they finished off the pepperoni pizza and most of the cheese, crackers, salsa, and chips. By the time the movie ended, the old year had less than sixty minutes left.

"The New Year has arrived in the most of the country," Chance said, turning to her.

"Not in Hawaii or Alaska yet," she said.

"Good point. Let's turn on live TV and see if we can find a ball dropping somewhere."

She turned the TV to a New Year's Eve show.

"Let's mute it," Chance said. "I'd like to talk to you, get to know you."

"Sure." He wanted to get to know her. That could be dangerous, to both of them, considering her bad luck on holidays. And her penchant for accidents around him.

He put his arm on the back of the sofa, his gaze locked on hers. Damn, he had the bluest eyes. She understood the old cliché of drowning in a person's eyes.

"There's something I've wanted to ask you all night," he said. Uh-Oh. "What is it?"

"Why is a beautiful, sexy woman like you alone on New Year's Eve?"

"Why is a hot guy like you alone on New Year's Eve?"

He laughed. "Touché. I deserved that." His eyes glinted. "You think I'm hot?"

"Puhleeze. You know you are. And you didn't answer my question."

"If I answer first, will you answer mine?"

"Maybe."

"Commitment phobic, I see." He shifted, sliding slightly away from her. "I moved to Vegas a month ago from Chicago, where I worked at a radio station. A buddy who works at KLVE here helped me get a job at that station. Other than him, I know very few people in Vegas. One of my co-workers invited me to a party tonight, but I declined. I suspected he wanted to fix me up with some woman. Holidays seem to bring me bad luck in the romance department."

Laney widened her eyes. "You have bad luck on holidays? I thought that only happened to me. Tell me about the worst thing that happened to you on a holiday."

His features tightened and pain flashed in his eyes.

Laney put her hand on his arm. "I'm sorry. I didn't mean to bring up anything painful."

"It's okay." He reached for the wine bottle. "Maybe we should have a little more of this now." He poured them each a half glass of wine and settled onto the sofa.

"What type work do you do at KLVE?" she asked.

"I have my own radio show."

She stopped with her wine glass mid-way to her mouth. "You do? You have such a great voice, it's no wonder you're on the radio. What kind of show do you have?"

"You think I have a great voice?"

"Stop fishing for compliments." Their banter provoked giddy-like pleasure through her. She couldn't remember the last time she felt so free to be herself with a man.

"I like getting compliments from beautiful women," he said. "It's good for my ego."

"I don't think your ego needs any help from me."

"You wound me." He put his hand over his heart. "To answer your question—I have a talk show from two to six in the afternoon, called By Chance."

"A political talk show?"

He shook his head. "No way. There are enough of those around. I keep my politics to myself. On my show, I talk sports, entertainment, and current events."

"Cool. I'm usually working then, but I'll try to tune into your show when I can." She dipped a chip into the salsa. "I would think Chicago is a bigger market than Vegas."

He set his glass on the coffee table and sat forward, his palms on his knees. "It is a bigger market, but something happened there that spurred me to leave."

"What happened? You don't have to tell me if you don't want."

He twisted to look at her. "I want to tell you. I had a similar show in Chicago, with my fiancée as co-host."

Fiancée? Of course he had a fiancée.

Not looking at Laney, he continued. "You asked about my bad luck on holidays. Last Valentine's Day, a guy called in to our show and wanted to talk to Naomi, my fiancée. She seemed very nervous when she heard his voice." Chance straightened and turned back to Laney. "He asked her when she was going to tell me about their affair." A disgusted look washed over his face. "The show has a nine-second delay to root out any inflammatory comments, but our producer liked controversy and let the call go through."

Laney put a hand to her throat. "What? You were outed on a radio show? And your producer let it happen?"

"Yup. All Chicago heard how I'd been cuckolded." His lips thinned. "We had great ratings for that show. Talk about your public humiliation."

"Chance, I'm sorry. Your story makes mine pale."

He settled onto the sofa, his attention on her. "With my contract coming up for renewal, I figured I'd get out of Chicago, start somewhere new. When Dennis, my buddy here, told me about the opening at KLVE, I decided to go for it. My agent got me a one-year contract with an escape clause. We're negotiating for a show in the L.A. area. It's one of the hottest markets in the country."

"You'll be here only a year?" A surprising ribbon of regret wound through her at the thought of his leaving.

"Could be less than a year, if I get that contract in L.A." His features relaxed and he smiled at her. "My public humiliation isn't the only lovelorn thing to happen to me on a holiday. Want to hear more?"

"If you want to tell me." She sipped wine and scrunched over into the corner of the sofa.

"In my senior year of college," he began, "the woman I'd

dated since freshman year broke up with me on Thanksgiving Day. We were supposed to spend the holiday with my parents outside Chicago, but at the last minute, Jen decided she'd rather go skiing with her friends. She said since we were close to graduation, she didn't want to be tied down and wanted to break up."

"Wow," Laney said. "That must have made for an uncomfortable Thanksgiving with your family."

"Tell me about it." His lips tilted in a wry smile. "Makes me sound like a loser, huh?"

"No." She would be the last to call someone a loser.

"I've broken up with a few women when things weren't working out, or they've broken up with me, but the two break-ups that hurt the most were the holiday ones. Maybe things affect me more on a holiday. I'm leery of them now."

"I get that."

"Your turn. Tell me why you're alone tonight."

CHAPTER FIVE

Laney sipped her drink slowly, gathering her thoughts. The rich red liquid warmed and calmed her as it slid down her throat.

"It started in first grade," she said.

Chance laughed. "First grade? We may need some food sustenance. Do you have more chips and salsa?"

"Always."

"Stay here and I'll get a fresh supply." Standing, he looked down at her. "I don't trust you to open another bag of chips."

Laughing at his words, Laney admired his long-legged gait as he loped toward the kitchen. His jeans hugged his firm butt and showcased muscular legs that went on forever. This might turn out to be her best New Year's Eve ever. No pressure. No worries. A few unfortunate mishaps, but nothing worse.

After munching on some fresh chips and salsa, Laney slid back to the end of the sofa and faced Chance. "It started in first grade on Valentine's Day. I had a huge crush on a boy named Ralphie. He liked me too. When he gave me a card, I went to pull the one I'd gotten him out of my pocket. The card got caught, and I fell forward. I fell on Ralphie and broke his arm. He never spoke to me again."

Laney could see Chance trying to suppress a laugh, and failing. When he'd finished laughing, he said, "Sorry, but that's a funny story. Are you sure it's not bad luck, and maybe you're accident prone?"

She lifted her chin in mock outrage. "I am not accident

prone."

He lifted his glass. "If you say so. To Ralphie. Poor sucker. Broken arm or not, he should have latched onto you and never let go."

Chance's compliments warmed her more than the wine. She touched her glass with his.

"That's it?" Chance asked.

"Nope. There's more. You'd better eat something first."

Chance grabbed a handful of chips. "I'm ready."

"In sixth grade," she said, "my mom made me go to an Easter dance with the son of one of her friends. I was angry with her for fixing me up with a boy I didn't know, but when I saw Nickie with his golden hair and green eyes, I forgave her. We had a good time at the dance. When we were leaving, Nickie went to kiss me. My first kiss. When he pulled me close, nervousness made me stumble. We went down together into a mud puddle. Ruined my pretty dress and any chance of having Nickie for a boyfriend."

Chance laughed and held up his glass again. "To poor, mud-splattered Nickie."

They toasted. "If this keeps up, we'll be drunk by midnight," Laney said.

"To midnight," he said, raising his glass to touch hers.

She shifted to a more comfortable position. "In eighth grade, I had a crush on Mattie. When he asked me to our school's Christmas dance, I was over the moon. My mom made me a beautiful dress. I'd not been feeling well all day but didn't tell her because I knew she'd make me stay home. Mattie and I were dancing when I got sick and threw up all over him."

"A double toast to that one," Chance said, laughing. "I hope you've got more. This is probably the most entertaining New Year's Eve I've ever spent."

His words triggered a surge of pleasure, heating her all over. "Glad I could entertain you," she said, trying to keep the tone light when she wanted to run her hands through his thick hair and kiss those delectable lips.

Instead, she said, "I had boyfriends in high school and college, and those relationships ended without incident. It seems only the guys I really liked were the ones I call 'bad luck holiday guys.' I fell in love with Jason my junior year of college. In our senior year, I thought he'd ask me to marry him."

Laney looked away from Chance's intense stare. After all these years, Jason's rejection still stung. "He called me Christmas Eve, said he didn't want to see me anymore and had fallen in love with a French woman, an exchange student he'd met at school."

"Maybe we shouldn't toast to that one," Chance said softly.

"Probably not." She glanced at the TV. Less than ten minutes to midnight. She turned on the sound, keeping it low. "Two more stories. I moved to Vegas from Philadelphia five years ago. Dated a few guys before I met Chris about three years ago. We got engaged after six months. On Valentine's Day year before last, he broke up with me by text. Said it wasn't working between us." She took a big gulp of wine to soften the bite of Chris's betrayal. "That Memorial Day, he eloped with one of the other lawyers from his firm. I found out later he'd been cheating on me with her for months."

"Shit, Laney. Sorry, didn't mean to curse. You've had some rotten luck."

"No kidding. See why I prefer to stay home New Year's Eve?"

"I get it now. What's your second story?"

She sighed. "I didn't date for over a year. A co-worker fixed me up with Darren last July Fourth. We weren't right for each other but I had fun with him. We attended a Halloween party this past October." She gave Chance a wry smile. "I found Darren and some woman in a closet making out during the party. Everyone there saw it. Talk about embarrassment."

Chance slid closer and cupped her face between his hands. "The fault isn't yours. You've been with some jerks. They're all fools for letting you go."

"You don't even know me, Chance."

"I know you're sweet and kind with a beautiful smile. And you're smart and sexy."

A shout came from the TV. The countdown had begun. Grateful for the distraction from the sexual tension that covered the room like confetti, Laney gripped her glass of wine and stood.

Chance plucked his wine from the table and stood too. He and Laney raised their glasses as the crowd on the TV shouted, "Ten, nine, eight, seven, six, five, four, three, two, one. Happy New Year!"

They toasted, then he took her glass and set it on the table, along with his. "Happy New Year, Laney."

He gathered her into his arms and kissed her, his lips soft. He tasted like wine and salsa. Laney wound her arms around his neck and kissed him back. His lips firmed over hers, devouring, feasting. A slow ache began to build in her.

The sound of fireworks cut through her sensual cloud. She pulled away from him, and immediately missed his heat.

Chance looked at her with an expression of wonder. "Now that's the way to ring in the New Year."

Fear mixed with caution spiraled through her. "As much as I enjoyed that kiss, I'm not ready for anything more. We're neighbors, maybe friends now. Nothing more. Agreed?"

"That kiss was way more than enjoyable. But agreed, considering our bad luck on holidays. We're neighbors, and I hope friends."

Disappointment, unbidden and surprising, tugged at her. On some level, she'd wanted him to tell her he wanted more than friendship with her. She should be glad he didn't. Instead, she felt...cheated.

Frowning, he looked toward the balcony. "I guess we're too far from the Strip to watch the fireworks."

"We are, and we're better off here than trying to fight our way out of Vegas later. There are fireworks in Henderson too. We can see them from here."

She opened the sliding glass doors and they stepped onto the small balcony, furnished with a white wrought iron table and chairs. Laney leaned against the wooden railing and inhaled the cool, crisp air. She pointed. "Over there. Fireworks."

Chance moved next to her, standing close. Not speaking, they enjoyed the dazzling show. When Laney shivered from the cold, Chance put his arm around her shoulders and held her close. Warmth blanketed her, and she melted into him and rested her head on his chest. Definitely the best New Year's Eve ever.

The fireworks over, they went back inside. She closed the

doors and turned to find him staring at her, his features serious. "What?"

"I have an idea," he said. "Do your friends try to fix you up with someone, especially on holidays? Like they can't stand the thought of you being alone on a holiday?"

"All the time. You too?"

He nodded. "I especially dislike the holidays with forced gaiety, like New Year's Eve and Valentine's Day, when everyone has to have a significant other or they're considered a loser."

Laney walked to the sofa and sat on the edge. "Me too. I hate it."

He moved closer, his blue eyes sparkling, and looked down at her. "Here's my idea. You and I pretend we're in a relationship so our friends will leave us alone. We go out to dinner Valentine's Day, Easter, Memorial Day, Summer Solstice, whatever, have fun and not feel any pressure. We won't have to worry about bad luck on holidays any more. What do you think?"

"A holidays-only relationship?" She tapped her chin. A pretend relationship couldn't hurt. Chance would leave in less than a year and she should be ready then to start dating again. "Let's do it."

He grinned. "It doesn't have to be only holidays. If we're invited to parties, or other functions, and we want to keep the matchmakers at bay, we take each other."

"I like the way you think."

"We'll call ourselves Bad Luck Partners." He held out his hand to her.

She stood and shook his hand. "To our partnership. Be warned. The partnership will dissolve if I find you in a closet making out with someone."

He gave her the three-finger Boy Scout salute. "Scout's honor. No making out in the closet." With a dimpled smile, he said, "Unless it's you I make out with."

"Not gonna happen." Despite their teasing, his words incited a thrill.

CHAPTER SIX

O n January 2, groggy from lack of sleep, Laney gripped her Styrofoam cup of coffee and stepped behind the concierge counter. The friend who had the key to Chance's place had called at one o'clock New Year's morning, and had come over shortly after with the key. She hadn't seen Chance since. She'd spent most of New Year's Day on her sofa, sluggish from over-indulging in food and drink. Her thoughts whirling with images of Chance, Laney hadn't slept much the past two nights.

The morning passed in a blur for Laney. Three of them worked the concierge counter, and they could have used three more. Tourists from around the globe flocked into the Augustus to see their world-famous conservatory and botanical gardens, decorated this holiday season with a Babes in Toyland theme. She'd be glad when things settled back to normal, or as normal as things got in Sin City.

She'd fallen in love with Vegas as a high school girl on her first trip there with her parents. She'd loved the vibrancy and excitement, even loved the summer heat and the desert. Several more visits convinced her she wanted to live there. She'd made a life for herself in Las Vegas, with a job she enjoyed and good friends. She never wanted to leave.

Except for the times she went home to Philadelphia, she didn't have to face her perfect brother and his perfect family or watch her parents fawn over them, while letting Laney know how disappointed they were in her choice of career and in her single status.

When Laney and Amanda met for lunch at the coffee bar that day, Amanda took one look at Laney and said, "Spill. Who is he?"

"What? Who is who?"

"The guy who put that dreamy look on your face."

"I don't look dreamy. I look tired."

Amanda tilted her head and studied Laney. "New Year's Eve was two days ago, and you're still tired? What did you do New Year's Eve?"

Laney moved her chicken salad around her plate with her fork before meeting Amanda's gaze. "My new neighbor got locked out of his place New Year's Eve. He couldn't reach his friend who had an extra key, so he spent the evening with me. No big deal. Just me being neighborly. We gorged on junk food and wine and watched a few movies. Not too long after midnight, his friend finally called and came over with the key." Laney tried to keep her expression neutral despite the knot in her stomach whenever she thought about Chance and that kiss. And the bargain they'd struck.

"Is this neighbor hot?"

"Very. Don't get any ideas. We're friends, that's all. Besides, you've seen him. Strange coincidence. He's the guy I bumped into here the other day."

"You've gotta be kidding me. Talk about karma." Amanda's brown eyes widened. "He could be *The One*."

"Let it go, Amanda." Although Laney didn't like keeping things from her best friend, she couldn't tell Amanda about the Bad Luck Partners. Or else Amanda would continue to try to fix Laney up with guys who weren't her type. She wondered if Chance could be her type, but dismissed the thought.

On the way home that evening, Laney tuned her radio to Chance's show. Caught up in his sexy, seductive, and mesmerizing voice, she almost ran a red light.

Home an hour, Laney had fed Ebony and changed into her in-home outfit of yoga pants and a long-sleeved top. She stood in front of her open refrigerator trying to figure out what to have for dinner when her doorbell rang. Frowning, she closed the refrigerator door and walked into the living room. When she looked through the peephole and saw Chance standing there, her heart did a little somersault. She brushed a hand over her hair and opened the door.

Chance smiled and held up a large bag. "You shared your food with me the other night and saved me from spending New Year's Eve in the hallway. I want to repay you."

"You don't have to do that." Despite her vow to remain only friends with Chance, her hungry gaze devoured him. His blue dress shirt, worn untucked, stretched across his broad chest. Indigo jeans hugged his muscular legs. His black motorcycle boots added to his bad-boy, hottie persona. The sparkle and warmth in his eyes gave frantic life to the butterflies in her stomach.

"I wanted to thank you," he said. "May I come in?"

"Sure." She stepped aside to let him enter and stumbled over Ebony who'd twined herself around Laney's ankles.

Chance grabbed Laney's elbow, steadying her. He slipped inside and closed the door. His lips tilted in a grin, and he said, "You look adorable when you blush like that."

She gave him what she hoped was a scathing look. He laughed.

Ebony rubbed against Chance's ankles. He bent to pet her, sending the cat into spasms of purring. Laney would purr too if Chance stroked her like that. Jealous of a cat! *You are losing it, girl.*

"What did you bring?" she asked, in an effort to tamp down her rising libido.

He held up the bag. "Subs, or hoagies as you call them in Philly. There's a great sub shop, Carlotta's, on the Strip. They started on the East Coast so the sandwiches are authentic. Thought you'd like one."

"I love Carlotta's. Whenever I feel a little homesick, I go there for a hoagie." She wrinkled her nose. "As good as they are, they can't beat the ones in Philly because Philly has the best sandwich rolls."

He grinned. "I'll remember that the next time I'm in Philly."

"You've been there?"

"Several times. Great city. Not too much sun though."

"Why do you think I like Vegas so much?"

"You're here to stay?"

"I am."

A short while later they sat at her dining room table, several selections of cut-up hoagies in front of them. Laney bit into her favorite, made with fresh turkey meat, mayo, stuffing, and cranberry sauce. Thanksgiving on a roll.

"Heaven," she said when she'd finished chewing. She reached for her glass of cold white wine.

"That's my favorite, too," Chance said. "How did you feel yesterday, after all those carbs and alcohol we consumed the night before?"

"I stayed on my sofa most of the day."

He laughed. "Wish I could have stayed on my sofa. Although I had the holiday off, I had to go into the station to take care of some business."

"I listened to some of your show today. I enjoyed it."

"Thanks. That means a lot coming from you."

They were silent for several minutes, finishing their meal. Finally, Chance set down his glass of wine and focused on her. "We need to come up with a plan if we're going to fool people, partner."

"What kind of plan?"

"Valentine's Day is coming up and we should make reservations at a romantic restaurant."

"Okay, but let's be sure we're in agreement. This is strictly a business arrangement. Neither of us likes holidays or fuss. It's a win-win, but we're nothing more than friends. Right?"

"Exactly." His eyes glinted.

"Why do I not believe you?"

"You hurt me, *partner*."

CHAPTER SEVEN

At the knock on her door, Laney smoothed a hand down the side of her short red dress and straightened her shoulders before opening to Chance. Her breath caught in her throat at the sight of him dressed in a well-tailored gray suit, white shirt, worn tieless, and with his hair slicked back. He'd turn more than a few female heads tonight.

He cradled a huge bouquet of red roses. "Happy Valentine's Day. Ready to meet our public?"

Laughing, she stepped aside to let him in. "I didn't realize this is our introduction to society." She inhaled his cologne, a subtle citrus scent. He smelled good enough to eat.

"Of course this is our introduction," he said. "The more people who see us together, the better." He held out the flowers. "For you."

Taking the bouquet, she sniffed their sweet fragrance. "You really didn't have to do flowers. It's not like anyone other than us will see them."

"When your friends and co-workers ask what your boyfriend gave you for Valentine's Day, you can tell them about the flowers, and you won't have to lie."

"Good point. One of my co-workers invited me to his place tonight to meet his brother. What a relief to tell him I already had a date. Let me put these in a vase and we can get going."

As she walked to the kitchen, he called out to her. "You look amazing, by the way. I'll be the envy of every guy at the restaurant."

She whirled to face him. "Thanks. You can save the compliments for when we're around others."

"I mean it. You look sexy."

She grinned and let her gaze trail over him. Two could play that game. "You look hot too."

Later, seated at a table overlooking the Vegas Strip, in an elegant restaurant owned by world-famous chef, Gloria Giovanni, Laney and Chance enjoyed a rich burgundy wine while waiting for their food.

"This place is beautiful," Laney said, admiring the modern room with white leather banquettes, white tiled floor, and tongue and groove ceiling, from which hung classy, understated crystal chandeliers.

"My new boss took me here when I arrived in Vegas," Chance said. "I guarantee you'll love the food."

"I love Gloria's show on the Food Network, and I can't wait to taste her food."

They shared appetizers of baby sweet peppers with goat cheese and olive tapenade, and fresh ricotta with honey, lemon, and peppercorn. Like two real lovers, they tasted each other's entrees—surf and turf with port wine sauce, creamy gorgonzola gnocchi and baby carrots for Chance; ravioli with lobster and white asparagus tips for Laney.

Through dinner, they traded stories of the crazy people they'd met at their respective jobs. Laney couldn't remember the last time she laughed so much.

"I love your story of the vegan who dressed up like a chicken to protest your deli meats sponsor. Then asked for your autograph when you walked outside," Laney said.

"And I liked yours about the woman who wanted you to find her a date because her husband was too busy at the blackjack table to pay attention to her."

"You should see the crazies we get at our counter when the moon is full."

He laughed. "Tell me about it."

As they were eating their dessert, a plate of assorted Italian cookies, and drinking espresso with toasted hazelnuts, whipped cream, and cocoa powder, Chance set down his coffee cup and caught Laney's gaze with his intense stare.

"What?" she said. "Do I have food on my face?"

"If you did, you'd be even more appealing. You're a beautiful woman, but you must hear that all the time."

Face burning, she set down the cookie she held. "Thank you, but, no, I don't get that all the time, or much at all. Please, Chance, we agreed we're holiday buddies, bad-luck partners. Nothing more."

"Just giving my dinner companion a well-meaning compliment."

"Don't."

Laughing, he took a cookie from the platter.

"Yes, yes, I'll marry you," a woman said loudly. Clapping and laughter broke out. Laney looked across the room to see a young couple embracing. The man slipped a ring onto the woman's finger as the restaurant patrons looked on and cheered.

A pang of regret twisted in Laney. At one time, she'd dreamed of marriage and children with a wonderful man. Chris destroyed that dream. She had no more illusions about love. Maybe she was better for it.

"It's nice to see others so happy," Chance said, pulling her attention from the recently engaged couple. "I guess it's nice to propose in public, but I'd prefer a more intimate setting."

"I would too, but since I may never marry, it's a moot point."

"You don't think you'll marry?"

"I like my life as it is."

As she picked up her coffee cup, she felt someone close by and inhaled the scent of heavy perfume that made her eyes water.

A sultry feminine voice said, "Chance. I'd hoped to see you. I've missed you."

Laney raised her gaze to the most beautiful woman she'd ever seen. Tall, with impressive breasts, barely concealed by the white halter top that exposed her tanned midriff, and with waist-length white-blonde hair, the woman's stunning looks froze Laney. A very short skirt showed off the woman's long, perfect legs. The blonde's green eyes stared at Chance with adoration.

"Hello, Naomi," he said, his voice tight. "What the hell are you doing here?"

She pressed her enhanced lips together in a pout. "Is that any way to talk to your fiancée?"

CHAPTER EIGHT

A tight ball of shock and frustration rolled through Chance. He stood slowly to face Naomi. With her high heels, she matched his height of six feet two inches. "You are not my fiancée." He kept his voice low, grinding out his words. "You gave that up when you cheated on me." Glancing around the large room, he asked, "Where's Wilson?"

"He and I broke up." She touched Chance's arm. "I've missed you, darling," she purred. "You look better than ever. Vegas must agree with you. I thought you'd be glad to see me."

"I'm not." He extricated himself from her, aware of Laney watching them closely. "What are you doing here, Naomi?"

She looked at Laney. "Aren't you going to introduce me to your date?"

He hesitated. Laney didn't deserve this confrontation. With a resigned sigh, he said, "Naomi, this is Laney."

Naomi studied Laney. With an expression of disdain on her beautiful, cheating face, as if Laney weren't worth her bother, Naomi turned back to Chance. "The station gave me the sports talk show after you...left. I'm in Vegas doing the play-by-plays for the American Wrestling League bouts at the Convention Center." She moved closer, her lips inches from his ear. "I'll be here for a week. I want to see you again. You're the best I've ever had. I still love you, Chance."

He stepped back. "You had a funny way of showing it. I have no interest in you."

"You can't stay away from me. We had something good."

"*Had* being the operative word. Good-bye, Naomi." Red-hot anger shot through him and he sat down, hoping she'd get the hint and go away.

Naomi rubbed her hand over his bicep. "Still working out, I see. I'm going for now. I know you'll call me." She sauntered away.

He forced a smile for Laney. "Sorry about that little scene. I had no idea Naomi was here."

Laney reached across the table and put a hand over his. "Don't worry about it." Withdrawing her hand, she said, "That's the fiancée you told me about, the one who had the radio show with you in Chicago?" She lifted an eyebrow. "Unless you have more than one fiancée."

"Trust me, one fiancée was enough, at least with a woman like Naomi."

Until Naomi showed up, Chance had been enjoying his time with Laney. Lovely in an earthy, real way, she intrigued him. He liked talking to her, liked the intelligence in her big amber eyes, the sweetness of her smile, her joy. Naomi had to ruin it. With Drama Queen Naomi, his life had been one spectacle after another. He'd been glad to leave all that behind.

He and Laney were quiet on the short ride back to their condo complex. When they got to her door, he bent to kiss her, something he'd wanted to do all evening.

She put up a hand, stopping him. "Friends don't kiss goodnight."

"Some do." He twisted strands of her long, silky hair around his finger.

"These friends don't."

Her beautiful, sweet smile took the sting from her words and made his pulse race.

"Thanks for the best Valentine's Day ever," she said. "Next date is my treat. Goodnight, Chance."

She slipped inside her place, leaving him alone in the hall.

He and Laney had an agreement, one she apparently intended to keep. He didn't know what had possessed him to come up with the Bad Luck Partners. Maybe he'd wanted a way to continue seeing Laney. She made him feel good.

He'd run away to Vegas to lick his wounds after his very

public humiliation. Determined to avoid relationships, he'd considered Vegas a stopover on the road to bigger and better things in his career. If all went well, he'd be in Los Angeles this time next year, and hopefully bringing his show to a national audience. He wouldn't open up his heart again. Love hurt, and he'd had enough drama and pain with Naomi.

Yet, a part of him wanted more than a friends-only relationship with Laney. He squashed that thought and went into his quiet, empty, lonely condo. He shut the door behind him, shutting out Laney and the possibility of love.

CHAPTER NINE

In the two weeks since Valentine's Day, the Augustus had been extremely busy with conferences, and Laney worked longer than normal hours. She saw Chance a few times in the hallway outside their condos, or going in and out of the parking lot. They exchanged pleasantries, but not much more. A vague sense of disappointment covered her. Try as she might to ignore it, a part of her wanted to see him, talk to him, have fun with him, and not solely on holidays.

Finally home after another long day, dragged out from putting in extra hours, Laney tramped across the parking lot to her building and took the elevator to her floor, her thoughts on Chance. No big holidays were on the horizon, no excuse to be with him.

He'd suggested they get together at other times. Maybe she should ask him to a co-worker's wedding the following weekend. Would he go if he and Naomi were a couple again? A few days after Valentine's Day, Laney had heard voices in the hall and looked out her door's peephole to see Chance with Naomi. Her heart had plummeted to the vicinity of her knees, and she'd turned quickly away.

Thankfully, she hadn't seen Naomi with him since.

Laney exited the elevator and walked the short distance to her condo. As she stood in front of her door, ready to put her key in the lock, Chance's door opened behind her. Pivoting to face him, she drank in the sight of him. His white T-shirt stretched over his broad chest, and his indigo jeans rode low on slim hips. His blatant sex appeal and his wide smile made her whole body tingle.

"Hey, Laney, we haven't talked for a while." He strode over to her. "Work has been demanding, and I was away at a conference three days last week. I've missed you."

She wanted to tell him she'd missed him too. She returned his smile, trying to project a nonchalance she didn't feel, and said instead, "It's been crazy busy at work for me. I saw you with Naomi a while ago. You getting back together?" The words had come out unbidden, and she wanted to bite them back. Chance and Naomi's relationship had nothing to do with her.

"Never." Anger dripped from his voice. "She's left Vegas, thankfully. She practically stalked me while she was here. I don't know how she found out where I live. She probably managed to get into the building by flirting with the guard. Funny how I once thought I was madly in love with her. I think my own shallowness had something to do with it. Having her on my arm stoked my ego."

Chance raked fingers through his hair, mussing it.

Fighting the urge to reach up and smooth his hair, Laney gripped the key in her hand until it dug into her flesh. "I don't think you're shallow."

"Hopefully, I'm not now." He stepped closer until they were a whisper apart. "I like being with you. I've missed our conversations. We don't have to go out together only on holidays or to special functions. Maybe we can go out once in a while, friends enjoying each other's company."

When she hesitated, he held up his hands. "If we want people to believe we're in a real relationship, we have to be seen together more."

"The more we're seen together, the less chance anyone will try to fix us up."

"You got it."

His sexy grin made her knees wobble. She backed up to lean against her door. "I'm invited to a wedding next weekend. A co-worker's. Want to go with me?"

CHAPTER TEN

"Laney, Chance is so hot. Every time he walks across the room, women practically salivate," Amanda said. The two women, sitting at the table they'd been assigned for their co-worker's wedding reception, watched as Chance, along with Ben, Amanda's boyfriend, made their way through a throng of guests to the bar.

"He's great looking, but he's also a decent guy," Laney said. "And fun to be with."

Amanda reached across the table to pat Laney's hand. "I'm so happy to see you in love. After what Chris did, you deserve a great guy. The way Chance looks at you makes me envious. Ben and I have a good relationship, but he doesn't look at me like he wants to devour me, the way Chance does you."

Ready to blurt out her true relationship with Chance, Laney looked down at the table. In control again, she smiled at Amanda. "Chance and I haven't known each other long. I'm not ready to commit to anything and neither is he. We have a good time together."

Amanda laughed and studied her with a smug expression. "Girl, you are in denial. You like Chance as much more than a friend. And he likes you."

The men came with their drinks, saving Laney from having to respond. During the delicious meal, she stole glances at Chance. He caught her gaze a few times and winked. When Laney saw Amanda watching them, she narrowed her eyes at her friend, causing Amanda to laugh. Laney refused to believe Amanda about Chance. Laney liked him as a friend only. It would be a long time before she let another man into her heart.

"Dance with me, Laney?" Chance asked as the band began playing dance music when dinner ended.

She shook her head. "I don't dance. I've never been good at it so I gave up trying."

"You can slow dance," he said. "Right?" He nodded toward the band. "They're playing a slow tune now. Let's go." He stood and held out a hand to her.

She had no choice but to put her hand in his and let him lead her to the dance floor. He gathered her into his arms and held her close as they swayed to the romantic ballad.

The soothing melody relaxed her and she laid her head against his chest, inhaling his scent of citrus aftershave. The fine wool of his suit brushed her cheek, and the steady beat of his heart further calmed her.

As they swirled around the floor, the soft silk of Laney's dress floated around her knees, making her feel like a fairy princess at the ball. She let herself imagine she and Chance really were lovers, and that he was everything she ever wanted in a man—loyal, smart, ambitious, gentle, caring, and with a sense of humor.

She liked Chance, and she liked their arrangement too. She could go out with him and be herself. She didn't have to try to impress him or worry if he liked her. And she didn't need to suffer through any more blind dates with guys who bored her.

The dance over, Chance looked down at her. "That wasn't so bad. We didn't step on each other's toes."

Her insides pulsed with the force of his sexual magnetism, and she turned to go back to their table, and safety. The highly polished floor and her mile-high strappy sandals fought with each other, and the shoes lost. Laney slipped.

"Whoa!" Chance grabbed her arm, helping her to balance herself. She gave him a sheepish smile.

"That's my Laney," he said. "You wouldn't be you if you didn't trip over something." His mouth quirked in a teasing grin.

She punched him in the arm, provoking a round of laughter from him.

Driving home after the reception, Laney laid her head back

on the smooth leather seat of Chance's Escalade. "I had fun today."

"I did too. I'm glad you invited me," he said. "Our arrangement is working out. We have fun together, and it's a relief to be able to assure my co-workers I have a significant other. I can concentrate on my career without anyone trying to help me find a woman and telling me I need to settle down. I'm perfectly happy being single."

"Me, too."

He glanced at her with a smile. "Next weekend, my station is having a party to celebrate their ten-year anniversary. Will you go with me?"

"Sure." It would give her something to do, and it would be fun. *And you'll get to spend time with Chance*, said a pesky little voice inside her.

He parked his car and they walked into their building together. At Laney's door, he cupped her face between his hands and skimmed his thumbs over her cheeks. Heat coalesced in the pit of her stomach and traveled lower.

"I tried to behave myself all evening," he said. "I really want to kiss you." He bent and took her lips in a tender kiss that electrified every part of her body. She dropped her purse and wound her arms around his neck. Heat sizzled through her like the desert sun at high noon.

He deepened the kiss, coaxing and teasing, urging her to give more. She opened to him. Their tongues mated in a fiery dance. She tunneled her hands through the thickness of his hair, reveling in his heat and masculinity.

After several passion-filled minutes, they pulled apart. Fighting her need to curl into his arms, Laney gathered her willpower around her like a shield and stepped away from him and temptation. "Goodnight, Chance. Thanks for going to the wedding with me." She grabbed her purse from the floor, unlocked her door, and slipped inside.

When she got to her bedroom, she threw her purse on the bed in frustration and stomped into the bathroom. She'd wanted Chance to do more than kiss her. Making love with him could ruin their budding friendship and leave her vulnerable.

She looked at herself in the bathroom mirror. "Damn it, girl, get hold of yourself. Chance isn't sticking around. He has plans that don't include you." She splashed cold water on her face.

CHAPTER ELEVEN

*W*e're coming out for a visit. Can't wait to meet your new boyfriend. Already booked the flight. Will call you tonight. On lunch break the Monday after the wedding, Laney stared at the text from her mom. She talked by phone to her parents once a week, and her mother always asked if Laney had a boyfriend. Last week, she'd told her about Chance, figuring her mom would leave her alone about finding someone.

What tangled webs we weave, she thought. Her parents came to Vegas once or twice a year to see Laney. They'd been out this past October. Crap. She didn't think they'd come again so soon, and to see her fake boyfriend.

"Hey, girl, why so glum?" Amanda asked, joining Laney at her table in the employees' cafeteria. The day had dawned cloudy, a rarity for Vegas. Tired from the weekend, and down because of the weather, Laney had packed a lunch today.

"Got a text from my mom," Laney said. "She and Dad are coming out here to meet Chance."

"So? What's the problem?"

Laney threw her friend a look. "I tell Mom I'm seeing someone and she immediately books a flight here. She didn't fly right out when I told her about Chris and Darren. Why now? Why Chance?"

Amanda settled back in her chair and gave Laney one of her signature *You'd better listen to me* glares. "Your mom must have picked up something in your voice that told her Chance is special. You can deny your feelings for him all you want, but your mama knows what's going on."

Laney stabbed her salad with her fork, her mood as gray as the storm clouds forming outside. "He's just a friend."

Amanda grinned. "If you say so."

<><><>

"So you're Chance's girlfriend?" The redhead with the hard green eyes scanned Laney as they waited in line in the ladies room at Mandalay Bay where Chance's office party was in full swing.

Laney looked at the other woman with what she hoped was condescension. "Yes. I am. He's a great guy."

"He's sexy as hell, and all the single women, and some of the married ones, wanted dibs on him. What's so special about you?"

Laney shrugged. "Chance and I fell in love the minute we looked at each other." She sighed and tried to put a dreamy look on her face. Maybe she should have been an actress. She enjoyed being someone she wasn't, a woman in love.

No wonder most of the women at the party ignored her or threw her daggers with their eyes. Guess she'd ruined their fantasies about Chance. Laney understood more clearly why he seemed so eager to make the deal with her. Probably tired of women chasing him.

Putting a bright smile on her face, she looked for Chance when she left the ladies room, and found him surrounded by several male co-workers. Laney went to him and slid her arm around his waist. Surprise flashed over his face for a millisecond, then he bent and brushed a whisper-soft kiss on her lips.

The men around him watched her with interest, some with lust in their eyes that made her press closer to Chance.

"I'd like another wine, Chance, please," she purred. Laney doubted she'd ever purred in her life, but after her encounter with the snippy redhead, she decided she'd pour on the lovesick act thick as she could make it.

"Sure, sweetheart," Chance said, getting in on the act. "Later, guys," he said, taking Laney's hand as they walked to the bar.

He whispered in her ear. "I expected you to start batting your eyelashes at me. What gives? Not that I mind this new, saucy Laney."

"Why not have fun with this?" She grinned up at him.

"Why not?" He leaned toward her again. "When I tell you how sexy you look, that's not acting. You're easily the sexiest woman here."

"Thanks." A sigh of pleasure escaped her at his words. She'd dressed carefully tonight, wearing her favorite "Little Black Dress," low-cut to reveal her cleavage, helped by her pushup bra. Her gold stiletto sandals made walking hard, but she felt oh-so-sexy. She'd had her hair done in an upsweep. Much as she tried to convince herself she wanted to make a good impression on Chance's co-workers, part of her knew she'd really wanted to knock him for a loop. And by the expression on his face when he first saw her, and the looks he kept giving her, she'd succeeded. Giddiness put a spring in her step. She wouldn't allow herself to fall in love with Chance, but she'd sure as hell enjoy their little con game.

"We're very lucky to have Chance," his boss said later to Laney as she and Chance sat at the head table with his boss and the boss's wife to enjoy their meal. Laney knew Chance being invited to sit with the station owner was a big deal.

"I agree," Laney said. "I listen to Chance's show every day. He talks about such interesting topics and has equally interesting guests." She rubbed a hand over his arm. "He has such a sexy voice."

Chance coughed and set down his wine glass. "Thanks, sweetheart. I love knowing you're listening." He skimmed her cheek with his knuckles, sending delicious shivers down her spine.

The other couple beamed at Laney and Chance. Uh-oh. Maybe she'd overacted the affection.

Later, alone at the table, Chance turned to her with a wicked grin. "You listen to my show every day, huh?"

She fingered the edge of her linen napkin. "I have listened to it when I'm free, and I do enjoy it." She frowned. "I'm coming on a little strong, aren't I?"

He laughed. "You are. I like it. It can't hurt with the boss."

"Do you think they believe we're in love?"

"Either that, or you worship me."

She hit him with her napkin. "When my parents come next

week, it'll be your turn to worship me."
  "Deal."

CHAPTER TWELVE

Her parents' flight arrived at eight the following Sunday night. Nervousness made Laney fidget as she and Chance stood in front of the luggage carousel. The bags from her parents' flight hadn't come down the conveyor belt yet, and the passengers from the plane hadn't gotten there either. She shifted her purse from one shoulder to the other, then back again.

"Relax," Chance said. "I guarantee I'll make them love me."

"Although you're very sure of your own charm," she said, giving him a wry smile, "I feel guilty passing you off as my boyfriend. I didn't think they'd come here so soon. I figured by the time they came to visit, I could tell them we'd broken up." She moved her bag to the other shoulder again. "Part of me is looking forward to finally getting Mom off my back about a boyfriend. Maybe she'll quit throwing it up to me that my brother has a perfect life." Laney winced. "Am I a bad person to think that?"

He put his arm around her waist and pulled her against him. "I understand how you feel. I hate fooling them too. Let's think about how we can tell them together."

She met his gaze. "It's good of you to offer. I'm the one who lied so I'm the one who has to tell them. I would have told them the truth before they flew all the way out here, but Mom had already booked the airfare." She glanced down. "I'm a coward. I couldn't admit to Mom that I'd lied about a boyfriend, and now I've made things worse."

"It'll all work out. Enjoy your parents while they're here."

The carousel bell rang, and the first bags appeared. Passengers began crowding around them. Laney stiffened.

Chance kissed the top of her head. "Relax."

"Laney!" Her mom's voice rang out above the thumping of bags coming down the chute.

Chance released Laney, and they both turned. Smiling, her brown eyes glowing, Laney's Mom approached them. Frowning, Laney's dad studied Chance as he walked.

Laney and her parents hugged, then she introduced them to Chance.

Her mom hugged Chance. "We're so glad to meet you."

The men shook hands.

"Nice to meet you, too, Mr. and Mrs. Sikora."

"Call us Lee and Sue," her mom said.

Laney smiled, forcing her tight muscles to relax. She could do this. She would do this, if her damn guilt weren't so overwhelming. She'd figure out the best way and time to tell her parents the truth. Just not right now.

After checking her parents into their suite at the Augustus, where Laney always secured them a discount, the two couples had a light meal together at one of the hotel's casual restaurants.

Through dinner, Chance showed a tender attentiveness to Laney that made warmth, with a tinge of longing, swirl through her. She wished she had a boyfriend who truly cared for her the way Chance pretended. The knowing looks her mother gave her told Laney that Chance had her mom fooled. A fresh dagger of guilt plunged into Laney's chest.

The following day, Laney didn't have to work. She had brunch with her parents, then sat outside with them by the heated pool. The March sun beat down on them. Laney lifted her head to the sun's rays, letting the warmth soothe and relax her.

"See why I don't want to move back to Philly," she said, turning to her parents. "We have sun here in March. It's warm. It's still winter back home."

Her mother patted her arm. "We miss you. If it weren't for your brother and his family, we'd retire out here." She shot Laney a sly smile. "We can't leave the grandchildren. However, if you were to marry and have children, maybe we could have a place here, too. Or you could always move home."

"Stop right there, Mom. Chance and I just met."

"Maybe so, but I can see you care for each other. I want to see you settled with a wonderful family, like your brother."

Laney turned her attention to her mimosa, letting the cool slide of the drink down her throat drown out the old, familiar hurt that rose in her. It always came back to Laney's older brother. A surgeon, Doug had been her parents' favorite when Laney was growing up. Although they tried not to show their favoritism, they didn't always succeed. Doug had done everything right. He'd been top of his class all through private high school, graduated from a prestigious university and medical school. Now, he had a thriving practice, a beautiful blonde socialite wife, and three beautiful, smart blonde children. He and his family lived in one of Philadelphia's most exclusive suburbs.

Her mom touched her hand. "We want you to be happy, darling."

"I am happy. Don't worry about me."

Laney knew she'd been a disappointment to her parents. They'd wanted her to go into insurance, like her dad. He owned a successful firm, and hoped Laney would someday take over. Laney had majored in hotel management, upsetting her parents. Five years ago, when Laney had gotten the job offer at the Augustus, her parents had been against her moving so far away. They grudgingly accepted her choice now, but they harbored the hope Laney would come to her senses and move home, take insurance classes, find an acceptable man, and settle down.

She'd planned to tell her parents the truth about Chance before they left. Her mother's mention of Laney's brother brought the resentment she harbored toward him to the surface and compelled Laney to rethink her plan. Truth be told, she liked seeing the happiness on her mom's face that Laney had finally found someone. Laney wanted to bask in that pleasure for a while longer. Her parents had liked Chris, and her mom had been disappointed when he broke the engagement. She'd never told them about Chris's infidelity. Maybe it would be better if her parents went home believing Laney and Chance were a happy couple. Later, she'd break it to them gently that she and Chance broke up.

"Too bad Chance couldn't be here," Laney's mom said, as if

reading her mind.

"He had to work today. He'll join us for dinner tonight."

Her mom's eyes lit up. "It's so exciting Chance has his own radio show. I've never known a celebrity before. We must catch his show before we leave."

"He's not a celebrity yet, but he will be someday. Chance is very good. He'll go places." Like Los Angeles, away from her. She pushed aside the thought and focused on the present.

"What are his intentions toward you?" her dad asked.

"Intentions?" Laney almost choked on the mimosa she'd sipped. "What is this, the nineteenth century? I've recently met him. I have no idea where this going with us."

Laney's mother gave her father a look that made him shut up. "I like Chance a lot," her mom said. "I'd always hoped you'd meet someone closer to home and move back."

Laney held up her hands. "Stop it, both of you. If Chance and I marry, or if I marry anyone, you'll be the first to know."

Her mother laughed. "I'm afraid you'll call and tell us you got married by Elvis at one of those tacky wedding chapels."

"That's not a bad idea," Laney said.

"It would certainly be cheaper for me," her father said. He glanced at his wife. "Don't discourage her from that, Sue. Think of all the money we'll save."

They all laughed, and Laney began to relax again. Things would work out.

CHAPTER THIRTEEN

"You're so quiet," Chance said two nights later, as he and Laney drove away from McCarron after dropping her parents off. "Miss your parents already?"

Laney stared out the windshield at the night sky, its darkness a reflection of the sadness she felt. "I always hate to see them leave, and I feel guilty I didn't tell them the truth about us." She shifted in the passenger seat to look at Chance. "I planned to tell them, then my mom mentioned my brother, and all the hurts came back. Besides, my mom looked happy I'd found someone, and I've disappointed her so much, I wanted to do something to keep the illusion going, even if for a little while."

"I can't believe you've disappointed them in any way." They stopped at a red light, and he glanced over at her. "What's the problem with your brother? Want to talk about it?"

"I don't think so." Despite her words, part of her wanted to unburden the heaviness that lay over her. She hadn't known Chance long, but felt he'd understand.

"Let's go have a drink and something to eat," he said. "We'll talk, but only if you want to."

"Well, I am hungry."

He laughed. "Way to make a guy feel good. You sound like I'm taking you to the dentist."

Her laugh joined his. "Sorry. Let's go to the Capri at the Augustus."

Later, seated in the Capri Bar & Grille, Chance and Laney enjoyed their drinks, beer for Chance and red wine for Laney, while they waited for their sandwiches.

Her mind whirled as she tried to rein in her jumbled thoughts. Seeing her parents always brought back her conflicting feelings about her brother.

Chance raised his longneck to his mouth and glanced around as he drank. Putting down his bottle, he met her gaze and said, "Everything I've seen at the Augustus is top-notch. You've worked here five years?"

When she nodded, he said, "Do you plan to make your career here or move to another hotel?"

"The Augustus is a good place. I hope to work my way up to management. If another hotel, one as good as this, makes me an offer I can't refuse, I might consider changing jobs."

"You want to stay in Vegas?"

"If I can. I love it here. The Augustus chain has hotels all over the world, so it's possible I'll accept a job at one of their other hotels in the future. And you'll most likely be in L.A. on the fast-track to your career before this time next year." She kept her tone light, but her chest tightened at the thought of never seeing Chance again.

"That's my plan, if all goes well."

The waitress brought over their roast beef sandwiches. They concentrated on their food, making small talk while they ate.

When he'd finished, Chance pushed his empty plate away and looked at Laney. "Do you want to talk about why you think you're a disappointment to your parents?"

He looked so sincere, as if he truly cared. She'd only shared her hurt with Amanda. Chance had become a good friend. Laney tossed back the last of her wine and set the glass away from her. Chance signaled the waitress for another round.

Laney nibbled a few of her house-made potato chips, gathering her thoughts before meeting Chance's gaze.

"My brother is eight years older than I am," she began. "He's brilliant. In high school, he graduated first in his class. He played quarterback on his school's football team and led them to the state championships his senior year. In college and med school, he made the Dean's List constantly."

She paused, drew a breath, and continued. "I grew up in his shadow. My parents doted on him and liked to brag about him to their friends. He's a successful surgeon, with a practice in Philadelphia and a mini-mansion on Philly's exclusive Main Line." She raised both hands in a gesture of surrender.

Picking up her fresh glass of wine, she took a sip, set down her glass, and gave Chance a wry smile. "I don't really care about making huge amounts of money. If I did, I wouldn't be in the hospitality business, but it grates that my parents consider money as a measure of a person's worth. Doug, my brother, and I aren't close, probably due to the age difference. His wife Sandi comes from old money. She's a society leader. Their kids, whom I adore, are beautiful and smart." She sighed. "The perfect family."

Chance put his hand over hers. "I see why your parents are proud of your brother, but that doesn't mean they're not proud of you."

His big hand over hers sent a jolt of pleasure rocketing through her. The encouragement in his blue eyes warmed her to her core.

She slipped her hand from his and continued. "My dad owns a successful insurance firm in Philadelphia. He wanted me to follow in his footsteps and take over the business someday."

"You didn't want to."

She smiled. "I love meeting people and I love to travel. My job is fun. Most of the people I meet are nice."

"Except the jerk who accosted you in the garage that night."

"Except him. I like helping people have a good time. When I travel, I get to stay at Augustus hotels at deep discounts. Cuts down on my expenses, and working here beats being in a stuffy office all day."

He lifted his bottle. "To having fun and staying out of stuffy offices."

She laughed.

"I know it's tough on you that your parents aren't happy with your career choice," he said.

"Mom keeps hoping I'll suddenly grow up, move back home, work at Dad's firm, and get married, not necessarily in that order. Dad doesn't say much, but I know he wants that too. They both want me to marry a successful guy with lots of money so I'll have a life like my brother's."

"You need to do what makes you happy, Laney."

"I'm doing that, but I feel guilty too."

As they walked out of the Capri after eating, Chance put his arm around Laney's waist. "I like your parents," he said. "I can see they love you very much. I get that growing up you felt in your brother's shadow. Your parents want what they think is best for you. Cut them some slack. They'll come around."

She looked up at him. "They know I'm happy and they come out to visit whenever they can. I've spent my life trying to please them, but I finally took my future into my hands when I got my hotel management degree. I love them and I want them to be proud of me."

"I know you do." He smiled. "Your mom likes me."

Laney grinned. "Don't get too full of yourself. Dad wasn't sure about you."

"Way to hurt a guy."

"You're too much." She laughed.

Several people in the hotel lobby turned to look at them, some giving them indulgent smiles. "You and I should be in Hollywood," Laney said. "We've got strangers believing we're a couple. Our little plan is working."

He grinned down at her. "This is the most fun I've had in a long time."

Laney felt like skipping. "Me too."

CHAPTER FOURTEEN

Because one of her co-workers called out sick, Laney had been forced to work overtime the day after her parents left. She'd lain awake most of the night before as images of Chance played through her mind like a streaming video. She liked being with him, liked it a little too much. She hoped to see him later today. Maybe she'd run into him at the condo, if she were lucky.

Finally, her long day over, Laney trudged up the two flights to her condo. She preferred the exercise rather than take the elevator. She yawned. Her lack of sleep had caught up with her.

As she got to her floor, she saw Chance at his door. He turned, and something hot and pulsing passed between them. His ruffled black hair and the light stubble on his square jaw gave him a macho hipster look that made her step falter. The sleeves of his white shirt were rolled up to expose muscled arms with a sprinkling of fine black hair. His dark jeans hugged his long legs. She gripped the railing.

"Hey, Laney."

"Hey, Chance." When she stepped onto the landing, her heel caught in the carpet and she stumbled. She would have fallen if Chance hadn't caught her.

His strong arms went around her, and he held her against his chest. His steady heartbeat pounded in her ears. She raised her gaze to his.

"You okay?" he asked, his voice thick.

Unable to find her voice, she nodded.

"Laney." His mouth descended on hers.

He tasted like coffee and mint. Hungry for him, she wound her arms around his neck.

He backed her up until she pressed against the wall. His tongue slid along the seam of her lips, and she opened to him. Their tongues twined, inflaming every cell in her body. She barely recognized her low moans of pleasure.

His lips, hot and intense, claimed her. Her body molded to his sculpted frame as if they were made for each other. Heat unfurled in her, warming her to her toes.

He slid his leg between hers. His hardness pressed against her belly. He wanted her as much as she wanted him.

When he left her mouth to trail kisses down her throat, she murmured his name, her senses on fire. He pulled her blouse from the waistband of her skirt. His large, warm hands spanned her midriff. Her hard nipples strained against the lace of her bra. He skimmed his fingers up her ribcage to massage her breasts until she was a puddle of need, pliable under his touch.

With a moan, he pushed away from her and buried his face in her neck, his breathing harsh. "I'm sorry, Laney. I shouldn't have, not here."

Embarrassment cooled her passion like ice water thrown in her face. She glanced around. "We shouldn't be doing this at all." Her ragged breathing matched his. "I don't know what came over me."

He gripped her shoulders. "I know. We want each other. We've been dancing around it for months."

Fear drove her to slide away from him. "We can't, Chance. We can't." With shaking hands, she dug inside her shoulder bag for her key. Heart pounding with humiliation and sexual frustration, she opened the door and slipped inside her apartment without looking back.

She didn't want a relationship now, especially with a guy who would soon leave for greener pastures. Her broken heart needed time.

CHAPTER FIFTEEN

Exhausted from a week-long conference in L.A. where he had to be "on" all day, Chance entered his condo, threw his suitcase on the sofa, and strode into his kitchen for a much-needed cold brew. It had been a week since the hot kiss he'd shared with Laney. Through the tiring workshops and craziness of the conference, she'd been constantly on his mind. During some of the more boring presentations, he'd pictured Laney's smile, her big amber eyes, the teasing way she looked at him.

At night, he dreamt of making love with her, of seeing her luxurious mass of hair spread on his pillow. Of worshipping her lush body and making her his. With his career beginning to take off, he didn't need any romantic entanglements now. Yet, there was Laney.

He'd texted a few times to let her know he was thinking of her and missed her. Her responses were terse, setting up alarms in his head. He'd come on too strong with her. He hoped he hadn't scared her away.

Twisting off the top on the beer bottle, he raised the bottle and took a long sip. His mind whirling, he sat at the kitchen island. He'd been a rising star in Chicago. He'd had it all, a sexy girlfriend, a top show, great money. Until Naomi had publicly humiliated him. He'd run, from Chicago, from Naomi, from the hurt and betrayal. Shame washed over him as he thought of his old life in Chicago. He'd been as shallow as Naomi, strutting around like a peacock, showing the world the hot woman he called girlfriend.

When he'd arrived in Las Vegas, he'd felt like a failure, that he'd come down in the world. The laid-back lifestyle here, the easy acceptance of everyone, the friendliness, had all worked on him until he'd begun to feel good about himself again. Now, with this chance for a show in Los Angeles, his career was back on track. He realized to his surprise the idea wasn't as important as it had been.

He took another swig of his drink and plunked the bottle onto the counter, his thoughts on Laney. Strong, sweet, honest Laney. She made him feel good, and accepted him for himself. Her friendship had begun the healing process for him, had helped give him back his confidence, had made him realize the hollowness of his previous life.

Deep inside where he locked away his most private desires, he wanted more than friendship with Laney. That wouldn't be fair to her. She had a career and a life here. He had to take care of his own career. For them to become involved could mean hurt for her, and maybe him. He'd never do anything to hurt Laney.

He heard her door open and close. Before he could change his mind, he stood. He needed to see her. Now.

<> <> <>

"Hey, Ebony," Laney said to the cat sleeping on the bed. "I'll feed you as soon as I get changed." Laney threw her purse on a chair and began to slip off her suit jacket. At the ringing of her doorbell, she froze. The rapid tripping of her heart told her Chance waited at her door. The guard hadn't called to announce a visitor. She adjusted her jacket and smoothed a hand down her skirt. For the past week, she'd rehearsed what she would say to Chance when she saw him again. She walked to the door with heavy steps. She wished things could be different, but she'd made up her mind.

When she looked through the peephole, she put a hand over her heart, as if she could stop its rapid beating. Chance. She'd missed him. Resolve stiffened her spine as she opened the door. She'd allowed herself to become vulnerable, opened her heart to him. He'd leave soon.

"Hi, Chance. How was the conference?" He looked tired, with dark circles under his eyes and stubble on his jaw. She moved away, putting distance between him and the temptation to throw her arms around him.

He smiled, and his dimples made an appearance. Not fair, she thought.

"The conference was good," he said. "Exhausting. May I come in?"

Nodding, she let him enter, then closed the door. "I just got home. Would you like a glass of wine?"

"Nah. I had a beer. You've had dinner?"

"Not yet."

"Let's get a bite to eat."

"Thanks, but I'm a little wiped out from work." She'd made up her mind to distance herself from him. Better now than later when she might have fallen in love with him. Seeing him here, so close, so appealing, her resolve began to waver.

"I'm sorry about what happened the last time I saw you," he said. "I wasn't lying about wanting you, but I know we need to take it slow."

She folded her arms across her chest, protection against his charm. "There's nothing to take slow. We had an arrangement. That's all. I've given this a lot of thought, and I believe it would be best to end our partnership." The lie stuck in her throat. Part of her wanted a lot more than friendship with Chance, but heartbreak lay that way.

He took a step back. "You're ending our agreement?"

"Things have gotten a little out of hand. I think we need to cool it all the way around. You'll be leaving soon. I don't want to be taken advantage of."

Anger darkened his eyes. "You think I'd take advantage of you?"

"I don't really know you that well. I need to be careful. It's best we don't see much of each other."

"I thought we were friends. I guess I was wrong. Friends trust each other. Good-bye."

He slipped out, shutting the door behind him, shutting her out of his life.

She'd done the right thing. She'd been harsh with him, but she had to protect her heart and her pride.

<><><>

With Memorial Day approaching, the Augustus hummed with

activity. Tourists from all corners of the world converged on Las Vegas, looking for fun, games, and maybe memories that would stay in Vegas. The concierge counter had lines from morning until night. Despite the guests who kept her busy, her thoughts strayed often to Chance, as they had every day in the three weeks since he walked out of her condo. And her life.

They'd run into each other a few times at the complex and said stilted hellos. She missed him. A lot. Funny how she could miss a person after knowing him such a short time.

Guilt had become her constant companion. Deep down, she didn't really believe Chance played her. Yet, her own fears of losing her heart when he left for greener pastures held her hostage and caused her to be unforgiving with him. Her mother's phone calls piled on the guilt. Whenever her mom asked about Chance, Laney said he was fine and changed the subject. She needed to apologize to Chance and tell her mom the truth. She should have done both a long time ago.

With a break in the activity at the concierge counter, Laney saw Amanda approaching, and groaned inwardly. She'd told Amanda about her falling out with Chance, and Amanda had her matchmaking mode in full throttle. Amanda rested her elbows on the counter. "Ben and I are having a pool party at his mom's house Sunday of the Memorial Day weekend. We want you to come. Ben invited some of his single friends."

"I don't know if I can make it, Amanda."

Her friend frowned. "Why not? It'll be fun. And you'll get to meet some hot guys. They'll take your mind off Chance."

"My mind is not on Chance."

"Yeah, right. You've been moping around like a lonely puppy dog for the past three weeks."

"I'll think about your party." Laney nodded to a couple waiting to talk to her. "I have to get back to work."

"Don't think too hard. Memorial Day weekend starts in three days." With a small wave, Amanda left.

<> <> <>

Later that day, Laney glanced at Chance's condo before entering her own. She'd listened to his show on her drive home and knew he hadn't come from work yet. She changed into yoga pants and a T-shirt and fed Ebony. Too nervous to eat, Laney paced her living room and waited until she heard Chance open and close his door. She marched across the hall and rang his doorbell.

He opened, frowning. "Hey, Laney, what are you doing here?"

"Can we talk?"

Nodding, he stepped aside to let her enter.

She twisted her fingers around the hem of her T-shirt and turned to him. "I came to apologize."

He stepped closer. The sexual excitement he always incited in her made her knees feel like unset gelatin.

"Apologize?" he asked.

"I miss our friendship. It meant a lot to me. I'm sorry I wouldn't listen to you that day, and I'm sorry I accused you of being a player. You've always been kind to me."

His smile warmed her like the sun peeking through clouds on a rain-filled day. "I've missed you," he said softly. Cupping her shoulders, he pulled her closer. "Can we be friends again? Go back to the Bad Luck partners?"

"I'd like that, especially the friends part."

His smile deepened, and those dimples winked. "Let's celebrate. I'll take you to my favorite Mexican restaurant. I have some news to share. I've missed talking to you."

News? Laney knew Chance's agent had been working hard to secure him a big contract in Los Angeles. Would Chance soon leave Las Vegas, and her? She put aside the thought for another day and returned his smile.

"Mexican sounds great. Give me a few minutes to change." With her hand on the doorknob, she turned to look at him. "Do you have plans for Memorial Day weekend?"

CHAPTER SIXTEEN

L aney hefted her carryall over her shoulder and locked her door behind her. Sunday had dawned stifling hot. She couldn't wait to dive into the pool at Amanda's party. As she waited in the hall for Chance, Laney rubbed a hand along the side of her shorts and told herself it was no big deal that Chance had agreed to go to the party with her. Going out together on a holiday was part of their deal. The Bad Luck Partners were back, and that made her smile.

The other night at the Mexican restaurant, Chance had shared that his agent was close to finalizing a deal that would bring Chance a lot of money, and, hopefully, a national audience. They were also in negotiations with the radio station in Vegas to let Chance use his escape clause to get out of his contract. At the thought of his leaving, gloom descended on her sunny day.

Chance's door opened, and with a smile for her, he stepped into the hall and pulled his door shut. Dressed for a casual afternoon in the sun, he wore khaki cargo shorts, black flip-flop sandals, and a blue T-shirt that stretched across his muscular chest and brought out the blue of his eyes. His long legs were straight with well-defined calves and a sprinkling of dark hair. She clutched her carryall tighter.

"Hey, Laney. You look great." He scanned her, his eyes gleaming with an appreciative light that made her throat go dry.

"Ready for a swim?" he asked.

"More than ready. The temperature is already 100 degrees."

"Let's go." He placed his hand on the small of her back. Her tank top had ridden up and he touched her naked flesh. His touch scorched her. The temperature outside had nothing on the heat radiating between her and Chance.

When they got to Ben's parents' house in an upscale gated Henderson community, they followed the music and laughter to the back.

Ben waved at them from across the wide lawn. Grabbing two beers from a large ice-filled tub, he sauntered their way.

"Hey, guys. Drink up." He thrust the beers at them.

"Hey, Ben," Chance and Laney said in unison.

"Where's Amanda?" Laney asked before taking a swig of her beer.

"She's flitting around here like a butterfly on steroids," Ben said. "I'll find her and let her know you're here."

He strode away.

"Looks like a fun party," Chance said.

"Amanda always has the best parties."

Chance lifted his bottle to his mouth, then stopped. Eyes wide, he glanced across the pool and stared. Turning to Laney, he said, "Is that the movie star and director Cole Lassiter over there with the gorgeous brunette?"

Laney followed his gaze. "That's him, with Analisa, his wife."

"You know a movie star?" His mouth dropped open.

She laughed. "Close your mouth. Vegas has almost as many celebrity sightings as L.A." She smiled and waved at Cole and Analisa, who waved back. "Analisa used to tend bar at the Capri. That's where she met Cole."

Still staring at the glamorous couple, Chance said, "I remember reading something about Lassiter marrying a bartender. Was in all the gossip rags for a while." Frowning, he looked at Laney. "Wasn't theirs a fake marriage?"

"It started that way. Now, it's very real, and they are very in love. They're a great couple. Cole, for all his celebrity, is a regular guy. They have the sweetest little girl. Analisa tutors disadvantaged kids here and in L.A., and she donates her salary to charity." Laney looked to where Cole and Analisa were laughing with some friends. A small pang of longing twisted in her gut. She'd always liked sweet, hard-working Analisa and was happy she'd found love with Cole. Laney wanted the same kind of happiness she saw shining from Analisa's eyes. Laney slid a look at Chance. Maybe she could find the love that had so far eluded her.

Amanda came running over, taking Laney from her introspection. "Welcome, guys." She gave them each a quick hug, then turned to Laney with raised eyebrows. "You little sneak. You didn't tell me you'd invited Chance."

"I hope you don't mind," Chance said.

"God, no. I'm happy to see Laney has come to her senses. Now I know why she's been smiling so much the last few days. You two are overdressed. The cabanas are empty. Go change into your suits. Now. That's an order."

"Yes, ma'am," Chance said, saluting her.

Laughing, Laney and Chance tramped toward the yellow and white striped cabanas set along the perimeter of the lawn.

Chance leaned over to whisper in Laney's ear. "What did Amanda mean about you coming to your senses, and about smiling more? Is it because we're together again?" He gave her a wicked grin. "Did you miss me that much?"

"It's nothing. And I'm smiling more because things have settled down at work."

He laughed. "You're a terrible liar."

CHAPTER SEVENTEEN

When Laney stepped out of the cabana, she found Chance waiting. He straightened when he saw her. His eyes, intense and hot, roamed over her, heating her as if he skimmed his fingers over her flesh. Her nipples swelled and tightened, aching for his touch. Warmth gathered low in her most intimate places.

His lips curved into a slow, sexy smile. "Wow! You're gorgeous."

The gleam in his eyes made her wonder if she should have worn her one-piece instead of her red bikini. She and Chance were friends. Maybe a little bit more she acknowledged to herself. She had the overwhelming impulse to grab him and drag him into a cabana where they could make crazy love.

Get hold of yourself, Laney.

Chance moved closer. "You okay?"

She found her voice. "I'm fine. You look good too."

Her eyes drifted over him, touching him where she longed to press her body. His black swim trunks rode low on his waist. Tall, broad-shouldered, he gave new meaning to the phrase "six-pack abs." A line of fine black hair disappeared into the waistband of his trunks. Her fertile imagination conjured up images of where that hair led.

"Hey, you two, time to play!" Amanda's shouted words pulled Laney from her erotic fantasies.

She looked over to where teams were forming to play water polo. A goal floated in the water.

"You game?" Chance asked.

"Why not?"

They jumped into the water. Laney dove under, letting the clear water cool her overheated body—overheated not from the one-hundred degree air temperature but from the naked desire she'd read in Chance's eyes.

They played for an hour—Laney, Amanda, and Analisa against Chance, Ben, and Cole. Another friend, Hal, acted as goalkeeper. The game become more and more boisterous as they were cheered on by others around the pool. Laney saw money changing hands and knew bets were placed. The players took frequent beer breaks, which added to the laughter and unruly play.

Ball in hand, Chance prepared to throw it toward the goal. Laney jumped up and knocked the ball away. Laughing, Chance grabbed her around the waist and dunked her. She pulled him underwater with her.

Chance wrapped his arms around her. Their nearly naked bodies molded to each other as they floated under the water, primal and alone, the world above far away. Despite the cool water, Laney's body felt on fire. When he bent to kiss her, she feared she'd melt away.

His lips touched hers briefly before they broke to the surface, gasping for air, to face the amused grins from their friends.

The rest of the day passed in a sensuously-fueled blur for Laney. Her whole body felt attuned to Chance. She barely remembered consuming a large hamburger, potato salad, and several bottles of beer. She made conversation and laughed with the others, Chance at her side. She wondered if the other guests felt the sexual tension that radiated between Chance and her. From the looks Amanda and Analisa gave her, she suspected they did.

At ten o'clock, the party wound down. Chance and Laney were silent on the short ride home. When they got to their complex, he went around the car to open the passenger door for her. At his touch on her elbow, she raised her gaze to his. In the pale moonlight, his eyes glinted. Her insides trembled.

"I want you, Laney," he rasped.

Consumed by his heat and her own needs, she nodded.

They sprinted to their building and ran up the stairs to her place. Hands shaking, she unlocked her door. As soon as they were inside, they threw their bags on the floor.

His eyes glazed with want, Chance gripped her shoulders and pulled her to him. His lips captured hers, hard, demanding, kissing her with a fierceness that shattered her control.

Moaning, Laney pressed closer and opened to him, inviting him to taste her. He deepened the kiss, tasting, sucking, igniting a fire in her. He backed her up against the wall, his lips never leaving hers. Hot, restless, her breasts tight, she thrust her fingers into his hair, reveling in its thickness.

Like two people possessed, they frantically undressed each other.

"Laney." His voice shook.

She took his hand and led him to her bedroom.

CHAPTER EIGHTEEN

The sun welcomed itself into Laney's bedroom, gently waking her. Smiling, she turned and patted the pillow next to her. When her hand felt emptiness, she jerked fully awake and sat up. Chance was gone. She pulled the sheet to her neck, a shield against the disappointment that settled over her. Gripping the edge of the sheet, she lay back down and stared at the ceiling.

Memories of their lovemaking rolled through her like an R-rated movie. Chance had been the lover she'd imagined he'd be, and more. Her whole body tingled now, satiated in ways she'd never been. Thinking of some of the things he'd done to her, of the things she'd done to him, fire blazed in her all over again.

A noise from the kitchen, followed by the scent of cooking bacon, brought her out of her sexual reveries. She hopped from bed.

Refreshed and dressed in shorts and a tank top, Laney entered her kitchen. The scene of domesticity that greeted her filled her with longing for a life she'd always wanted. Chance stood at the stove, dressed in his cargo shorts, shirtless, his back to her, stirring something in a frying pan. She stood still, admiring the ripple of his muscles as he stirred.

In the far corner, Ebony lapped water from her bowl. Bits of food remained in the cat's food bowl, and Laney knew Chance had fed her.

Laney went to Chance and wound her arms around his waist. With a contented sigh, she rested her head on his broad back. "You're taking a chance being shirtless while cooking bacon.

I'm not complaining. I like seeing you almost naked."

He turned and gathered her into his arms, slanting his lips over hers in a tender kiss. "Morning, Princess. Did you sleep well?" he said when they drew apart.

She laughed. "You know I hardly got any sleep. Someone kept me up most of the night."

"I hope losing sleep was worth it." His voice had thickened.

"Very worth it."

He kissed her again, deeply this time, with an almost desperate hunger. She returned his kiss with all the longing and desire that filled her. Her skin, partially bared by the tank top, melted into his firm flesh. With the intensity of the desert sun, the truth hit her. She loved Chance. Fear and joy squeezed her chest. She loved him.

Today was a holiday. Maybe her bad luck holiday curse had finally broken.

The bacon sizzled, as sensual sparks sizzled and popped between them. Chance ended their kiss to reach over and turn off the heat under the pan.

"The food can wait. I can't."

<><><>

They had breakfast on her small balcony, the sun high in a cloudless sky. The food filled her, as Chance had filled her last night and this morning. With a contented sigh, Laney sipped her hazelnut cream coffee.

Chance set down his fork and met her gaze.

"I guess things have changed between us," he said.

"You think?" Uncertainty caused her to sound flippant. "I didn't mean it like that."

He chuckled. "Yeah, I think things are different now. What are we going to do about it?"

Laney wrapped her hands around her mug. "I don't know. Now that we've...I don't know if we can go back to being friends only."

"I don't want to be friends only with you, or friends with benefits. I haven't for a long time. I like you a lot. We've both got issues, and maybe things won't work out between us, but I want to give us a chance."

"I'm not sure what I want. I hadn't planned on this." She

couldn't tell him she loved him. Her feelings were still so new, so raw. And she didn't know how he felt.

He smiled and relaxed into his chair. "Most people don't plan on whatever this is we're doing." He raked fingers through his hair, his smile gone. "I have things going on with my career. I don't know how much longer I'll be in Vegas."

A boulder seemed to settle in her chest, crushing some of her happiness. "I've always known that, but I guess on some level I'd hoped you'd stay here."

His eyes lit. "Do you mean that? You'd like me to stay?"

"I would, but your career is important to you. I get that. I wouldn't want to hold you back."

"We can still see each other if I'm in L.A. It's only a four-hour drive to Vegas and a one-hour plane ride."

"I don't want a long distance relationship, Chance. I wasn't planning on any relationship right now."

"We don't always get to pick the right time," he said softly.

She gripped the chair arms, fighting the need to go to him, to hold him close, and never let him go.

A shadow came across his face. "I have something to tell you, Laney."

The seriousness of his tone and features made her shiver. "What is it?"

His steady gaze continued to hold hers. "Negotiations for the new gig in L.A. are going well. The station there wants me to guest host for a month as a tryout for them and for me. I leave later today."

A rushing noise filled her head. "You're going away for a month?" Anger replaced her shock and propelled her from her seat. Breathing hard, she looked down at him. "When were you planning to tell me? You made love to me, and now you tell me you're leaving today? I thought you were a decent guy. You're no better than the others." Tears threatened and she looked away. "This is another holiday disaster. I think you'd better leave."

His chair scraped as he stood. When he touched her arm, she jerked away, not looking at him.

"Please, Laney, it's not like that. I've wanted you for a long time, but I would never use you. We can be together. Over the next month, I'll come back here every chance I get and you can come visit me in L.A. We can make it work."

Red-hot anger sizzled through her as she turned to him. "That's not what I want in a relationship. I want a man who is always honest with me, a man who doesn't hold anything back. Leave now, Chance. The Bad Luck Partners is officially dissolved for good, and so is our friendship or whatever you want to call it."

He stepped toward her. "I could say you used me, that you use your bad luck holiday curse to keep men at a distance. When things don't go your way, you pull back. I call that selfish. This is a good career move for me, and I thought you'd be supportive. You're not the friend, or the woman, I thought you were. Goodbye."

He turned and walked out of her apartment, out of her life. For the final time.

CHAPTER NINETEEN

Chance greeted the doorman at the luxury apartment complex in Santa Monica and strode toward the elevator leading to the penthouse apartment where he'd lived for the past three weeks. The radio station had pulled out all stops to lure him into signing with them. They'd put him up in a beautifully furnished apartment with a view of the ocean. They'd taken him to dinners and Hollywood parties and introduced him to the movers and shakers in the entertainment industry.

The station owners had tried to set him up with beautiful, sexy rising young actresses desperate for publicity. Chance had refused any offers to date the women, leading one of the owners to try to set him up with young men.

Hollywood! Chance entered his spacious apartment and threw his keys on a table. The only woman he wanted was in Las Vegas. He missed Laney more every day. In his anger and hurt that she seemed so willing to cut ties with him, that she didn't share his enthusiasm over his career move, he'd said things he now regretted. He hadn't heard from her since Memorial Day when she'd told him to get out of her life. Many times he'd started to text her, but stopped, afraid she wouldn't respond, a sure sign she wanted nothing more to do with him. He didn't want to face that. Not yet. Maybe he'd read her wrong, and she had no lasting interest in him, or maybe he'd hurt her with his harshness. Regret over lost chances pounded him like the ocean waves outside his apartment building.

To the chagrin of his agent, Chance had begun to rethink his whole career strategy. His thoughts swirling, he went into the kitchen and pulled a beer from the professional stainless steel refrigerator. Back in the living room, he sank onto the white leather sectional and turned on the TV to a cable news show.

Settling back, he barely noticed the TV screen. As he drank his beer, his mind traveled two-hundred seventy miles to Las Vegas. He'd really screwed up with Laney. He should have told her about his gig in L.A. before they made love. Once he'd seen her in that red bikini, his libido had chased away his common sense.

He'd been a jerk. He knew how Laney felt about holidays, and he'd gone ahead and seduced her anyway, wanting her without considering her feelings. To be sure, she'd wanted him as much as he'd wanted her. That didn't change the fact that he should have been upfront with her about his leaving. He needed to make it up to her, but it might already be too late.

Kept busy with his radio duties and the endless round of parties necessary to advance his career, Chance hadn't had time for much else. He'd come to one very important realization in the past three weeks. He knew now what he wanted to do with his career and his life.

<><><>

"Laney, don't forget your friends on your way up the corporate ladder," Amanda said.

"You guys will always be my friends," Laney said, smiling. "Of course, if I meet a hot movie star, like Analisa did, and head to Hollywood, all bets are off."

The others laughed as Laney looked around the table at the Capri. Her best friends in Vegas—Amanda, Analisa, and Patti—had taken her for a night on the town, ending here in their favorite place, to celebrate Laney's promotion to head of the concierge department at the Augustus. When Stu, her boss, got promoted to the chain's flagship hotel in New York City, he'd recommended Laney as his replacement.

Stu's glowing review of Laney's work ethic, her knowledge of Las Vegas sights, her leadership qualities with her co-workers, and her ease with customers all helped her get the coveted promotion. The feeling of loss she'd carried in her heart since the day three weeks ago when she'd sent Chance away tempered her happiness.

Laney's smile faded, and she looked down, running her fingers over the rivulets of water on the outside of her glass of club soda.

Amanda reached across the table and put her hand over Laney's. "What's wrong? Thinking about Chance?"

"No. He's not in my life anymore and I rarely think about him."

"Liar," Analisa said gently. "You haven't been your smiling self for weeks now, even with this promotion."

"She's right," Patti said. "I miss the old, cheerful Laney who could always make me smile."

"Why don't you text Chance?" Amanda said. "Reach out to him."

Laney sipped her club soda, her mind on Chance, as it had been for most of the past three weeks. She missed his laugh, his smile, their good-natured banter, their friendship, their lovemaking.

She met Amanda's concerned gaze. "I told you the cutting things he said to me before he left. Called me selfish. He knows how I feel about holidays. He used me, then walked out."

"I think you *were* a little selfish," Amanda said in a soft voice. "Maybe he wanted you to be more supportive of his career."

"It doesn't sound to me like he used you," Analisa said. "He didn't seduce you. You wanted him too. His career is important to him. You should understand that. Maybe he wanted it all, you and a career. Cole and I live between L.A. and Vegas. Mom and her husband Bennett live in both places too. It works for them and for us. Sometimes when Cole is shooting a film he works long hours and I don't see much of him. When he's on location, Miranda and I go with him whenever we can." Analisa smiled. "She loves to watch her daddy play make-believe or direct a scene."

"You're married, Analisa, and Cole loves you. Chance has never said he loves me."

"And you never told him you love him," Patti said.

"Maybe you didn't give Chance a chance," Amanda said.

Laney rolled her eyes. "Please, no puns."

"You've got to get over this obsession about bad luck in the romance department on holidays," Amanda said. "You're letting it rule you. I don't want to hurt you, but maybe Chance had it right that you use the so-called holiday curse to push men away."

Laney rubbed her forehead where the makings of a headache stirred. "You're my friends and I love you all, and I know you want to help." She looked down at the table. "I miss Chance more than I thought I would. I was so scared of being hurt again that I pushed him away. I was a little selfish too, wanting him to stay here. Tomorrow I'll text him and see what happens."

"That's our girl," Analisa said.

Surrounded by her friends, and missing Chance, needing him, some of Laney's fears and hurts began to dissolve. The time had come for her to put aside the holiday curse.

She hoped it wasn't too late for her and Chance.

CHAPTER TWENTY

The next day, Saturday, Laney had the day off work. Almost as soon as she'd awakened, she'd texted Chance, *How R U? I've missed you.* By two in the afternoon, she hadn't heard from him. His silence spoke volumes. Regret and sadness hovered over her like a black cloud.

She tried to keep busy, but found it hard to focus. She kept picking up her phone to be sure she hadn't missed a call or text from him, despite the fact that her phone had been silent.

She sat on her sofa now, a book opened on her lap. In twenty minutes, she'd read one page. Her doorbell rang, making her pulse jump. Frowning, she set down the book. The guard hadn't called from the gate to announce a visitor. She jumped up from the sofa and hurried to the door. When she looked through the peephole, her pulse ratcheted up a few more notches, and she pressed a palm to her stomach.

She opened to Chance. Not speaking, they stared at each other. Wearing black jeans and a black T-shirt, and with a scruff on his firm jaw, he looked like a gunslinger come to town to steal her heart. He wouldn't have to take her heart because she'd give it to him willingly.

As she stepped aside to let him in, he said, "I got your text. I'd already packed to come here. What I need to say, I have to say in person."

He stood so close she inhaled his unique scent of light citrus. He didn't touch her as she closed the door.

"You just drove here from L.A.?"

He nodded.

Ebony came running over to Chance. He picked up the cat and held it close, rubbing his chin on its fur. "I've missed you, Ebony." The cat responded by purring. "I've missed your mommy even more." He set the cat down and met Laney's gaze.

Buying time to settle her frazzled nerves, she said, "How about some wine? Something to eat?"

"Do you have chips and salsa?" he asked with a grin. "And guac? Like our New Year's Eve."

Her heart soared that he remembered their first holiday together. "I always have chips, salsa, and guac."

"I'll help," he said. "Someone has to make sure you don't spill something or trip." He looked down at Ebony, winding herself around his ankles. "Better stand back, Ebony, before Laney falls over you."

Laney narrowed her eyes, shooting him a look, trying to hide her joy that Chance was here and that they'd picked up on their bantering as if he'd never left. Chuckling, Chance followed her into the kitchen.

Fifteen minutes later, food spread on the coffee table before them, they settled on opposite sides of her sofa each holding a glass of wine.

Chance cleared his throat. "We have to talk."

"I know."

"My four-week gig in L.A. is almost over," he said.

Her heart seemed to sink to her knees. She sipped wine. The liquid that slid smoothly down her throat couldn't dislodge the constriction in her chest. "I guess you'll be moving to L.A. permanently. I wish you a lot of luck."

"Thanks, but I'm not going anywhere."

She dropped the chip she'd just picked up. Setting down her glass, she said, "What?"

He put his glass next to hers on the table and slid closer to her. "I've missed you something fierce, Laney."

"I've missed you too. More than I thought possible." She looked down before meeting his gaze again. "What do you mean, you're not moving to L.A.? I know how important that move is to your career." She reached out and touched his arm. His muscles flexed under her fingers. "I'm sorry I wasn't more supportive, Chance, that last time we were together."

He placed his hand over hers. "I said some things I shouldn't have. I was hurt, and I lashed out at you. I've had weeks to think things through, and I know now what I have to do." His sapphire eyes met hers. "And what I want."

She pulled her hand from his and put distance between them. She couldn't think straight so close to him. "If you're not moving to L.A., what are you doing?"

"I'm staying in Vegas."

"Why? What happened in L.A.?"

He moved closer until his warm breath fanned her face. "What happened in L.A. is I realized I want you in my life. I love you, Laney Sikora. No amount of money they offered could keep me away from you."

"You love me?" she managed.

He took both her hands in his, his gaze steady, sincere, hopeful. "Can you forgive me, Laney? I didn't mean to hurt you. I've been a fool. I had stars in my eyes. I wanted the whole Hollywood scene, the money and the glamour. The job in L.A. would have given me that, but Vegas changed me. You changed me. You've made me realize what's important in life—love with the right woman. Nothing else matters. Please tell me you can learn to love me."

"I have something I need to say. I want your forgiveness too," she said. "I've loved you for a long time, but I was too afraid to admit it, even to myself. I let my fear of being hurt again blind me to opening my heart fully to you and trusting you. I pushed you away out of a misguided attempt to protect my heart. The whole bad luck on holidays obsession began to take over my life."

His eyes glinted. "You love me?"

When she nodded, he gathered her to him and kissed her with tenderness as if she were the most precious thing in the world. When their kiss ended, she saw tears glistening in his eyes. She blinked back her own tears.

"You gave up the job in L.A. for me?" she asked.

"The money was more than I'd ever thought I'd make. They wined and dined me and set me up in a luxury apartment. And it all felt empty without you."

She squeezed his hand. "What will you do now?"

He chuckled. "My agent is upset with me. He lost a bucket of money too. He renegotiated my contract here. The station is so happy I'm not leaving, they offered more money, and they're taking my show national, something L.A. dangled over me and never delivered."

"Chance, that's terrific. You'll be famous."

He skimmed his finger over her bottom lip. "We'll be together. That's all that matters."

"That's all that matters to me, too," she said softly. "I have news of my own. I've been promoted to head of our concierge group."

He grinned. "Good for you. I know that's what you wanted." His features sobered. "With my work, I may at some point need to relocate. Would you be okay with that?"

"I think so. We'll face that when we come to it. I may need to relocate also if I'm offered a better promotion."

He placed a light kiss on her lips, then slid off the sofa to kneel on one knee before her, and took both her hands in his again.

Her heart pounded so furiously, she thought her chest would explode.

"Laney, I can't imagine a life without you. Will you marry me?"

Her voice shaking, she said, "Yes, Chance, I'll marry you."

He stood and pulled her gently up, then gathered her to him and kissed her hungrily. She returned his kiss, pouring out her love.

When they pulled apart, she looked deeply into his eyes, the eyes of the man she would love forever. "July Fourth is coming soon. Let's have a party to celebrate the breaking of our curse."

"Good idea." He brushed hair back from her face and hooked strands behind her ears. "I have another idea. Let's get married on a holiday. How about New Year's Eve?"

"Yes! New Year's Eve."

He picked up both their glasses and handed hers to her. Lifting his glass, he said, "To the Bad Luck Partners. It's been a mutually satisfying partnership, but time to move on."

They toasted, each taking a sip of wine. Lowering her glass,

Laney stood on tiptoe to touch her lips to his. "To love-filled holidays the rest of our lives."

***

A VERY VEGAS CHRISTMAS

CARA MARSI

A Very Vegas Christmas

A Las Vegas event planner in need of luck meets a mysterious guy who might be her winning ticket. Will his secret split them apart?

Can things get any worse for Las Vegas event planner Amanda Moreau? Her boyfriend dumped her for a stripper; she's arranging a Christmas wedding for a Bridezilla; and her mother is playing matchmaker from 2000 miles away. When she meets hunky and ever-so-sweet Erik, who's in town for a conference, she begins to hope her luck is changing. But Erik has a secret that threatens to split them apart.

CHAPTER ONE

*I*t's Malcolm E. Hamilton. From Greenview High School. Your mom gave me your number. I'll be in Vegas December 15 for a convention. Want to meet for a drink?

Amanda Moreau read the text and groaned before setting the offending phone back on the table.

"Bad news?" Amanda's best friend, Laney Sikora Carlisle, asked. The two women sat in the employees' cafeteria of the Augustus Hotel and Casino in Las Vegas where they worked.

"My mother is playing matchmaker from 2,000 miles away." Trying to tamp down her annoyance, Amanda stabbed a piece of grilled chicken with her fork and put it in her mouth. Chewing slowly, she glanced around the crowded room. Her co-workers laughed and talked together as they ate. She'd been working at the Augustus for five years, since moving from Indiana. She usually loved the nonstop exuberance of Las Vegas. Lately, not so much.

Inhaling the delicious, calming aromas of chicken, burritos, and sizzling veggies, she turned back to Laney. "That was a text from a guy I haven't seen in twenty years. My mom gave him my number."

Laney wagged a finger at her. "You shouldn't have told your mom you broke up with Ben. Now she's on a quest to get you married off."

"I refuse to pretend we're still together," Amanda said. "The rat bastard left me for a stripper, and to make it worse, she's in the music revue at the Augustus."

"You were too good for him. You deserve better. What does the text say?"

"Malcolm's going to be in Vegas for a convention and wants to get together."

Laney laughed. "His name is Malcolm?"

"It fit him. In high school, he was a total gamer and Trekkie, a real geek. Straggly hair, freckles, thick glasses, chubby."

"Maybe he's changed."

"I hope so, but I doubt it. He put his middle initial in his text."

"What's the problem with meeting him while he's here?"

"I don't have time to entertain anyone, especially a guy I haven't seen in twenty years. I'm up to my neck in work. It's only four weeks until Christmas and Bridezilla's wedding. She and her mom are plucking my last nerve. Sometimes I wish I hadn't taken the job as event planner and still worked in reception."

"You're a great event planner, the best the Augustus has ever had," Laney said. "Spill it. There's another reason you don't want to meet this Malcolm."

Amanda sighed. "Guilt. I broke his heart when we were fourteen and I still feel bad about it. I knew he had a crush on me. When he asked me to the end-of-school dance, I told him no, humiliating him in front of a group of classmates. I hadn't meant to humiliate him. I was in my Goth phase then. If I'd gone to the dance with him, my Goth friends would have shunned me. They were the only group that accepted me in high school. Thankfully, his family moved away after freshman year so I didn't have to face him when school started again. My mom and his Aunt Flo are still friends."

Amanda stirred her iced tea. "Soon after I moved here, Mom told me Malcolm had left Indiana and started his own company, but I was too busy getting settled to pay much attention."

Laney laughed. "Wait a minute. Back up. You were a Goth?"

"Complete with purple hair and black lipstick."

"Oh, my God. I would love to see a picture."

Amanda winced. "All pictures have been destroyed."

"Going to answer him?" Laney asked, with a nod toward Amanda's phone.

"I guess I should be polite." She texted, *Love to see you, but very busy. Will let you know when I'm free.*

Another text from him. *Sounds good.*

"That's that." She put her phone down. "If I'm lucky, maybe I can avoid seeing him."

<><><>

His texting with Amanda over, Malcolm Hamilton slipped his phone into his jacket pocket, his mind on the girl he'd called Mandy. He recognized a brush-off. Too bad. He'd checked her out on her hotel's website and saw a recent picture. Always pretty, at least to him, she'd turned into a beauty with long, thick black hair and those big brown eyes he'd never forgotten. As a fourteen-year-old, he'd found her purple hair sexy.

"Mr. Hamilton, your table is ready."

Smiling at the hostess in the elegant New York City restaurant, he slipped her a fifty dollar bill. "Please show the rest of my party to my table as soon as they arrive."

She gave him a flirtatious smile. "Certainly, Mr. Hamilton." He followed her to his usual table in a quiet corner. He'd be glad when things settled down in his company and he wouldn't have to make so many transatlantic flights. At the moment, he had to focus on business. He had tons of work to do as he prepared to take his company public.

His potential investors came in soon after. They shook hands all around, and he ordered several bottles of wine, the best the restaurant offered.

"Hamilton, we want to know what investing in your company can do for us," the group's leader said.

"Let me show you." He drew papers from his briefcase and fanned them out on the table. While the others studied his proposal, his thoughts went back to Amanda. She'd thought him a gaming nerd, totally unacceptable to her and her Goth friends at age fourteen. If she only knew how lucrative gaming could be.

CHAPTER TWO

"Our design team has outdone themselves this year," Amanda said to her assistant Phillip as they walked through the world-renowned conservatory and botanical gardens at the Augustus, a must-see for the tourists.

She consulted her tablet, then looked at Phillip. "Can you mesh your decorations for the Fischer wedding with this design?" She wrinkled her nose. "I can't believe Bridezilla wanted live doves flying over her guests during the ceremony."

He shuddered. "Can you imagine the cleanup afterwards, with bird poop everywhere? I can handle the decorations, provided the Fischers don't want more glitter and gold. Garish seems to be their middle name."

Amanda put a finger over her mouth, signaling him to be silent. "Don't let anyone hear you. You never know if someone will report back to Mr. Gordon."

The hotel allowed some weddings in the conservatory, but they were very selective about who they approved. They'd never before had a wedding on Christmas or another holiday. Since Lisa Fischer was the niece of one of the owners, she could have her wedding wherever and whenever she wanted. Phillip and Amanda had to walk on eggshells around her and her mother.

"Those silver snowflakes should be all the glitter they need," Amanda said, glancing up at the spectacular giant snowflakes and silver Christmas ornaments suspended from the glass-dome ceiling.

"We'll put a white carpet on the center path," Phillip said.

"But it's a shame to cover up the mosaic. The canopy of silver icicles is perfect for the ceremony."

"If we can convince the Fischers we don't need much more in the way of decorations, this might be a classy wedding after all."

Phillip rolled his eyes. "We can only hope."

Amanda lowered her tablet as she and Phillip turned to leave. "It's bad enough this wedding is causing me sleepless nights, but now my mom is playing matchmaker. She gave some guy I knew twenty years ago my number. He's coming to town and wants to see me."

"My mom does that all the time. Keep making excuses why you can't meet this guy. He'll give up."

"Something tells me it won't be that easy."

Amanda's phone dinged, signaling a message. As she had for the past week since she'd heard from Malcolm, her pulse jumped every time a message came in. She didn't want to see him, felt guilt over her treatment of him all those years ago, and yet a frisson of excitement filled her at the thought of seeing him again. Truth be told, she'd had a secret crush on him, but she'd been too much of a coward, desperate to stay a member of the high school's Goth clique, to have admitted it.

The message was a reminder of a meeting she had in thirty minutes with clients interested in having a wedding reception at the hotel. Relief, mingled with a vague sense of disappointment, slowed her steps.

CHAPTER THREE

J *ust got in town. Free for drinks tonight? M.*

Amanda stared down at the text from Malcolm. Ten days before the Fischer wedding, and she was swamped with work. She could honestly tell Malcolm she couldn't meet with him.

Swamped with work. Another time?

OK.

She set her phone on her desk. That was easy.

At nine that night, exhausted from a long day, and starving, Amanda stopped in the Capri Bar & Grille, her favorite of the hotel's many eateries. The place was crowded, and she stood in the doorway, looking for a seat at the bar. Her friend Patti, the bartender, pointed to an empty seat at the far end. Amanda threaded her way through the tables and slid onto the barstool.

The man sitting on the next stool turned to her with a smile. Excitement and surprise made her stomach flutter. Damn, he was hot! His gold-green eyes, framed by thick black lashes, studied her with undisguised interest. With his longish black hair that gave him a hipster look, and the light stubble on his square jaw, she could picture him in an ad for a macho cologne. His white dress shirt stretched across broad shoulders, and his rolled-up sleeves exposed a light smattering of black hair on tanned, muscled arms.

"Hi," he said holding out his hand. "I'm Erik."

"Amanda." They shook hands, his large, calloused one engulfing her much smaller one. His firm handshake signaled his confidence, and his calloused hand told her he did physical labor.

A thrill shivered through her. A confident man who wasn't afraid to work with his hands. Sexy!

Too busy for even the slightest relationship now, her confidence had taken a huge hit when Ben dumped her for the stripper. A little harmless flirting with hottie Erik might help her restore some of that confidence.

Patti, a knowing smile on her face, came over to take Amanda's order.

"A glass of pinot grigio and a crispy chicken sandwich," Amanda said.

"Put that on my tab," Erik said.

Amanda shook her head. "Oh, no, please. You don't have to do that. We don't know each other."

He leaned closer, his eyes locked on hers. "I hope to change that," he whispered, his voice smoky.

Amanda wanted to fan herself. "Okay, then, and thanks."

As the crowd in the Capri thinned out, Amanda and Erik sat at the bar, talking and laughing. Erik lived in Los Angeles and worked for a software company. He was in Vegas for a convention at the Mirage.

Amanda sipped from her second glass of wine and let her imagination dwell on all the possibilities between her and Erik. She pictured well-defined abs under that shirt, and imagined his long, slim fingers trailing over her naked body. Her temperature went up a few degrees, and she drank more of the cold wine. He'd told her he wasn't married, and she saw no sign of a ring indentation on his finger, yet she'd be careful.

A woman's laughter drew her attention to the doorway. Her ex, Ben, stood there with a blonde whose legs looked as long as Amanda's entire five foot two inch frame. She recognized the stripper from the Augustus dance revue.

Ben looked around. He'd spot Amanda alone at the bar, like a pathetic loser still pining for him. She turned to Erik.

"Kiss me. Now," she said.

He blinked, then his full lips curved in a slow, sexy smile. He touched her chin with his fingers and took her lips in a tender kiss that soon turned hot and made her entire body tingle. Lost in his seductive power, Amanda wrapped her arms around his neck and kissed him back, hungry for more of him.

He tasted of beer and salsa. His clean scent of soap filled her nostrils. Low groans came from her. The bar, Ben, his stripper girlfriend, all disappeared in the heat of Erik's kiss.

After several passion-filled minutes, they pulled apart. Their breathing ragged, they stared at each other.

"Wow," she breathed.

"Wow is right," he rasped.

"You two need some privacy?" Patti said with a smirk, coming up to them.

Amanda looked around. The other patrons stared at her and Erik, grinning. Ben and his stripper were nowhere around. Amanda burned from her neck to her forehead and she knew she blushed.

"I-I need to go," she stammered, sliding off her stool. She reached under the bar for her purse hanging from a hook.

"Wait." Erik touched her arm. "I want to see you again. Can I have your number?"

Aware the others still watched, Amanda nodded. Erik handed his phone to her and she punched in her number. With a mumbled "good-bye," she marched out of the bar.

CHAPTER FOUR

"**I** can't believe I kissed a stranger," Amanda said to Laney the next day. "I saw Ben with that stripper and I went momentarily crazy. I wanted to show him I'd moved on." She rubbed her temples where the makings of a headache stirred.

The women sat in their favorite coffee house on the Strip. Laney had first seen her husband, Chance, here almost two years ago. Married last New Year's Eve, Laney and Chance were deliriously happy. Although delighted for her friend, Laney's happiness only emphasized Amanda's yearning to share her life with someone special.

Laney stirred her coffee and took a sip before answering. "What was it about this guy that made you order him to kiss you?"

Amanda put out her hands in a gesture of surrender. "I don't know. He was hot?" She blew on her latte, cooling it, then took a sip, going through in her mind everything that had happened from the minute she'd sat next to Erik. Setting down her coffee, she met Laney's gaze. "There was something about Erik, something familiar, like I knew I could trust him." She shrugged. "Maybe it was my lucky night. At least he wasn't Malcolm."

"Don't worry about it," Laney said. "You got one on Ben, and who knows, Erik might call you. Go out with him. Have fun."

"Fun? What's that? Less than ten days before Christmas, and Bridezilla and her mom call me constantly with one harebrained idea after another. Their latest was pink bows tied on all the exquisite flowers our design team labored over. I convinced them it wasn't a good idea, but it's exhausting trying to find different, polite ways to tell them no. Not to mention all the holiday parties my staff is coordinating at the hotel."

Laney put a hand over Amanda's across the table. "Stop and breathe for a while. Relax."

"If only."

<><><>

Ready to finally leave work, Amanda stuffed papers into her briefcase and snapped it shut. Her phone signaled a text. Thinking it might be Erik, her pulse ratcheted up, only to crash when she saw Malcolm's number.

Have some time tonight. How about a drink? M.

Drat. She really didn't feel like seeing him, not now.

She texted, *Very busy. Another night?*

Sure. Let me know.

As she turned off the light in her office, another text came it. When she looked down and saw Erik's number, she smiled.

Free for dinner tonight? he'd texted.

Yes. Where and when?

Meet you in your hotel lobby in fifteen.

Great.

Guilt hit her like a stab in the solar plexus. She'd made an excuse not to see Malcolm, then jumped at the chance to see Erik.

Amanda walked out of her office and slammed the door shut behind her, trying, and failing, to shut out her guilt. With the kind of day she'd had, she deserved to be with Erik, and not Malcolm, she rationalized.

CHAPTER FIVE

"**B**usy day?" Erik asked as he and Amanda sat at a small, intimate table in a French bistro just off the Strip.

The restaurant was one of Amanda's favorites, for the good food, and also because there weren't many tourists.

She chuckled as she set down her glass of red wine. "My title should be firefighter. It seems that's what I do every day, put out fires. But I love it."

"I'm impressed you handle all the big events at the Augustus."

"Thanks. I don't do the conventions and conferences. That's another department. What type of software company do you work for?"

He cleared his throat and sipped wine, then met her gaze. "We design programs we sell to larger companies."

"You're a designer?"

He hesitated, and she wondered if he'd answer.

Finally, he said, "I'm one of many designers."

The waiter came with their food then, stopping their conversation for a while.

Dinner over, they strolled the Strip. When Erik took her hand in his, she didn't pull away. As usual, the Strip vibrated with excitement, even at this late hour. They had to shoulder their way through the boisterous, loud crowds. Amanda didn't mind. She loved the non-stop excitement of Las Vegas. The multi-colored festive Christmas lights glowing from the hotels and businesses added to the cheerful atmosphere. She inhaled the cool desert air and looked up at the three-quarter moon, pale gold in a black sky strewn with twinkling golden stars. She'd needed this evening with Erik, free of stress, free of work.

When they got to the Augustus where she'd left her car in the parking garage, a sliver of regret passed through her. The night was ending. Wanting to extend her time with Erik, she pointed to the 65-foot LED Christmas tree in the middle of the Augustus' circular drive. Lit with thousands of small lights, the tree changed colors, going from white to Christmas red, and nearly every color in between, during nightly shows throughout the holiday season.

"Let's watch the tree," she said, tugging on Erik's hand. "We can get a better view across the street."

Her hand in his, they stood across from the Augustus and watched the shimmering light show. When Amanda shivered, Erik put his arm around her shoulders and drew her against him. Sighing, she rested her head against the side of his firm chest. She hadn't felt this sense of peace and security in a long time.

When the tree had gone through the color spectrum, Erik squeezed her shoulders. "I guess the evening is over."

She wondered if she imagined the note of regret in his voice.

When they got to her car, she unlocked the door, then turned to him. "Thanks for dinner and a great evening. I needed this tonight after the stress of the last few days."

"I'm glad I could help the little lady," he said in a John Wayne voice that made her laugh.

She opened her car door, threw her purse onto the seat, and started to climb in, but he grabbed her hand, stopping her. She raised her gaze to his. The raw desire she glimpsed in his eyes heated her insides.

"I've got a full day tomorrow," he said. "I'll try to text you during our breaks. I'm supposed to have dinner with some...some co-workers, but I'll try to find a way to see you if I can. Okay?"

Amanda wondered about his hesitation when he mentioned his co-workers, but she pushed that aside and nodded. "I'd like to see you again."

He stepped closer and skimmed his thumbs over her cheeks. When he bent toward her, she raised her face to his.

His lips touched hers, soft and warm, seducing her with promise. His tongue teased her lips until she opened for him. She rose on her toes, molding herself against his taut frame, and ran her hands up his shoulders to curve around his neck. He slid his fingers into her hair, massaging her head and sending swirls of ecstasy through her.

Shivers danced along her skin. She leaned into him, hungry for his heat. She'd found heaven, and she never wanted to leave.

Loud voices and laughter, followed by the roar of a car's engine, finally permeated her sensual paradise. She reluctantly pulled free.

Erik looked down at her with an expression of wonder. He reached out to twist strands of her hair around his finger. "I'll hold onto that kiss until I see you again." He took her elbow and helped her into the car. She backed out of her spot, then looked at him in her rearview mirror as she drove away. He stood watching her, the look of wonder still etched on his face.

<><><>

"Earth to Erik." Erik blinked and scrubbed a hand down his face, his attention back on his co-designers. They sat in one of the Mirage's conference rooms, reviewing Erik's presentation scheduled for later that day.

"Where were you just now?" Matt asked.

"Sorry, guys, and lady," Erik said, nodding toward Sally, an older woman who'd become an essential part of their team. "Just tired, I guess." Tired covered a fraction of how he felt. He'd been unable to concentrate on the morning workshops and talks because, like a streaming video, his mind kept going back to that kiss, that amazing kiss, with Amanda last night.

Grinning, Sally said, "Got a woman on your mind, Erik? I hope so. You're too much of a workaholic."

"No time for a woman." He shuffled the papers in front of him. "Let's get back to work."

<><><>

His presentation over, Erik could breathe easier. The talk had gone well. Lots of influential people heard him this afternoon, people he had to impress.

As he left the theater where he'd given his talk, his thoughts again went to Amanda. He neither needed nor wanted any romantic entanglements now. His work consumed him. This was the deal of a lifetime and he couldn't get sidetracked. Work commitments had to be the focus of his attention.

He strode toward the bank of elevators, wishing he could see Amanda tonight, especially after the great time they'd had last night. He'd call her as soon as he got to his room. He had to hear her voice.

CHAPTER SIX

It had been two days since her date, and that kiss, with Erik, and Amanda's elation had turned to disappointment. She wondered if she'd see him again. He'd called her last night. Although they only talked a few minutes, as Erik had dinner plans with clients, hearing his voice had covered her with a blanket of warmth that incited erotic dreams about him.

He'd texted her again this morning. With meetings and client dinners, he didn't know when he'd be free to see her again. Her disappointment spiked.

After a morning spent fielding calls from desperate people trying to find last-minute venues for their holiday office parties, Amanda ate lunch at her desk. She'd been able to accommodate smaller groups, but had to turn away others. Turning away potential clients was a part of her job she didn't enjoy. That, and dealing with spoiled brides and their demanding mothers.

She was halfway through her Cobb salad when Phillip knocked on her office door and peeked inside. "The Fischers are here."

"What? I wasn't expecting them."

Phillip slipped into the room and shut the door behind him. "Bridezilla has that look, the one where she's ready to stamp her foot and demand changes."

"Damn! Give me a second. I'll be right out."

Phillip left, and Amanda stood, smoothing her hands down the sides of her black skirt. With a longing look at her unfinished lunch, she went out to meet the Fischers.

"Hello, Mrs. Fischer, Lisa. What can I do for you?"

Mrs. Fischer lifted her chin. "We were just in the conservatory again looking at the Christmas display where the wedding will take place. It just won't do. You *will* change it."

Behind her, Phillip coughed. Amanda shot him a look before turning back to Mrs. Fischer. "Change in what way?"

Lisa stamped her foot. "I want my gown to look like Glinda, the Good Witch in The Wizard of Oz. I've told my bridal consultant to have extra material put in the skirt of my dress, and extra crinolines to wear under it. The path I'll walk to the altar is too narrow. Take out the flowers and make the path wider."

"Don't forget the confetti, dear," Mrs. Fischer said.

"That's right," Lisa said. "I want glittery gold confetti to fall over me as I walk."

Phillip choked and sputtered. Amanda ignored him. With effort, she kept her features expressionless. "I've seen a picture of your gown, Lisa, and it's lovely just as it is."

Mrs. Fischer huffed. "If Lisa wants to look like Glinda, that's what we'll do."

Amanda took a deep breath, resisting the urge to look at Phillip. "Mrs. Fischer, that conservatory was designed by the award-winning design team here at the Augustus. Everything for this year's holiday display, down to the smallest detail, was carefully planned out a year ago. We'd like to accommodate you, but I'm afraid we can't change the conservatory. If we could, I'm not sure it would be done in time for the wedding."

Lisa folded her arms and pouted. "You have to change it."

Could this day get any worse? The Fischers interrupted her lunch, and tonight no Erik.

CHAPTER SEVEN

After a quick microwaved dinner, Amanda slipped on her pajamas and grabbed her ereader, prepared for an evening of reading and relaxing before she went to bed.

She'd convinced Lisa to keep her wedding gown the size it was, but as a concession, Amanda had agreed that confetti would fall on the wedding party as they walked along the white carpet to the canopy of silver icicles. Amanda smiled, remembering Phillip's inspired cursing when she told him the news about the confetti.

Disappointment made her shoulders sag as she walked into her living room. She'd been subconsciously waiting all day for Erik to call or text.

Damn it! She would text him. As she picked up her phone, it rang. When she looked at the ID, her heart flipped.

"Erik," she said when she'd connected the call. Her voice sounded breathless.

"Hey, Amanda," he said, his velvet voice covering her in sensuous heat. "I've missed you."

Smiling, she pressed the phone to her ear. "I've missed you, too. How's the conference going?"

"Good, but busier than I'd anticipated. We're trying to put together a big deal, and it's kept us hopping."

"Isn't the conference over soon?"

"In three days."

"Oh, then you'll be going back to L.A.?" A twinge of regret wound through her at the thought of his leaving.

"I need to get back there, but let's not think about that now." He paused. "I know it's a little late, but I'd like to see you."

"It's not that late. I'd like to see you, too."

"I've had dinner, and I imagine you have. Is there someplace we can go to just have some fun?"

"Have you been to Fremont Street yet?"

"What's that?"

"Fremont Street is the original Strip, the site of some of the oldest casinos in Vegas, and where the first hotel was built in 1906. It has an amazing overhead light show that plays every hour. The Fremont Street Experience is tacky, trashy, and totally fun."

He laughed. "Sounds like my kind of place. Can I pick you up at your apartment?"

"How about if we meet in the lobby of the Augustus? It'll be easier for you." And safer for her. She trusted Erik, but she'd only recently met him.

Erik parked his Jag in a seedy parking garage a few blocks from Fremont Street. He cupped Amanda's elbow as they walked. Her stilettos made negotiating the uneven pavement difficult, but she didn't regret wearing them. They made her legs look longer in the skinny jeans. She'd put on one of her favorite sweaters, a deep red number that hugged her chest and made her breasts look larger. She'd topped the outfit off with her favorite black leather jacket and a red cross-body purse. She'd wanted to look sexy for Erik. From the jaw-dropping look on his face when he'd seen her, she'd succeeded.

When they got to the crowded pedestrian mall, Erik snaked his arm around her waist in a protective gesture. She felt safe with him, as if she'd known him all her life.

"Why are all the lights in the buildings dimmed?" he asked.

"They're getting ready to start the show. Let's pick a spot to watch."

They found a clear spot in front of one of the casinos. "Up there." She pointed to the canopy that ran the length of the mall. "It's the largest screen in the world, the size of five football fields."

He grinned. "The enthusiasm in your voice tells me you love Vegas."

"I love it, and I get a little excited at times."

Chuckling, he pulled her closer. "There's nothing wrong with that."

Loud music blasted, getting their attention. The light show began, a spectacular vision of changing pictures with accompanying music. Staring up, the crowd ooh'd and aah'd at the colorful display.

Psychedelic colors flashed to a rock and roll tune; colorful fish swam by on blue-green water. Banners in pinks and blues floated by to the strains of a Doors' song, along with pictures of famous rockers, including Elvis. The show ended to cheers and claps. Lights came on fully in the casinos and restaurants.

Erik stood looking up for a few more seconds. "That was amazing."

Amanda laughed. "Told you so."

He looked down at her. "Let's have a drink and try our luck at the slots."

They went into Binion's, one of the oldest casinos in Vegas. Feeling like she'd stepped back in time to the 1950's, Amanda looked around at the diversity of patrons in the retro casino. Elderly women kept guard over several slot machines at once, ready to challenge anyone who dared use one of their machines. Middle-aged men with large paunches stretching their T-shirts, walked by carrying bottles of beer. At one of the roulette tables, a crowd had formed, cheering and clapping the action. Young men, probably college kids on break, staggered by, holding oversized glasses of beer. Women, dressed for a night out, teetered on sky-high heels.

"There are some interesting people here," Erik said.

"Sure are. Let's find two open slot machines. I don't usually gamble, and I can't at the Augustus or any of its affiliates. If we gamble, we get free drinks."

"Free is good. Let's go."

Forty dollars poorer, they left the casino arm-in-arm.

"We're pathetic gamblers," Erik said, laughing.

"We are, but you're fun to lose money with."

"So are you." He grinned down at her.

She couldn't remember the last time she'd enjoyed herself so much. They'd had two beers each while playing the slots, and ribbed each other on their bad luck. When she was with him, even the most routine, familiar things took on a new vibrancy.

As they walked slowly back to the garage, he held her against him with his arm around her waist. They came to a small side street, and he took her arm, pulling her along with him. He backed her up against a building. His eyes sparked gold fire in the glare of the street lights. Anticipating his kiss, she licked her lips.

"God, you're beautiful," he whispered before his lips descended on hers. With a low moan, Amanda wrapped her arms around his waist, pressing against his muscled body. His urgent, hungry kisses sent jolts of pleasure through her to rival Fremont Street's pulsating light show.

His large hands spanned her ribcage, electrifying every part of her body. His hard erection pressed against her, sending delicious heat to her stomach and lower. Her nipples hardened and pushed against her tight sweater.

"Get a room!" someone shouted.

Erik pulled back and stared down at her. "That's not a bad idea," he rasped.

Amanda blew out a few breaths to settle her racing heart. "I'm tempted, Erik, but it's too soon." She skimmed fingers over his high cheekbones and full lips. "We've only known each other a short time, yet I feel I've known you much longer. I don't want to mess this up. Let's give it time and see where this goes."

He gathered her to him and held her against his chest, rubbing his hand up and down her back. "You're right. You're becoming important to me, and I don't want to pressure you to do anything you're not ready for. Come on, it's late. You need to get home."

CHAPTER EIGHT

The next morning, nursing her second cup of strong coffee, her mind on Erik and last night, Amanda lifted her head at the knock on her office door. "Come in."

Phillip opened the door and stepped inside. "Want to take a walk with me to the Mirage? I just hung up with Bruce." He named the event planner at the Mirage Hotel and Casino. "He has a confetti machine we can borrow so we won't have to rent one."

"I'll go with you. I'm not getting much done this morning anyway." Amanda finished her coffee and stood. "That's decent of Bruce and saves us the hassle of hunting one down."

Plus Erik's conference was being held at the Mirage. Maybe she'd see him.

<><><>

As Amanda and Phillip entered the Mirage and walked through the domed atrium filled with tropical foliage resembling a rainforest, adrenaline rushed through her, and she looked around expectedly as if Erik would suddenly appear.

They took the elevator to the floor that held the conference rooms and event planning offices. As they headed down the wide hallway, Amanda froze and backpedaled. She'd seen a poster with Erik's picture on an easel outside one of the rooms. The door was closed but she could hear voices.

She stared at the poster, disbelieving, then put a hand to her throat as anger and confusion stifled her breath.

"What's up?" Phillip asked, following her. He squinted at the poster. "Malcolm Erik Hamilton. Who is he?"

"Not who I thought he was." Her voice sounded strangled. She read the glowing description of Erik, founder and CEO of World Scope Gaming Company, the hottest startup in California. She guessed all those years of being a geeky gamer paid off.

"Looks like he's got some good creds," Phillip said. "I'm impressed." He looked over at Amanda. "What's wrong?"

"I've been had. That's what's wrong. Wait until I see him again, if he has the nerve to face me."

"Oh. Tiger Lady. I like that."

She shifted her purse to her other shoulder, feeling like a soldier on a mission. "Come on. Let's go get that confetti machine."

The rest of the day, Amanda went through her work routine on auto pilot. Soon it would be Christmas and the Fischer wedding. There were a thousand details to handle, yet, overwhelmed by a sense of betrayal, Amanda could only think of Erik.

She couldn't understand why he'd hidden his real identity. He'd played her. Underneath her hurt, she had to admit Malcolm Hamilton had turned out okay. More than okay. The nerdy gamer had become a hunk and a successful business owner. She'd hurt his feelings when she turned down his dance invitation all those years ago. She wondered if his lying to her now was his way of getting even. Yet, the Malcolm she remembered, and the Erik she'd come to know, and was falling in love with, didn't strike her as a vindictive guy.

When six o'clock came, as she prepared to leave work, a bell on her phone signaled a text.

With a flutter in her stomach, she looked at her phone and saw Erik's ID.

Last night was great. Can't stop thinking about you. Late night with clients. Can we get together tomorrow night?

She responded before she could talk herself into ignoring him.

OK.

<><><>

Erik read the text from Amanda again as a sinking sense filled him. Uh-oh. Her terse reply told him something was wrong. After last night, he could no longer deny he'd fallen for her. He raked fingers through his hair and blew out a breath. Life had just gotten more complicated.

Guilt reared its head. He needed to tell her the truth.

He'd always been good at compartmentalizing the diverse layers of his life, but his feelings for Amanda overrode everything. This convention was the most important of his career, and all he could think about was Amanda, wanting her, being with her. Her laugh, her smile, her sparkling brown eyes, her warmth, her intelligence.

"Ready, Erik?" Matt walked up to Erik where he stood outside the conference room. "We're all set to leave for dinner."

Erik slipped his phone into his pants pocket. "Ready as I'll ever be." But he wasn't ready for Amanda to cut him out of her life. He hadn't been honest with her. That had to change if they ever had a chance at a real relationship.

CHAPTER NINE

The next night, Amanda sat at a table in a far corner at the Capri, nursing a glass of wine. She drummed her fingers on the table while she waited for that lying Malcom/Erik to appear. He'd texted her and asked her to meet him.

When he walked in the door and looked around, her traitorous heart jumped for joy at the sight of him. She twisted her fingers around the stem of her wine glass. No matter how attractive she found him, or how appealing, or that she had begun to fall for him, she would not let him off the hook for his deception.

He saw her, and smiling that sexy grin of his, strode over to where she sat. Before taking his seat, he leaned down to kiss her. When she flinched and drew away, confusion flitted over his face.

He sat slowly and signaled the waitress for a beer. "What's wrong, Amanda?"

She flared her nostrils. "Maybe I don't like being lied to, *Malcolm*."

Closing his eyes, he took a deep breath. When he opened his eyes, anguish darkened them. "How did you find out?"

"I was at the Mirage yesterday and saw a poster board with your name and picture. CEO of the hottest startup in California. Another thing you conveniently forgot to tell me."

"I can explain, Mandy."

"The name is Amanda now. No one calls me Mandy."

"I've always thought of you as Mandy, and I've thought of you a lot over the years."

She waved a hand. "Spare me. Why did you do it, Erik, or should I call you Malcolm? Why weren't you honest with me from the first?" She tried to keep her voice calm so he wouldn't know how much he'd hurt her.

The waitress came over with his drink. Erik took a swig of his beer and plunked the bottle onto the table before he met Amanda's gaze again. "I'm sorry, Amanda. It was never my intention to fool you or hurt you. Things got out of hand. I planned to come clean before I left."

"A little late for that, isn't it? You lied to me."

"It wasn't technically a lie."

"Don't weasel out of it. A lie of omission is a lie." She clasped her hands tightly on her lap to control the anger that simmered in her and threatened to boil over. "You played me. You even texted me from two different phones. Sounds like premeditation."

"I'm not proud of myself. When you brushed me off, I figured you didn't want to see Malcom, thinking I was that same nerdy, annoying guy who used to tease you all those years ago."

He released an audible sigh. "As for the phones, I keep one for personal stuff and one for business. I sent the original text from my personal phone. I had my business one when we met here that first time. That's the one I handed to you so you could put in your number. I continued to use that whenever I texted as Erik. I admit to feeling guilty about it, but as things went on, I couldn't suddenly start texting as Erik from Malcolm's phone."

She stared down at the table then back to him. "You should have told me who you were that night I sat next to you here."

"When you gave me that incredible kiss?" he said softly.

"You let me kiss you, and you still didn't tell me the truth."

"If you'd known I was Malcolm, would you have kissed me?"

His words released a nugget of guilt that thickened her throat. "I don't know. I'm ashamed to say I didn't want to see Malcolm. I would have for my mom, although I'm annoyed at her for playing matchmaker."

"She didn't play matchmaker. I had Aunt Flo ask her for your number."

"Why?"

"I had a crush on the fourteen-year-old Mandy. When I knew I'd be in Vegas, I wanted to see you."

"If that's supposed to make me feel better, it doesn't. What were you doing in the Capri that night, anyway?"

He raked fingers through his dark hair, ruffling it, and making himself look completely adorable. Amanda rubbed her fingers over the tabletop, as if the cool wood could help resist his pull.

"I had some free time so I came over to the Augustus with the idea of looking you up. I came into the Capri for a drink." He gave her a wry smile. "I needed to shore up my courage to meet you. Imagine my surprise when you walked in."

"How did you know it was me? We haven't seen each other since we were fourteen. I had purple hair the last time you saw me."

His lips formed a tentative smile. "I liked your purple hair. I checked you out on your hotel's website where they list all their management employees." He wrapped his hands around the beer bottle and locked his gaze with hers. "I always thought you were beautiful, but now you're gorgeous."

She held up a hand. "Stop with the flattery. You're not going to get out of your dishonesty that way."

Hurt shadowed his green-gold eyes. "Please hear me out. After our kiss, and your response to it, I wondered if I'd have a better chance with you if you didn't know my true identity. I wanted you to get to know me as I am now. I was afraid if you knew who I really was, all you'd see was that geek who lived for games. The next day, when I texted you as Malcolm, and you said you were too busy to meet then agreed to meet Erik right after, it reinforced that you had to know me as Erik."

She looked down as guilt melted some of her anger. Raising her eyes to him, she said, "You're right. I wasn't being fair to Malcolm. I did think of you as that same nerdy guy from all those years ago. I owe you an apology too. I wasn't very nice to you that time when you asked me to the dance. I wanted to go with you because I thought you were fun to be around, and I liked you, but I wanted to get in with the Goths, and—"

He held up a hand, stopping her. "We were kids. It's not a big deal. I admit I was hurt for a while, but I've long since gotten over it." He reached across the table to take her hand. At the sincerity in his eyes, she didn't pull away. "Amanda, please give me another chance to make things right. I want to be with you and see where this goes."

She shifted in her seat. She had to let go of the past. He wasn't the geeky guy she remembered, and she was no longer the purple-haired Goth.

"I'm sorry I wasn't straight with you," he said. "Things happened, and before I knew it, I was in too deep and didn't know how to get out of the mess I'd created." Releasing her, he sat back and scrubbed a hand over his face. "This isn't an excuse for my actions, but I'm taking my company public, and the amount of work and time I've had to put in has been overwhelming. Spending time with you was a much-needed break. I didn't want anything to spoil that or come between us. I enjoy being with you, and I selfishly wanted to hold back the truth a little longer."

Gathering her thoughts, Amanda studied him. His chiseled features, with his sharp cheekbones and square jaw, bore little resemblance to the chubby-faced boy she'd known. His black T-shirt stretched across his broad chest and couldn't disguise his well-defined muscles. "I didn't recognize you, although there was something familiar and comfortable about you from the beginning. Your hair is styled and you're no longer wearing glasses. What happened to your freckles? You are most definitely not nerdy looking now."

He laughed. "I found a good hair stylist, and I wear contacts. The freckles disappeared on their own, along with the baby fat. And I discovered rock climbing. I need the physical stuff to help control my stress. My mom and co-workers accuse me of being a workaholic, something I'm trying to correct. Don't let my new looks fool you. I'm still the nerdy gamer you knew."

"I liked nerdy Malcolm, although I hid it." She frowned. "Erik now and not Malcolm?"

"I dropped the Malcolm when I got into college, in an effort to appear less of a geek and attract girls."

"How'd that work out for you?"

Shrugging, he said, "The girls still didn't pay attention to me. When I moved to Los Angeles and started my own company, and began to make money, suddenly Erik was very popular with women. Malcolm was gone forever."

"Sounds like you've built a successful company."

He nodded, pride evident on his face, the face that was coming to mean a lot to her. "My love of gaming paid off, big time." He smiled. "You would never have expected that, would you?"

She smiled. "I guess not." She glanced away and stared at a painting of the Isle of Capri hanging on the opposite wall. Feeling calmer, she turned back to him. "I'm still hurt you weren't honest with me."

"I'm sorry I hurt you."

"I'm sorry I ignored Malcolm."

His sexy grin made heat pull low in her belly. "Now that we've gotten the *mea culpas* out of the way, what are we going to do?" he asked.

"I don't know. Give me time. I had a bad break up last year that made me question my judgment." She ran her finger over the rim of her glass. "We've both done things to each other we regret. I have a lot to think about. Total honesty in a man is important to me."

He took her hand again and traced a circle on her palm with his finger, inciting warmth to swirl through her.

"I want to stay here, to see you every day, to prove how much I want to be with you," he said. "But I have to go back to L.A. tonight. A work emergency. We've hit a glitch in our plans to go public. I'll be back as soon as things settle down." His eyes, almost pleading, held hers. "Think about us while I'm gone. Will you give me another chance?"

She chewed her bottom lip, gathering her thoughts. "I want to, but I have to be sure."

His smile lit his face. "Thank you. I promise not to pressure you, but I'll miss you." He glanced at the wall clock. "I have to get on the road." He stood, pulled his wallet out of his jeans pocket, drew out some bills, and slapped the money on the table. He held out his hand to Amanda and she took it, allowing him to help her stand.

He placed his hand on the small of her back as they walked out of the bar and into the hotel lobby. They stopped, and he gripped her shoulders to turn her to face him.

"Good night, Amanda. I won't say goodbye." He leaned down to place a tender kiss on her lips. With one last look at her, he strode away.

Amanda watched until he disappeared from sight. She had a lot to think about. As she hurried to the elevator that would take her to the garage, hope put a smile on her face and a spring in her step.

CHAPTER TEN

Christmas morning dawned sunny and clear with a fall-like crispness in the air. Amanda had to get to the Augustus early to see to last minute arrangements for the Fischer wedding, scheduled at two that afternoon.

As she drove to work, her thoughts went to Erik, as they'd done the past five days since he'd left. He'd called and texted a few times to say he was keeping killer hours trying to straighten out problems with bringing his company public. He told her he missed her. She missed him more as each day went by.

She'd done a lot of thinking through many sleepless nights, and decided she wanted him in her life.

Yesterday he'd sent her a bouquet of two dozen red roses with a card wishing her a Merry Christmas. He hadn't said when he'd be back in Vegas. Despite the flowers, she wondered if he might have changed his mind about wanting to pursue a relationship with her. Anxiety squeezed out some of her hope.

<><><>

Ten minutes to the start of the Fischer wedding, Amanda stood at the back of the conservatory, tablet in hand. Wedding guests sat in chairs along the wide paths leading to the canopy of glittering silver icicles where the minister waited. Curious hotel and casino guests strained behind velvet ropes, their cameras snapping shots of the shimmering fairyland. An excited hum rode over the crowd as the groom, best man, and groomsmen took their places near the minister.

Seeing Mrs. Fischer, on the arm of one of the groomsmen, approach from the hotel lobby, Amanda unlatched one of the velvet ropes so they could walk down the white carpet set over the Italian-mosaic path. The mother of the bride wore a long gown in varying shades of green. The usually overdressed woman looked classy and understated today. Mrs. Fischer smiled at Amanda as she passed. Amanda couldn't help but smile back.

The violinist standing off to one side played a variation of the traditional wedding march as the mother of the bride sat. The bridesmaids, dressed in Christmas green, followed by the maid of honor in bright red, entered from the lobby and began their walk down the white carpet. Phillip gave Amanda the thumbs-up as he started the confetti machine. Gold flakes fell on the wedding party and the guests. Some of the guests looked up and frowned as they tried to keep the flakes away. Amanda closed her eyes for a few seconds, imagining the clean-up crew's job.

Finally, the bride made her appearance, almost floating across the lobby on her father's arm. She easily fit down the flower-lined path in her white wedding gown, overlaid with shimmering transparent gold. Amanda sighed with relief. Thank God she'd talked Lisa out of making her gown wider. In addition to her bouquet of white and gold roses, Lisa carried a large gold wand, much like the one Glinda, the good witch in Oz, carried. A gold crown, like Glinda's, topped the bride's long lace veil. The crowd behind the velvet ropes ooh'ed and aah'ed as cameras clicked. No doubt the gossip rags would cover the society wedding.

Amanda smiled at Phillip. They'd done it. The wedding might not be what Amanda would have chosen for her own ceremony, if she were ever to marry, but Lisa seemed happy, and the guests and onlookers seemed to love it.

Duties over, Amanda had the rest of the day to relax and enjoy the holiday. The hotel's head of catering and the Fischers' bridal consultant would handle everything now. As Amanda turned to go back to her office to close up, she bumped into something hard and unmovable. She raised her eyes to Erik's intense gaze.

She stumbled, and he gripped her upper arms, steadying her. "What are you doing here?" she asked, her voice shaky as joy washed over her.

Expression sober and his eyes dark, he looked down at her. "I got here as soon as I could. Please, can we talk?"

"Let's go to my office where we can have privacy."

When they got to her office, Amanda went to her desk and

sat, needing the sleek black glass between them as protection from flinging herself into his arms. She had to maintain her cool in case he'd changed his mind about having a relationship with her. Erik perched on the edge of a chair in front of her. She folded her hands together on the top of the desk.

"Thanks for the roses," she said. "They're beautiful."

"You're welcome."

His brief reply twisted a knot of anxiety in her chest. "Is everything okay now with your company?" she asked.

He nodded. "We're good. We're ready to go public on the first trading day of the New Year."

"I'm glad."

He shifted in his chair and brushed a hand over his hair. Her heart softened at the dark circles under his eyes and the several days' growth of stubble on his square jaw. The urge to comfort him prompted her to start to rise from her chair. She sat and pressed her palms on the desk. They needed to talk first. "You look tired."

His brittle laugh hovered in the room. "No sleep will do that to a person."

"Yet you came all the way here today when you could have been resting."

He leaned forward, his hands on his knees. "Despite working almost around the clock, you were never far from my thoughts. I had to see you. I know I hurt you and I hope you can forgive me. I want you in my life, Amanda."

She read anxiety on his tight features. "Do you mean that?"

"With my heart and soul. I promise to never lie to you again or hide anything from you. Will you give me another chance?"

Amanda plucked a pen off the desk and rolled it between her fingers, letting the rapid beating of her heart settle. Drawing a long breath, she set down the pen and looked into his eyes. "I thought about us a lot in these last five days. I've missed you more than I could believe. I want you in my life, too. I want to see where this goes with us."

His head fell back and he closed his eyes. When he looked at her again, his eyes shone. "You want me in your life? You want to see where this goes with us?"

She smiled at his questions that echoed her.

When she nodded, he stood and came around the desk to gently pull her up. He cupped her face between his large hands and looked into her eyes. "I'm falling for you. I need you."

"I-I need you too." Her voice trembled.

"No more hiding anything from each other," he said softly.

"No more."

He took her lips in a tender kiss. She wound her arms around his neck. With a groan, he deepened the kiss and pulled her closer. Like a hungry man, he devoured her with his lips. His long fingers traced her midriff and higher to massage her breasts through the thin silk of her blouse.

She moaned softly and gave herself over to his scorching lips and hands. When they pulled apart, he rested his forehead on hers. Their ragged breaths were the only sounds in the quiet room. He gathered her close and held her as if she were the most precious thing in the world to him.

She rested her head on his chest. His steady heartbeat reverberated through her, secure and calming. After a few minutes, she drew away and ran her finger lightly over his lips. "Merry Christmas, Erik."

"Merry Christmas, Amanda."

She smiled. "I'm really glad you sent that first text."

"You mean the one you brushed off?"

"I'm happy you ignored the brush-off."

He grinned. "I'm a determined man."

Still held in the circle of his arms, she frowned. "How will we make this work? I can't leave my job."

"I can work anywhere. I'll buy a place in Vegas and set up a second office. How does that sound?"

"Amazing." She wound her arms around his neck. "We'll have our own very Vegas Christmas today."

"And for many more Christmases," he whispered before taking her lips in a sweet kiss that promised days and nights of love and passion.

***

Thank you for reading *Gambling on Love*. I really appreciate your purchase.

ALL ABOUT CARA MARSI

An award-winning and eclectic author, Cara Marsi is published in romantic suspense, paranormal romance, and contemporary romance. She loves a good love story, and believes that everyone deserves a second chance at love. Sexy, sweet, thrilling, or magical, Cara's stories are first and foremost about the love. Treat yourself today, with a taste of romance.

When not traveling or dreaming of traveling, Cara and her husband live on the East Coast of the United States in a house ruled by two spoiled cats who compete for attention.

*Read more about Cara's books and sign up for her newsletter at her website www.caramarsi.com. She's on Facebook, Twitter, Goodreads, and Pinterest.
She's always interested in making new friends.*

BOOKS BY CARA MARSI

A Catered Romance
A Cat's Tale & Other Love Stories
(All stories in this anthology are available separately)
A Cinderella Christmas
A Groom for Christmas
Accidental Love
Capri Nights
Cursed Mates
Her Forever Husband
Her Snow White Christmas (Snow Globe Magic Book 1)
Her Frog Prince Holiday (Snow Globe Magic Book 2)
Her Red Riding Hood Valentine (Snow Globe Magic Book 3)
Snow Globe Magic Holiday Boxed Set
Logan's Redemption (Redemption Book 1)
Franco's Fortune (Redemption Book 2)
Luke's Temptation (Redemption Book 3)
The Redemption Series Boxed Set
Love Potion
Loving Or Nothing
Murder, Mi Amore
Storm of Desire
Sweet Temptations
Sweet Temptations Boxed Set
The One Who Got Away
The Ring
Wedded In Vegas (Gambling On Love Book 1)
Love By Chance (Gambling On Love Book 2)
A Very Vegas Christmas (Gambling On Love Book 3)
Gambling On Love Boxed Set
Wedding Dreams Boxed Set

Multi-Author Boxed Sets

Brandywine Brides: A Blackwood Legacy Anthology
Desperate Measures Boxed Set (Coming January 2018)
Entice Me: Luscious Love Stories
Holiday Magic

Letterbox Love Stories Boxed Set, Volume 1
Season of Magic Holiday Boxed Set
Season of Promises Holiday Boxed Set
Season of Surprises Holiday Boxed Set
Sizzling Summer Boxed Set
The Marriage Coin Boxed Set

Read excerpts at www.caramarsi.com
All books available at online booksellers

A Catered Romance, A Groom for Christmas, Brandywine Brides: A Blackwood Legacy Anthology, Capri Nights, Cursed Mates, Franco's Fortune, Gambling On Love, Logan's Redemption, Loving Or Nothing, Luke's Temptation, Murder, Mi Amore, Seasons anthologies, Snow Globe Magic, and The Marriage Coin, are available in print
***